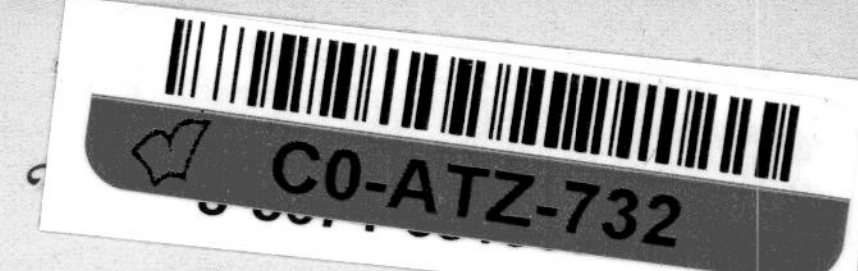


"I was listening to your ham radio tonight and it said that your police car was involved in a shootout."

Ali lay his head on top of hers. "It was. But as you can see, I'm okay," he said. His voice was muffled in the fullness of her hair.

"What happened?" She did not move away from his rock-hard form.



"[illegible] along with anot[illegible] for s[illegible] the [illegible] was [illegible] for a [illegible]



"Were any cops killed?" she whispered.

Ali didn't respond for a moment and then answered, "No, Davis was injured but he'll survive."

"Thank God," Solange said, relieved. "I have never been so afraid in all my life. I tried to call the precinct to find out what was going on and they wouldn't tell me because I'm not your wife." Tears were beginning to fill her voice.

Smoothing her hair, Ali said, "Well, then we'll have to do something about that."

"I agree."

Suddenly she pushed herself away from Ali and dropped down to the floor on one knee. Taking his left hand and looking up at him she said, "Ali Marks, I've known for some time how much I love you, but it wasn't until tonight that I realized how different my life would be without you. I want you for now and for always. Will you marry me?"

# *UNCLEAR AND PRESENT DANGER*

*MICHELE CAMERON*

Genesis Press, Inc.

INDIGO LOVE SPECTRUM

An imprint of Genesis Press, Inc.
Publishing Company

Genesis Press, Inc.
P.O. Box 101
Columbus, MS 39703



ISBN: 13 DIGIT : 978-1-58571-408-7
ISBN: 10 DIGIT : 1-58571-408-9
Manufactured in the United States of America

First Edition

Visit us at www.genesis-press.com
or call at 1-888-Indigo-1-4-0

# *DEDICATION*

I dedicate "Unclear and Present Danger" to my paternal grandmother, Maggie Cameron, of Camerontown, South Carolina. May you Rest in Peace . . .

Church mother of the East Lake City Church in Camerontown.

Birth mother of Rosalind, Rudolph, Jesse, Dallas, Henry, and last but not least my father, Philip Cameron of Palm Ray, Florida.

# *ACKNOWLEDGMENTS*

I would like to take this time to thank Deborah Schumaker, Brian Jones, Diane Blair, Valerie and all the other nameless faces that work at Genesis Press, Inc. and do whatever they can do to make my novel the best that it can be.

# *CHAPTER 1*

With a long sigh, Solange Montgomery threaded her hand through long, golden-highlighted hair. Then she wearily put her head down on her desk. After closing her honey-brown eyes, she tried to relax from the frustrations she'd experienced that day as corporate manager for Microsystems Computers.

For the last week she'd had back-to-back exit interviews with laid-off employees. Many of the older employees had been ready to go, but she knew when she saw the tears that they unsuccessfully tried to quell that there was a difference between resigning and feeling as if you weren't needed.

Employees that weren't on the list averted their eyes from their fellow coworkers as they'd made their way to Solange's office. When she happened to venture into the production area, her entrance had immediately curtailed hushed conversations. The still-employed had scurried back to their stations as if they had huge stockpiles of work and they were so valuable she needed to keep them around. True, with the changing of the guard and a Democratic president and Congress, revenue had picked up, but it had been a slow recovery for Microsystems Computers after eight years of double-digit nonprofitability.

It had been a grueling day. She had been forced to finish laying off one third of her employees. She sat up and propped her chin on her hand as she allowed herself to drift into an uncharacteristic feeling of self pity as she mulled over the last employee she needed to lay off.

She'd deliberately put this off as long as possible, but she couldn't put it off any longer. She looked at her list for the umpteenth time and then, stiffening her upper lip, picked up her telephone and hit the intercom button for Jane.

"Yes, Ms. Montgomery. What can I do for you?" Her secretary's voice sounded morose, and Solange knew that Jane, too, had been affected by the queue of people that had filed in and out of her office.

"Teresa Benedict was supposed to be here for her appointment over ten minutes ago. Will you find out what's keeping her?"

There was a slight hesitation before Jane said, "I saw her talking to her son Arnold earlier. I'll go see if I can find out what's keeping her."

Solange quickly hastened to say, "No, don't do that. I'm sure she'll be here soon."

Then, before Solange disconnected, Jane whispered to her through the phone line, "Here she comes."

"Show her in." Quelling the slight feeling of nausea she always felt at the beginning of each exit interview, she stood and, with outstretched hand, walked over to Teresa Benedict. The return handshake was lukewarm, to say the least. Motioning for Teresa Benedict to sit down, she resumed her position in her chair behind the desk.

Without preamble Solange looked directly at her and said, “I'm sure that you know why you're here.”

Teresa Benedict didn't attempt to hide the surly look on her face as she replied hoarsely, “Yep, you're gonna fire me.”

Solange held her hand out in denial and said, “I'm not firing you. I'm laying you off.”

Teresa's eyes snapped and her nostrils flared with anger. “What the hell's the difference?”

“The difference is you'll get a severance package that includes your regular paycheck for the next six months. That should give you financial stability while you look for another job. Also, if you invested in company stocks, you can sell them without paying any fees.”

Teresa Benedict glared at Solange and said, “I don't have no money invested in this place. I never had enough money left over from my paycheck for that.”

Solange replied in a somber tone, “I'm very sorry to hear that. But at least I'm able to keep your son. Maybe he'll be able to help you out.”

“Humph,” she retorted bitterly, “ever since his wife took off and left him, I'm the one that's been helping him out.”

Solange cleared her throat. “I hope you know, Teresa, that this is not by my choice. You know that companies all over the world have to cut production and expenses.”

Teresa cut across her, “But you chose me. Why didn't you pick one of your *sisters*?”

Immediately Solange bristled at the insinuation of racial favoritism, but because extenuating circumstance, she decided to let it go. "As you know I have no sisters that work here. I chose who I needed to lay off on the basis of what's best for the company."

After Teresa Benedict left, Grace left her office and went to the watercooler and filled her favorite mug. Then she walked over to her secretary.

"Jane," she said, handing her a ten-dollar bill, "would you please go and get me a turkey and Swiss with lettuce and tomato on white bread from the deli next door? I'm going to walk down to the manufacturing floor and check things out."

A flash of irritation crossed Jane's face before she replied in a somewhat surly tone, "Sure."

Solange drew herself up short and asked, "Is there something going on with us that I'm not aware of?"

"No," she denied quickly. "It's just been a tough month."

Solange gave Jane a frank stare and said, "But it's been better for you than one third of the other people here, hasn't it?"

Solange Montgomery threw her half-eaten sandwich in the garbage can underneath her desk, stared out the window of her office and watched the security guard escort Teresa Benedict to the front gates. Once Rodney Willis, the security supervisor, took Teresa's badge and threw it on the pile with the others, Solange Montgomery went back to her desk, sank into her leather chair, laid her head on her arms and wept.

When she pulled into her driveway and hit the remote for her garage door to open, Solange was relieved when she saw Ali's Explorer parked inside. Hurriedly, she shut off her engine and entered her townhome. Ali's back was to her. She was sure he couldn't hear her over the din of the music he was playing on her stereo. She sneaked up behind him and put her hands across his eyes. "Guess who?"

Ali stopped stirring the contents inside the frying pan and replied, "I don't know, but whoever you are, my girlfriend will be home any minute, so if you intend to seduce me you better stop playing games and get down to business."

Solange dropped her hands from his face and encircled his neck with them. "Don't you know you're playing with fire when you say something like that to me? I've had a horrible day, and I'm sure no jury would send me to jail if I suddenly snapped."

Ali made pretend choking sounds, and once Solange released her hold on him, he turned around and planted a long kiss on her mouth. Solange returned his kiss with the fervor of pent-up love, tiredness, and gratefulness. Once they freed each other's mouths, Solange buried herself in his arms, breathing in the scent of him that wafted to her nostrils. No words were spoken as Ali allowed her to lean on him, giving as much of his strength to her as he could.

Finally releasing him from her embrace, Solange stepped back and passed a weary hand across her face before giving him a tremulous smile.

"Tough day, huh?" Ali said, reaching over to ruffle her shoulder-length hair.

"You bet. But I think that's it. At least I hope so."

He picked up a remote off the counter and aimed it at the stereo system, and immediately an atmosphere of peacefulness flowed throughout the room. Ali pointed to a chair at the kitchen table. "Sit," he ordered softly.

Solange gratefully acquiesced and watched Ali go to the refrigerator and pull out a bottle of wine. "I thought that you said that you would be able to wrap things up today."

"I did," she said.

Ali handed Solange the full wine glass as he sat down. She genuinely smiled for the first time that day as she watched him gulp in one long draught half a glass of the wine he'd poured for himself.

Feeling the need to change the subject, she said, "What's for dinner?"

"Hamburger Helper beef stroganoff." He smiled.

Solange shook her head chidingly. "Ali, you are the worst Arab ever."

"Don't I know it," he mocked.

Suddenly Jane's sulky countenance flashed in front of her face, but then it was gone. "I got attitude from Jane today."

"You did?' Then Ali shoveled so much food in his mouth at one time that for the second time that day, Solange smiled.

"I sure did. I asked her to get me some lunch and she acted like it was an imposition."

"Maybe it's not about you. Maybe she's having problems with her boyfriend."

"She doesn't have a boyfriend," Solange responded with conviction.

"You don't know that," Ali said as he eyed Solange's delicate features.

"If Jane had a man, I and everyone else would know about it. She would regale us with every insignificant detail from what she wore on the first date, to what he wore, what they ate and daily updates as to how," Solange put her fingers up in the "quote unquote" gesture, " 'the relationship' was progressing. That's her history."

"Maybe she's decided in the future to keep it quiet until she knows that the relationship is going to last."

Solange made a snort of denial. "I doubt that. She's a chatterbox. After holidays with her family, she comes back to the office with every minute detail that her nieces and nephews did. It bores me to death, yet I quietly suffer through it praying for a phone call to interrupt her tales."

"Maybe that's why she's changed. By the way, I called you three times today and your office number went straight to voice mail."

Solange's eyebrows moved up in surprise. "It did? That shouldn't happen. And you're not the first person to tell me that. Also, now that I'm on a roll, Jane disappears and I kind of thought she was saying goodbye to her friends," Solange said. "Now I'm not so sure since most of her friends are gone. You could have been someone important calling me about business," she added.

Ali retorted with mock affront, "I'll have you know that I am important and I was calling about business. I wanted to know what you wanted for dinner, but since I couldn't reach you I made the decision. I figured something on the stove was better than nothing."

"For which I'm very grateful." Solange reached over and patted his hand consolingly. Then she eagerly picked up her fork and dug in. "Mmm," she said after swallowing a mouthful of food, "I never knew Hamburger Helper could be so tasty."

"It's comfort food." Ali gave Solange a perceptive look. "I knew this evening you would need some comfort. Besides, it's my favorite, too. When I was growing up, my mom would make this all the time."

"So that's why it's your favorite?"

Suddenly a flash of nostalgia crossed his face. "It was my dad's favorite also. That and ribs. Oh, my God, don't let me get started on some fried chicken."

Solange gurgled. "Didn't your mom ever make dishes from her native country?"

"No. Once she married my dad and left Iraq, she left all that behind her," Ali said after swallowing a mouthful. "Do you feel like going to Brooklyn on Sunday?"

She grinned. "It depends. What is your mom cooking?"

"I don't know, but she said we should be there around five o'clock."

"Tell her I'll bring the dessert."

"Sounds like a plan."

Solange reverted back to their former topic. "If Jane disappears again and doesn't have a good explanation as to where she is, I'm going to write her a warning."

All Ali said was, "You're the boss."

Later that evening, as she allowed her sunken tub to fill with water and dissolve the bath salt she'd emptied inside it, she stared at her naked body in the bathroom mirror. Since she and Ali had been together, she'd filled out considerably. Her breasts were so full, she'd been asked several times by envious females if she'd had a boob job and could tell by the look of disbelief of their faces when she'd proudly responded with, 'No, this is all natural, darling,' that they didn't believe her. Her long legs were a smooth honey brown, and her long neck made her head look like it was on a pedestal. Leaning closer to the mirror, she scrutinized the corners of her almond-shaped eyes looking for crow's feet. *Not yet.* Still she grabbed a jar of wrinkle and cellulite cream and placed it on the counter, poised to slather it on her body after her time in the bathtub.

Solange turned the faucet knobs on the bathtub, shutting off the water before gingerly immersing herself in the steaming hot soapy water. She quickly scrubbed her body before breathing a sigh of relief and laying her head back on her bath pillow. Feeling the effects of the wine, she closed her eyes. Burrowing herself deeper into the heat of the water, she felt her body totally relax.

As Solange drifted in and out of sleep, she felt a sudden stirring of the water in the tub and, opening her eyes, found the bathroom in total darkness except for a small candle. She smiled at Ali as he sat opposite her. His shoulders and sleek black hair glistened as he cupped handfuls of water and drenched his upper body. His pecs, matted with wavy, black hair, flexed, and she immediately felt a warmth flutter in her abdomen.

Solange let her legs fall between Ali's thighs and, taking one foot, she slid her foot up to his manhood. She began to massage his balls with her toes as if she was playing with the keys of a piano.

Ali opened his legs wider and slid closer to her in the water so she could have full access to his slick genitals.

Once Solange got tired of the first course, she stopped her movement. "Turn around," Ali softly ordered.

Solange had to stand up to do as she was told and, once she stood over him, Ali took his middle finger and slid it inside her. She eagerly spread her legs, and when his fingers began to explore her, she had to plant her hands on the tile walls to keep from losing balance from the feel of his touch. Solange threw her head back and closed her eyes from the pleasure, and the only sounds in the room were those of her deep moans of ecstasy. When she felt his touch withdraw from her, she opened her eyes and slid into the water, practically sitting on his lap.

Ali began to massage her shoulders. He worked her neck, shoulder blades and back, kissing the knots he loosened. Then he reached around and cupped her breasts. His hands found the hardness of her nipples and gently squeezed them. Not being able to wait for him to fully satisfy her any longer, Solange got out of the tub. After handing Ali one of the towels, she quickly dried herself, let her towel fall to the floor, and, with one beckoning look over her shoulder, walked into the adjoining bedroom. The room was dark.

When Ali joined her in the bed, he needed no light to find her as he slipped between the sheets. He leaned over and gathered her close. "I love you more than life itself." Before Solange could respond he kissed her. His kiss was tender but then it grew passionate as their tongues leisurely danced inside her mouth. When Ali withdrew his mouth, she made a small sound of denial until she felt the path of his lips down through the peaks of her breasts to settle on her belly button. He inserted the tip of his tongue into its center and she felt heat flow from her hairline to her toes.

Solange took the palms of her hands and pushed his head down. Instinctively he knew what she craved, and once his tongue entered her, she arched her back, giving him as much access to her as she could. Ali took his hands and placed her legs over his shoulders and devoured her.

From the midst of her passions, Solange didn't know exactly when Ali withdrew his mouth, but in the deep recesses of her mind, she felt her legs being lowered and then spread before he entered her.

"Thank you, Ali," she panted as he drove his long, hard member into her.

"For what?" he whispered.

"For loving me," she gasped right before she came.

Since they had been dating, Solange and Ali made the drive to Brooklyn at least once a month. Solange encouraged Ali to spend a lot of time with his mother. She was a widow and he was her only child. Solange knew that his mother was very dependent on Ali for company. Once they pulled up to the brownstone, a look of consternation crossed Ali's face when he saw that there were no parking spaces close to his mother's house. He double-parked next to a car in front of the brownstone.

"You know you're not supposed to park like this on the street," Solange chided.

"We're already late, and you know how Mom is if her dinner sits for too long," Ali said sheepishly. Then he reached into the backseat of his SUV and picked up his strobe light and set it on the dashboard. "That ought to keep me out of trouble for a couple of hours."

Solange reached for the cheesecake in the backseat. "I ought to make a citizen's arrest."

"I wouldn't mind as long as you handcuffed me. That way we'd both get a thrill." Then he grabbed the bottles of wine he'd purchased, and with Solange following him, he walked up the cobblestone path, took out his key and unlocked the door. "Mom, we're here."

Solange watched Ali's mother regally descend the staircase.

At five feet, five inches, Amira Marks was short in comparison to her son, who stood over six feet. Her tawny skin and sleek, black hair weren't the only physical characteristics that her son had inherited from her. Dark eyes, a full bottom lip and high cheekbones made them look like Arab royalty. To top it off, their mannerisms were identical and people immediately knew that they were mother and son because they each had a way of tilting their heads when they were listening to what someone was saying, and furrowing their brows when they were annoyed by what they'd heard.

When she reached them, Amira lifted her cheek as was her practice. Solange bent her lithe form and dutifully kissed her on the cheek.

Taking the wine bottles from Ali, she went into the kitchen so that he and his mother could greet each other in private. As she put the dessert in the refrigerator, her attention was drawn by a picture on the refrigerator door. It was one she'd never seen before. A young Arab woman, dressed in a veil and long, flowing black dress, was holding a baby. Judging by the terrain she was obviously in Iraq.

"Hmm. I wonder where she got that from," Solange murmured.

"My cousin Anah sent it to me."

She heard from behind the voice of Ali's mother that now only had a slight tinge of an Iraqi accent. "It is my mother holding me as a baby. I am deeply indebted to her for sending it to me. The name Anah means 'answer to my prayers,' and she is."

Then Amira took her hand and led Solange out of the kitchen and into the living room. Once Amira released her hand, Solange sat close on the sofa, with Ali's arm resting behind her. They waited for her to spill the news that had her beaming.

"My cousin Anah found me on the Internet," Ali's mother said, finally.

With an unfathomable look on his face Ali said, "That's great news, Mom. I know for years you've wanted to connect with your family in Baghdad."

"I know. I'm so excited." Amira practically clapped her hands gleefully as if she was a small child.

"Is there a particular reason why, after all this time, Anah contacted you?" Solange asked.

"They're thinking about making a trip over here next year because her daughter, Farrah, wants to go to Syracuse for medicine, and she cannot travel alone. I can't believe after all this time I will be seeing my family."

Ali asked, "Did Anah mention your parents?"

Suddenly the light in Amira's eyes lessened and she responded slowly. "No, she didn't. I think they still have not forgiven me for eloping with your father and coming to the States. They feel that I betrayed them because they had already chosen a husband for me." She gave Solange a look. "His name was Yusef and our parents were business partners. We had been friends since we were children, but I did not want him to be my husband." Now she focused solely on Ali. "And then I met your father." Amira's eyes misted over with tears, and she didn't try to blink them away. Then she redirected her eyes on Solange. "When I see the way you look at my son, it is the same look that I had from the moment my eyes rested on Ali's father."

"I thought that arranged marriages between families were pretty much the norm," Solange said. "Weren't you afraid to break tradition?"

"Yes, I was, but my need for Malik was stronger. My family was considered wealthy because we had a strip mall. Anything one needed could be found there. I loved to go there after school because it was so much more interesting than going home and cleaning. We had a clothing store, Laundromat, grocery store, and money exchange store. That is how I met Ali's father.

"He would come every week and exchange money to send home to his family. Sometimes my father, Hakim, would be at one of the other stores and I would wait on him. We became friends, and whichever store I was at he would wait until my father left and then he would come and talk to me." Amira's expression became dreamy. "He was the most interesting man I had ever talked to and I was fascinated by his thirst for knowledge. Malik would buy the newspaper and explain things to me that I didn't understand."

"I'm surprised your father left you alone in the store."

"But he didn't," Amira said. "My cousin Anah would be with me, but she didn't care because she was having a secret relationship with a boy who was not considered good enough for her to marry."

"Oh, so you were cohorts committing crimes," Ali commented dryly.

"Not committing crimes." Amira pinned her son's eyes with hers. "Why is it considered a crime to follow your heart?" A heavy silence filled the room. Then once again Amira redirected her focus to Solange. "This went on for a year and then Malik was told that he was being sent to protect another region. My heart was broken until he asked me to marry him. I was petrified, but I was more afraid of him leaving me and what would become of me, so I pretended that I was at Anah's house and we eloped.

"We went to nearby Sadr City and found an old man who was tired of Iraqi ways, and he married us. We stayed hidden for three days, and by the time they found me it was too late because I was no longer chaste and no good Arab man would marry me. My father disowned me and didn't even give me the clothes at my house. I have not worn a hijah or abayah since."

"I'm surprised no one killed Ali's father."

"There were plenty of other men that wanted Malik's position in the army." Amira clucked her tongue. "Once Malik and I returned to Baghdad, he was discharged from the military, so that was his punishment. That was his only way to feed his family, and that was why he was fighting for a cause that he didn't believe in. But at least he got an honorable discharge, and that is why he was able to become a policeman. But our history followed him throughout his career."

"Is that why you moved to the States?"

A look of sadness settled on Amira's face. "Malik's family was wiped out in a bombing. After that, he wanted to leave and I had no reason to stay."

"Did Anah get in trouble for helping you?" Solange asked, fascinated by the love story.

A guilty expression crossed Amira's face. "Yes. I heard she was severely beaten and was not allowed to contact me. They married her to my intended, Yusef, the week after I married Malik." Then excitement reappeared on Amira's face and she said, "But finally, after all these years, I've heard from her. I am very indebted to her."

On the drive home, Ali's jaw was clenched, and glancing at his stern profile, Solange knew that he was displeased. "Maybe if they do come, your mom will feel less of the void for family," she said.

Ali shot her a look full of resentment. "I can remember as a little boy, my mom would receive packages from Iraq. When she would get the large envelope, each time before she opened it, she would clutch it to her breast and bend her head, quietly praying. Then she would excitedly open the envelope and one of her unopened letters would fall out. She would go to the room and I would hear her sob for hours."

"Why did they go to the trouble to repackage it? Couldn't they just write on the envelope 'return to sender'?"

"No, because it was mailed out of the country. After my dad died, it was worse. I was all she had left then, and I'm all she has left now. She thinks that she wants a relationship with these people, but they're strangers to her."

# CHAPTER 2

Early Saturday morning, the sound of the telephone ringing made Solange roll over. She glanced at the clock and saw that it was eight o'clock. "You better be sick," she said drowsily.

Grace's tinkling laughter on the other end of the phone made Solange sit up with resignation. She knew that meant her best friend Grace was in a one of her "I'm gonna talk your ears off and there's nothing you can do about it" moods.

"Did you go out last night? Is that why you're so grumpy?"

"No, I did not go out last night. I don't go out any night. I'm too old for that."

"You're crazy if you think thirty-two years of age is too old to go out. Age is a mind thing, girl."

"If that's the case, I'm thinking I feel about forty."

"That bad?"

"No, not lately. I did the last of my layoffs last month, so things are going more smoothly."

Grace said in a cajoling voice, "Do you feel like a road trip?"

"I don't know. What's the occasion?"

"Jet and I are having Livingston and Ebony baptized the weekend after Christmas, and we thought that if you came for the holidays, we could have the ceremony with you as godmother at the same time. I really want to finalize the paperwork before the new year comes in."

"Christmas is only a month away. Thanks for the notice."

"I know, but I wasn't sure that I could get Pastor Greene to agree to do it at that time, but he did. Please come down," Grace wheedled. "We haven't had a Christmas together in years."

"Okay, I'll come. Corporate is shutting us down for a week this year. I'm really looking forward to it."

"Can you stay the whole week?"

"I wish I could, but I don't know what Ali's situation is. As it is, I'll probably have to talk him into taking four or five days off. He's trying to get ready for his detective exam, so he's kind of pressed for time."

"That gets me to my next question. How do you feel about me asking Ali to be the children's godfather?"

"I don't know," Solange said. "I guess that's up to you."

"Not really. You see, the godparents need to be able to work together and raise our children if something happens to us, and the two of you aren't married yet. What I'm really asking is, do you think that the two of you will end up together?"

"Yes," Solange answered without hesitation.

"Okay. Then let me talk to him."

"He's not here. Ali stayed at his place last night. He had to work late and be there early, so there really was no reason for him to take the train that late at night out here to White Plains."

"Tell him to call me when he gets a minute."

"Okay, I'm sure he'll be thrilled. He loves family."

"Have the two of you decided if you're getting married?"

"He's brought it up several times, but I'm dragging my heels. You know how my childhood was. My parents fought all the time. Only after they got much older and went to counseling did they get their act together. I just don't want to go through that."

"I'm not going to even bother to ask if the two of you love each other because I've seen you together. But the test is, do you think that you want to see him every day?"

"Yes, I do. Last night when he wasn't here, I tossed and turned all night."

"Would you want him even if he became sick with a debilitating disease?"

"Of course, silly, that doesn't change the heart of a man."

"Do you enjoy spending time with him?"

"Yes. You know sometimes we'll be at his place and we won't even be talking. He'll be watching a game on television and I'll be in the other room reading a book, but I feel happy knowing that we're in the same house."

"Do you have the same goals and ideals about the difference between right and wrong?"

"Absolutely," Solange responded with heartfelt meaning.

"Then marry him. There's not one reason in the world why you shouldn't. You are not your parents."

"He's never formally asked me," Solange said.

"Then ask him. He's probably afraid of getting shot down." Grace added teasingly, "You are a formidable adversary."

"I will not ask him."

"All right, you old-fashioned girl, but the next time he hints around," Grace ordered, "put an amiable smile on your face. In other words," she paused deliberately for effect, "don't be you."

Solange smothered a laugh and said, "Yes, dear."

Ali Marks walked out of the shower and, after grabbing a towel, walked over to his locker and began to vigorously dry his wet body. The muscles in his arms rippled as he dried his six-pack. Just as he finished and wrapped the towel around his waist, he spied his partner, Randolph Vernon, enter the room and go to his locker.

After opening his locker, he stepped back and shouted, "What the hell?" Then he turned around and glared at the other officers in the room, who studiously kept their heads bent, finishing whatever they were in the process of doing as they pretended they didn't hear or notice Randolph's anger.

Ali padded over in his shower shoes and stood next to Randolph. His body stiffened from anger and his eyes hardened when he saw what Randolph was shouting about. A half-eaten watermelon was in the bottom of his locker.

Randolph screamed, "Whoever put this shit in my locker, when I find out, I'm going to fuck you up!"

"Calm down, man." Ali attempted to put his hand on Randolph's arm, but his friend angrily pushed it away.

Now the men in the locker room stared at Randolph's locker sheepishly. Ali's attention was drawn to Eric Pritchard, the newest cop on the beat. He had flaming red hair that made him look like the devil. One of the policemen in the unit had secretly nicknamed him Lucifer, and that name had been bandied amongst the men. Eric stood apart from the rest of the men, and with narrowed eyes, observed the scene with keen interest. Abruptly, Ali's attention was drawn from Randolph and diverted back to his coworkers. They were quietly filing out of the room, and one or two gave Randolph an apologetic look before they left.

Once they were alone, Randolph started kicking the locker in anger as Ali quietly observed him.

After Randolph was done and there was silence in the room, Ali said, "Don't let them get to you."

"That's easy for you to say, man. They didn't do this shit to you!"

"They'll just continue if you let them know that it upsets you. Whoever did it is just pissed off because you passed the exam to become a detective."

Randolph glared at Ali and pointed at the watermelon. "Do you know who did this shit?"

"Hell, no, man. If I did, I would tell you. But it's obviously they are just jealous. Just cool it. You'll be out of here in a couple of weeks with a better position and making more money. Soon you'll be leaving all this shit behind. Some of these beat cops, this is what they are and this is what they'll always be."

"When are you going to take your test?"

"In January. But even if I don't pass the test, I want the hell out of this precinct. Shit ain't right down here."

"I hear you, man." Then they bumped fists. "But if I find out, I'm going to get him or them . . ."

"Hey, man," Ali said. "Let's get ready for our shift."

Later that night, Ali and Randolph sat quietly in an unmarked car. The air around them hung heavy as they waited. Suddenly their radio went off and Randolph hurriedly answered it, whispering. "Randolph Vernon, here." Ali and Randolph listened to the voice from the other cop car at the end of the street.

Randolph said, "I think that there are more people in the warehouse moving stolen goods than we thought."

Ali said, "I have a bad feeling about this."

Then he heard Lieutenant Heath, who was listening in from the precinct, say, "We're sending more backup."

Then they heard the voice of the other officer in the car ask and Ali recognized the voice of Eric Pritchard, "How long must we stand down on our position?"

"There are two black and whites in the vicinity. All of you hold your position until they get here," Heath responded.

"Affirmative." Ali and Heath recognized the voice from the other car. It was David.

"Affirmative," Randolph responded, but before he could hang up, they heard a succession of popping sounds followed by rapid gunfire.

"Get out, and get down," Ali ordered as he opened his car door and slid to his knees in the darkness.

Randolph did the same and crawled to Ali's side of the car for cover.

"Radio for a bus," Randolph croaked. "I think one of the guys in the other patrol car was hit."

"Will do," Ali said as he picked up his radio. "This is Ali Marks, and our location is 69 East Fifty-third Street. We need an ambulance. I believe we have an officer down and backup is on the way, but we need more. There are shots being fired from a warehouse window. No visual has been made at this time."

"This is Captain Heath. Do not leave your position. Once again, do not leave your position."

Then, all of a sudden, shots were fired out of the warehouse at the stationary cop car on the other side of the street. The officers returned fire and all of a sudden the building exploded into flames. Two people came running out of the building and toward the second police car.

"Cover me," Randolph ordered as he bounded from his position. "This is the police. Stop or I'll shoot!" One of the men fleeing the area stopped and put his hands in the air, while the other continued to run.

"Put your weapon down and lay face down on the pavement," Randolph shouted.

The man made a quick movement towards Randolph and he aimed, shooting the man in the thigh and bringing him down to the ground.

Ali watched from his position from behind the car door as Randolph kicked the man's legs apart and bent to handcuff him. As he watched Randolph bend to retrieve the weapon, Ali saw from the corner of his eye a dark, shadowy figure sneaking along the wall inching closer to Randolph. Then he saw the glint of a gun barrel being aimed at Randolph.

As if in slow motion, he aimed and fired his pistol. The next thing he saw was the assailant double over and fall to the ground in a shattered mass of a dead body.

Three fire trucks were pumping water as they tried to douse the inferno that was burning on East Fifty-third Street. Solemnly, Ali watched the unknown assailant in the body bag being lifted onto a gurney and slid into the back of the medical examiner's van. He quelled the urge to vomit, knowing all eyes were on him. He had just killed his first perpetrator. Another ambulance with its siren going full blast tore out of the parking lot with the injured police officer while Ali and Randolph stood quietly watching the blaze, hoping any occupants left in the warehouse would be saved.

Randolph nodded his head at a cluster of people around the back of the ambulance. He watched Eric Pritchard having his blood pressure checked by EMS. "I didn't know until tonight that Eric Pritchard was teamed up with Jonathan Davis."

Ali cocked his eyebrow at Randolph and said, "You know that they usually pair a newbie with a veteran."

"I know that. But Davis is at the top of the totem pole. Every newbie would like to train under him. Why does Pritchard rate?"

Ali looked at Randolph in surprise and said, "I thought you knew that he has connections. His dad is Captain Lyle Pritchard. You know Daddy's going to look out for his little boy."

"You mean to tell me that Pritchard is Lyle Pritchard's son?"

"Yes, but I don't think that he wants anyone to know who his connections are."

"No, just use it to his advantage," Randolph responded bitterly. "Any person who trains under Davis moves up the ranks in a hurry."

Ali added dryly, "I'm just glad Pritchard didn't get killed. Can you imagine the second-guessing that would lead to? Somehow we would be called on the carpet for it."

"We saved his life tonight. I bet we don't get any recognition for that."

Next, a detective car drove up and Ali and Randolph immediately bristled when they realized it was Internal Affairs.

"Here we go," he whispered to Randolph. "They're here to see if we messed up."

"They're here hoping we messed up," Randolph corrected him with a somewhat worried look on his face. "If cops always did everything right, then they would be out of a job."

"Yeah," Ali muttered sarcastically.

An insipid short man walked towards them and once he reached them, he flashed his badge. "I'm Franklin Petty from Internal Affairs. What happened here tonight?"

Randolph and Ali looked at each other. "Do we have to do this now? It's been a long night and my partner and I are exhausted," Randolph said.

Franklin Petty swung his head around and surveyed the chaos that was still in motion. "Of course. There's just one thing. The two of you were asked to remain in position. Why did you not follow orders?"

Randolph responded with deliberate sarcasm, "I saw two armed men fleeing the building heading to a car full of fellow officers and felt the need to act quickly."

"He probably saved their lives because of his quick thinking," Ali added with just as much sarcasm.

Franklin Petty's eyes bored into Ali's as he took in his distraught expression that he was unable to mask. "But not everyone made it out okay, did they?" He nodded his head to the ambulance that was slowly leaving the scene. "But I guess if we have to choose," he shrugged his shoulders nonchalantly, "the right one will live, right?"

Before Ali could answer, Franklin Petty closed his small notebook and put it in the inside pocket of his jacket and said, after handing them each a card, "You're both on desk duty until further notice. Each of you is to report to me at Internal Affairs for a statement tomorrow. Marks, you come at eleven-thirty, and Vernon, ten."

"What an asshole!" Ali watched as Franklin got back into his car.

"You give him a compliment by calling him that," Randolph said bleakly.

As they watched Franklin Petty drive away they saw Eric Pritchard walking towards them. Once he reached them, he held out his hand, first to Ali and then to Randolph. Solemnly they each shook it.

Eric cleared his throat and said, "Thank you guys for tonight. You not only saved Davis's life, but mine also."

There was an awkward silence for a moment and then Ali said quietly, "We're part of a brotherhood. We have a common bond and we're supposed to have each others' backs."

Then Randolph added, "You're thanking us for doing the right thing. I would like to think if our positions were reversed, you'd look out for us, too."

Eric Pritchard stared at Randolph, his eyes bleary with emotion. "I just hope one day that I can be half the policeman that you two guys are. You put your lives on the line tonight." Then he looked at the ground and looked up again, staring only at Randolph. "That watermelon joke in the locker room today, that wasn't funny, was it?"

Randolph gave a start of surprise when he heard the words.

Eric continued in a voice filled with remorse, "I'm positive nothing like that will ever happen to you again. Sometimes when people are new to a job, their insecurity makes them do things that they normally wouldn't do.

It's a way to deflect attention away from themselves and their shortcomings."

The air around them was now filled with tension and smoke. "I'll see you at the precinct," Eric said and he turned and walked back to Cpt. Heath and the others.

Ali turned to Randolph and noted a smirk that appeared to be a combination of derision and satisfaction.

At three o'clock in the morning Ali tiptoed into Solange's dark house. He hoped the garage door hadn't awakened her as he quietly placed his keys down on the kitchen counter. Immediately a bright light flooded the room, temporarily blinding him. Startled, he turned around the see Solange rising from the occasional chair that was positioned in a corner of the den. She strode towards him and took her hands and placed her palms on the side of his face. Then she traced his features. Gingerly she moved her fingertips across his high cheekbones and took her index finger and traced the line of his straight nose. Then she moved her hands down his body, touching him in the way a mother traces the limbs of her newborn baby, checking him to see that he was unharmed. Once she was satisfied he was okay, she slid her hands around his waist and buried her head deeply into his chest, holding him tightly.

Ali took her in his arms and gathered her to him closely, giving her a hard squeeze.

"I was listening to your ham radio tonight and it said that your police car was involved in a shootout."

Ali lay his head on top of hers. "It was, but as you can see, I'm okay," he said. His voice was muffled in the fullness of her hair.

"What happened?" She did not move away from his rock-hard form.

"Randolph and I were on a stakeout along with another patrol car. Supposedly, the warehouse was a front for stolen goods. All of a sudden all hell broke loose and the perpetrators started firing their guns. Once gunfire was returned, the warehouse exploded. It was also a cover for a methamphetamine lab and we didn't know it."

"Were any cops killed?" she whispered.

Ali didn't respond for a moment and then answered dejectedly, "No. Davis was injured but he'll survive."

"Thank God," Solange said, relieved. "I have never been so afraid in all my life. I tried to call the precinct to find out what was going on and they wouldn't tell me because I'm not your wife." The sound of tears was beginning to fill her voice.

Smoothing her hair, Ali said, "Well, we'll have to do something about that."

"I agree." Suddenly she pushed herself away from Ali and dropped down to the floor on one knee. Taking his left hand and looking up at him, she said, "Ali Marks, I've known for some time how much I love you, but it wasn't until tonight that I realized how different my life would be without you. I want you for now and for always. Will you marry me?"

Ali looked down at her and said, "Are you sure about this?"

"Positive," she answered emphatically.

Ali dropped down to the floor and, taking both of her hands in his, he stared into her honey-brown eyes and said, "Yes, Solange Montgomery, I will marry you." Then he lovingly kissed her on the mouth.

Ali stood in the shower and let the hot, pelting force of the water wash over him. With his hands placed on the wall in order to steady himself, the events of the night crowded his memory. Unknowingly he shook his head as the mental vision of the body destroyed by the bullet fired from his gun falling to the ground surfaced. A feeling of queasiness filled his stomach and he suddenly lurched forward, emptying his insides of the cheeseburger he'd eaten earlier that evening. Disgusted, he reached his hand up and aimed the shower head at the remains, making sure the mixture dissolved down the drain. Turning off the water, he left the shower and, after toweling himself off, walked into the darkened room. He slid in beside the sleeping Solange.

Once she felt the weight of his body next to her, Solange turned over and snuggled into Ali's arms. "Hold me tight," she ordered softly. As soon as he did, Solange felt Ali's manhood rise. Smiling sleepily, she reached down and caressed him. Then she moved her hands across his abdomen and, suddenly, Ali switched position, pinning her to the mattress. In the darkness of the room, Solange saw a cat-like glow in Ali's eyes. It was a look she'd never seen before. She greedily reached for him and closed her hand around his penis. Then he lowered his mouth to hers and kissed her hard. When his mouth released hers she whispered, "I'm so proud of you, Ali. What you did tonight was so heroic. You're my brave man. You did good tonight."

All of a sudden, Solange felt Ali's penis go flaccid in her hand as he lost his erection. A look of fury crossed Ali's face and he said through gritted teeth, "I'm a cop. We do what we do out of necessity, not because we want to. And that's not always something to celebrate." When he saw the astonishment on Solange's face, he added, "I killed a man tonight." Then he threw back the covers and, naked, stalked into the bathroom.

Solange lay in bed stunned by Ali's revelation and the look of rage on his face when he heard her words. Then it dawned on her. *No cops died, but someone did and he feels responsible.*

Solange slipped out of bed and went to the bathroom. Tentatively, she knocked on the door. "Ali, may I come in?"

There was no answer. Taking a deep breath, she slowly opened the bathroom door. After venturing inside she leaned against the wall and watched Ali, and he vigorously brushed his teeth. Once he was done, he straightened and stared at himself in the mirror. Solange could see that he was staring at his reflection as if he'd never seen himself before.

"What happened?"

"We were told to hold our positions and then suddenly shots were fired. Randolph and I got out of our patrol car and went for cover. Shots were returned and all hell broke loose. The perps were fleeing and someone was heading towards the other cop car and Randolph pursued them. He ended up shooting one in the leg, and while he was handcuffing him, I saw a shadow. There was someone sliding against the wall taking aim at Randolph, and I didn't think that he saw him so I aimed, shot, and hit my mark. I killed him."

"So you saved your partner's life," she said softly.

"Yes, but I took another," he answered morosely. "What if that man had a wife or children?"

"I'm sorry for them if he does. But he did that to them!" She pointed at Ali. "Not you. It was up to him to protect his family. It's not your fault that he's dead, it's his."

"But children are innocent. They don't pick their family," Ali whispered.

Solange gently tried to reason with him. "Randolph also has three children and a wife who loves him very much. And I know when they hear what happened tonight that they're going to be very grateful that things turned out the way they did."

"I guess you're right."

"If you were in the same position again, what would you or could you have done differently, Ali?"

Ali was quiet and Solange watched the myriad of emotions cross his face as he wrestled with his feelings.

Then he shrugged his shoulders and held his hands out, saying, "I don't know. I'd probably react the same way."

"That's how you know you did the right thing." She walked up to him and once again slid her arms around his middle. "And you know deep in your heart that I'm right. There was nothing else you could do."

Ali squeezed her then released her.

Now Solange gave him a look of stern chastisement. "As your fiancée, I demand that you don't keep things like this from me ever again. I'm going to be your wife and that means that I promise to be a rock for you if you need it. You and I," she pointed at him and then herself, "we're in it for the long haul."

"Yes, ma'am," Ali said, giving her a sheepish look. "Can I please have a minute alone?"

"Of course," she replied softly.

When Ali rejoined her in the bedroom, he walked towards her like a stallion. Solange had turned on the small lamp on her nightstand and, in the soft glow, his hand snaked out and the next thing she knew the room was bathed in total darkness.

The mattress dipped from the weight of Ali's body. Impatiently pulling her towards him, Ali grabbed her legs and positioned her spread-eagled on the bed. Then moving over her, he tilted her chin up and pressed his lips to hers, at first tenderly, but then his kiss became more powerful.

Even though she was unaccustomed to the fierceness of his kiss, she felt a flood of liquid saturate her body.

Ali took his hand down and fingered her and once he found that she was ready, he stilled his movements and stared down into her face.

Solange gave him a nod of acceptance and, seeing this, he plunged into her. She gripped his shoulder blades as a way of holding onto him, and in the deep recesses of her mind she realized that her nails were like talons, yet Ali seemed to relish the pain she was inflicting and didn't hesitate as he began to ravish her. His tempo as he thrust inside her was long, hard, and fierce, and she moaned.

"Ali, harder, harder, harder," she moaned.

He obliged and then suddenly released all of his pent-up frustrations, anger, and hurt before exploding and then collapsing on top of her.

# CHAPTER 3

Solange rolled over to her side, picked up her phone, and hit number two on her phone log. After several rings, she heard Grace's voice.

"Hello."

"Girl, Ali gave me some real good lovin' last night."

Her words were met with a cackle of laughter that made it seem as if her best friend was in the room with her instead of Lake City, South Carolina.

"I'm very happy for you, Solange," Grace replied dryly.

Solange sat up in bed, pulling the sheet up over her naked body. "It's the first time he's been so, let's just say aggressive. I mean, I've never had any complaints before. Sexually, Ali's always been the master in the bedroom, but last night, it seemed as if he almost lost it. He was just like a character in an erotic movie, but in a nice way," she added as if an afterthought.

"Maybe his conversation with my man last week got him all revved up."

"What conversation?" Solange asked.

"Oh," Grace answered. "Ebony had a doctor's appointment and when I got home Jet was on the telephone with him."

"Hmm, Ali didn't mention that he talked to him."

"I think they discussed the fact that you guys are going to be Ebony and Livingston's godparents."

"Oh, good." Quickly changing the subject, Solange said excitedly, "I have some really good news." Then her exuberance changed to moroseness. "Brought on by a tragedy."

"Tragedy?" Grace gasped. "What happened?"

"Last night, Ali killed a man in the line of duty."

"Oh, no! How is he doing?"

"Okay now, I think. But he took it really hard. We talked and I told him how he didn't have a choice. It was either that guy or of his fellow officers."

"How are his partners?"

"They're fine, thanks to Ali," Solange said with pride.

"But you think he feels guilty."

"I know he feels guilty. It'll probably take him a while to fully accept that his actions were right. But I do know that whenever there's a shooting, the police officer has to go see the department's psychiatrist. Hopefully, this will help him in his acceptance and give him the ability to forgive himself."

"Gee, that's too bad. I'll make sure and tell Jet and when you guys come down for Christmas, I'll get him to talk to him."

"Only if he's ready to," Solange warned. "If there's one thing I've learned about Ali, it's that he holds things inside."

"Okay, then. Now I'm ready for your good news."

Solange took a deep breath, waiting, teasing Grace by taking her time telling her. "Ali and I are getting married."

"Hallelujah!" Grace laughed. "How did Ali ask you to marry him?"

"Actually, I asked him," Solange said slowly.

Grace shrieked, "You asked him? I can't believe it!"

"Grace, last night when I was knew that Ali was in trouble and couldn't get any information because I'm not his wife, it was the worst hours of my life. The thought of him not coming home to me one day was something I couldn't even comprehend. When I got my hands on my man, I knew that I needed to lock him down and make sure that he would always be a part of my life and I would have the rights of a married woman and be able to assert my rights for him if I was ever needed to."

"You finally get it, Solange. That's how you know that you have a lasting love."

Ali sat across from Joy Goody, the department's psychologist. He had never met her before, but he knew from his peers that her notepad could make or break a policeman's career. He had to be sure to gauge the effect each of his answers would have on his future with the department.

"How do you feel today, Mr. Marks? Or do you want me to call you Ali?"

*Oh, God! She's trying to set me at ease as if we're friends or something.*

"Whatever you feel the most comfortable with," he replied smoothly.

Ali gave the woman facing him a quick but thorough perusal. When she smiled, she revealed a set of perfect white teeth. Her brown hair was cut in a perfect bob, and she wore a perfect navy blue suit. *She looks like she's in complete control.* Then Ali gave himself a mental shake. *Don't be fooled by appearances. I'm sure that she doesn't know what I'm really thinking. If this stranger decides that I have psychological damage from the shooting, I'll be on desk duty until doomsday.*

"Mr. Marks. How do you feel about being a police officer?"

"I love it," Ali stated honestly.

"How do you feel when you fire your weapon?"

Ali shrugged.

Goody started writing furiously, and this made Ali feel compelled to say, "I never fire my weapon unless it's absolutely necessary."

"I see," Goody said. She gave Ali a measured stare. "How do you feel when innocent people are caught in the crossfire and lose their lives?"

"That's never happened to me."

"I know that you were involved in a deadly shooting. How do you feel about that?"

"How do you think that I feel?" he replied curtly before he could stop himself.

Without any apparent ruffling of her feathers, Joy Goody responded obliquely, "I don't know. That's why I asked."

Ali didn't respond for a few seconds. "Any time there is loss of life, that's a tragedy," he said.

"You're a police officer. Didn't you ever think when you went to the police academy that this would happen to you one day?"

"But we hope that it never happens."

"Are you having trouble sleeping at night?"

"No," Ali lied. Then he felt that he came across too cold and amended his response. "I did the first few nights, but once things settled down, I was okay."

Goody raised an eyebrow. She was absently tapping her pencil on the pad that she was jotting notes down on. "Since the shooting, do you think about the man's life that you took?"

"Of course I do. I think about him every day. I also think about his family left behind." Then Solange's words came back to him. He looked into the psychologist's eyes. "But then again, I think about my partner's life, which I helped save, and I revel in the fact that his wife, Madison, and his three children still have him."

Goody gave Ali a look of appraisal. "That's a good answer," she said as she closed her small notebook. "I don't think that I need to set another appointment for you. But if you need anything at all, don't hesitate to call and I'll fit you in." She reached inside her desk drawer and handed him a small notebook. "This is for you. I won't ask you for it. Write down anything that you might be thinking or feeling in regards to the shooting. Then, later, reread what you wrote. It's a technique I like to use because sometimes people are better at expressing themselves on paper instead of one-on-one conversation."

Ali hesitantly reached for the notebook and without opening it he placed it in the inside pocket of his jacket. He stood and held out his hand to her. "Thank you. I'll make sure and do that if I need to."

After Ali left the office he leaned back on the door with relief.

For over an hour, Ali had sat across from Franklin Petty. Petty had a yellow pad and had written down everything that Ali had said in regards to the shooting.

"If you could have done anything differently, what would it be?"

"Absolutely nothing," Ali replied with certainty. "I had a choice. It was either the criminal or my partner."

Petty gave Ali a long look, then scribbled down what he said.

"But you and Vernon were told to remain in position. You disobeyed orders," he coldly answered.

"When Captain Heath instructed us to do that, shots weren't fired, the warehouse wasn't ablaze and criminals weren't making a beeline for two other police officers. We didn't have time to call and ask for permission to do our job and protect each other."

Petty said brusquely, "You'll be on desk duty until you hear from Internal Affairs. You may go. Make sure you keep that appointment for the police psychologist. It's mandatory after a shooting incident."

"I already did," Ali said over his shoulder before he left.

When Ali entered the locker room, he found Randolph doing push-ups on a mat that was part of the locker room equipment.

Randolph stopped his movements and sat up, saying, "How are you doing, man?"

"I just finished with Petty," Ali said.

"No kidding. How'd you do with the shrink?" Randolph said.

"I'm good," Ali said. "She said that she doesn't need to see me again, but her door is open."

"Well, as far as I'm concerned she can go ahead and shut it," Randolph commented dryly. "Anyhow, this is just a bunch of bull. They're just covering their asses."

"I know. In case they're sued. The victim's name is Howard Dennings, a career criminal with a rap sheet as long as my arm."

"So I heard. He's unmarried, but his mother has already gotten a lawyer and is no doubt going to sue the department on behalf of his children." Randolph said dryly, "Parents certainly don't see their children for what they are. She's acting as of he was just in the wrong place at the wrong time. Forget about the fact that he was running a meth lab."

After a moment of silence Randolph changed the subject. "Do you know what desk job you're going to be given?"

"Not yet. I'm going in to see Heath in a minute. What'd you get?"

"I'll be down in SVU pushing papers. Talk about seeing mankind at its worst."

"Don't I know it?"

"At least we'll be working days for a while. I know that our women will be glad for that."

"You really can find a silver lining in every cloud." Suddenly a bright smile lit Ali's face. "By the way, speaking of Solange, we're getting married."

Randolph slapped him on the back. "Congratulations, man. So she finally accepted."

"Actually, this time she asked me," Ali said and laughed. "She was so upset about what happened, she proposed to me when I got home. I was shocked as hell."

"Hey, man, since she proposed, that means she ought to pay for the ring."

"I think not," Ali said, grinning. "Besides, I already have the ring. I was walking down Fifth Avenue and saw it over a month ago. We're driving down to South Carolina for Christmas, so I'll give it to her then."

Solange banged her hand down on her desk, then rubbed her tired eyes with her fists. For hours she'd been poring over the inventory reports for the last six months and she couldn't get the figures to jibe. The cash flow at Microsystems Computers was off. Every deposit was accounted for, every withdrawal had a notation, yet something wasn't right. "Is anything wrong, Ms. Montgomery?"

Solange looked up and saw Jane standing nervously in her office door. "No, why would you ask?"

Jane cleared her throat. "Well, you're talking to yourself and banging your fist on your desk."

Solange hesitated. "Come in and shut the door, Jane."

Jane turned around and closed the door with a decisive click.

"How's the general morale of the employees at work since we had that huge layoff?" Solange carefully scrutinized Jane's face, more interested in what she didn't say than what she did.

"Well, they don't talk to me like they used to," Jane said guardedly.

"Why?" Solange asked bluntly. "Do they consider you an enemy because you're my secretary?"

"I wouldn't say enemy," Jane replied cautiously, "but they do stop talking sometimes when I approach."

"So they're afraid that you're going to report back to me. Do they resent me for laying people off?"

"I think they know that you had no choice." Now it was Jane's turn to scrutinize Solange's face. "I mean it was that or go completely under, right? What I mean to say is that was your only choice, wasn't it?"

"Of course it was," Solange declared vehemently. "I saved as many jobs as I could."

Jane's gaze slid away from hers. "Well, then, that's all there is to it. You did what you had to."

Solange took sudden notice of Jane's physical appearance. Even though it was winter time, there was a rosy color to her cheeks. Then Solange looked at Jane's clothes. She was wearing a black skirt that fell right below her knees and a white scooped tank top. She'd had her mousy brown hair highlighted with blonde and evenly cut to fall just below her shoulders. "You look very nice today, Jane," Solange complimented her.

Jane blushed, making her rosy cheeks even rosier. "Thank you, Ms. Montgomery. I'm going out after work tonight with a friend and I don't have time to go home and change." Jane gave a self-deprecating look. "I bought this outfit especially for the evening."

"Well, I hope that you enjoy yourself, and you can leave a half hour early so you won't be so rushed. I'll lock up," Solange said.

"Are you sure, Miss?" Jane beamed.

"Positive," Solange answered.

"Thank you, miss. If you don't need anything else, I'll just go and straighten up my desk."

Solange hid a smile, knowing Jane was going into the bathroom to do what every woman does at the outset of an evening that is much anticipated. She was going to the nearest mirror to stare at her butt from all angles.

Two hours later, Solange was riding the elevator from the twelfth floor to the fifth floor in the parking garage. The creaking sound made it seem as if the elevator shaft was on its last leg and was going to burst into flames any minute. Suddenly the motion of the elevator stopped.

Nervously, Solange began banging on the panel of buttons to try and get it moving again. As she did so, she had to stamp down the ball of fear that was suddenly lodged in her throat as one of her phobias came to the surface. "Help! Help! Can anyone hear me?" Solange shouted. Then pounding on the alarm button, no sound was emitted, but all of a sudden the elevator began to move. It stopped at the seventh floor of the parking garage. The elevator doors slowly opened, and once they did, Solange shot out of them like a cannonball. Stumbling in her haste, she turned her ankle on a curb and fell. She landed on the sidewalk that had small pebbles of parking lot gravel. Hoisting herself up, she brushed her bloody knees with her hand and leaned against a pillar. As she clutched her stomach, she tried to still the beating of her heart.

Looking to the left, she saw the stairwell and limped towards the entrance, weighed down with her briefcase in one hand and pocketbook in the other. Once inside the staircase, Solange held onto the railing in the semi-darkness and thought she heard footsteps. She stopped. Not hearing anything, she continued her descent to the fifth floor. Again thought she heard footsteps and stopped. Forcing bravado she didn't feel, she called out. "Is anyone out there?"

All of a sudden, Solange heard a low, sinister-sounding chuckle and she broke into a run. She fled down the rest of the steps and threw open the door that led to the level where her car was parked. Only then did she look back over her shoulder. Once she was sure that no one was pursuing her, she dug quickly into her purse for her keys. She opened her car door, and after throwing her pocketbook and briefcase on the passenger seat, slid in and manually locked her car doors. Looking in her rearview mirror, she shifted her car into reverse, gunned it and sped out of the deserted parking garage.

Once she was safely in traffic, she called Ali using her cell phone.

"Hey there," he said, obviously happy that she'd called.

"Someone was chasing me!" Sheer terror echoed in her voice.

"Chasing you! Who the hell was chasing you?"

"I don't know. I was in the garage and the elevator broke, so I had to take the stairs and someone was in the stairwell following me."

"Are you okay?"

"I turned my ankle and it hurts," she said just as she burst into tears.

"Solange, calm down. How far are you from home?"

"Twenty minutes," she replied, trying to sound less hysterical.

"I'll be home in less than an hour. Okay?" His calm, soothing tone helped settle her fears.

"Okay," she whispered.

When Ali entered Solange's townhome thirty-five minutes later, she was laid back on the couch with a hot water bottle planted on her forehead.

"I didn't know it was possible to get here from your precinct that quickly," she said as she smiled weakly at him.

"I used my strobe light," he said gently.

"I ought to make a citizen's arrest," she replied, making an attempt at humor.

"Go ahead and call the law. My woman needed me, so I broke it. You know what they say, 'Don't do the crime if you can't do the time.' " Ali sat down on the small space on the couch that was left and with a worried expression. "Are you okay?"

"I am now," she said.

"What happened?" Ali asked, probing her features with his eyes.

"First of all, the elevator broke and then . . ." She screwed up her face as she tried to make sense of what happened. "I don't know. It was like adrenalin pumping through my body because everything happened so quickly. I thought I was being followed, and then I heard someone laughing. It scared me to death."

Ali took her hand and touched her cheek. "Why were you alone at night in a dark garage in the first place?"

"I stayed later than intended, and Jane left early because she had a date."

Ali gave Solange a look that held censure. "Jobs come and go, but people don't. I don't want you staying late alone anymore. Don't you have a security guard?"

"The building cut back on security because of the recession. There are blocks of time when no one is on watch."

"Then during that time you won't be leaving by yourself, either. If I have to come and escort you out of there to make sure you're safe, I'll do that."

"Honey," Solange said, "that's not necessary. Believe me, I won't be caught alone like that again."

"Good," Ali said. "Your ankle is really swollen."

"And it hurts, too," Solange whined forlornly. "Along with my knees."

Ali got up and went to the kitchen. He took a cold compress out of the freezer, walked back to Solange and gently laid it on her ankle.

She winced from the pain. "Ouch, that hurts," she said and she tried to sit up and remove it.

"Leave it alone," Ali ordered. "You're going to have to get used to it. I need to do this every twenty minutes to bring the swelling down. No heels for you for at least a week, young lady."

"Yes, Daddy." She settled back against the couch cushion and grinned, loving the way Ali was able to take charge of every situation. He let her show her weaknesses about things and didn't show impatience with her when she did.

"Lie there and I'll make dinner." Standing in front of the refrigerator door, Ali eyed the sparse contents, cocked an eyebrow at her and asked, "How do franks and beans sound to you?"

"Like a meal fit for a queen."

As they finished the remains of their dinner, Solange leaned over and, with a napkin, tenderly wiped sauce from the corner of Ali's mouth.

Ali grabbed Solange's hand and kissed it, making her smile at his gentlemanly gesture. "When do you want to get married?" he asked.

"I don't know," she responded, suddenly bashful. They were discussing the biggest step in their lives over hot dogs and beans, she thought. "I have two weeks vacation in July. How does that sound to you?"

Ali beamed. "That sounds like a plan. Let's do it during the Fourth of July weekend. I think it's kind of ironic to get married on Independence Day when I'm losing mine," he joked.

"Very funny," Solange grinned. "Next thing I know you'll be referring to me as the old ball and chain."

Ali looked Solange in the eyes and said, "I look forward to being able to say that. I feel as if I'm the happiest man alive."

"And I'm the happiest woman." Then she said with heartfelt feeling, "Ali, I want something small. Not all that craziness that I've seen at a lot of weddings where it seems as if the vows take a backseat to all the trimmings."

Ali looked horrified. "I hope you're not suggesting that we go to the courthouse. My mother would kill me!"

"I know you're right. I don't think my family would pleased with that, either. But my circle of friends is small, so out of necessity a small wedding party. Of course Grace will be my matron of honor and Ebony my flower girl. Livingston is too young to be anything. He'll probably just sleep through it anyhow," Solange said, laughing agreeably.

"When we go to Lake City for Christmas, I'll ask Jet to be my best man."

"That sounds like a plan." Then they bumped fists.

# *CHAPTER 4*

The next day at work, Solange dialed Microsystems's corporate headquarters. "Please connect me to Mr. Seth Dickerson," Solange said briskly when the operator came on the line.

"Just one moment, please," the voice answered.

She waited a few seconds.

"Seth Dickerson here."

"Hello, Mr. Dickerson, this is Solange Montgomery out of the White Plains office."

"Hello, Miss Montgomery. How are things going up there?"

"They're going," was Solange's noncommittal response. "I called because I know that money is tight, but I would like authorization to have a Christmas party for my employees."

"Oh, I don't know about that." Seth Dickerson's voice had considerably cooled since the outset of their conversation.

"I think that it would be good for the morale of the employees. I think that in the long run showing them a little appreciation for their hard work would go a long way."

"How much money are you talking here?"

"I want to do a buffet, which is the cheapest way to go, but I can't give you an exact dollar amount."

"No friends or family. Only workers should be allowed to attend."

"Yes, Mr. Dickerson." Solange readily agreed because she knew before she made the phone call that part of the plan was a bit of a stretch.

Then Dickerson added snidely, "This might cut into your Christmas bonus."

"I can live with that," Solange countered smoothly. "Having camaraderie with the people that work for me will make my life easier in the long run."

Seth Dickerson's only answer was a grunt. "Is anything else you need to talk to me about? I've been pulling your numbers, and it's good to see that at least your division isn't working in the red."

Solange hesitated before answering. "Things could be worse," she said.

"They are worse for some. We're going to have to trim the fat again at some of our other divisions. I'm just waiting until after the first of the year to make the cuts. But your branch doesn't have anything to worry about because you're solvent. Now if there's nothing else, I have to go because I have another call. Put in a requisition for how much money you need."

After Solange hung up the phone, she looked up and saw Jane standing there. She looked good again and Solange couldn't help but say, "How did your cocktail date go the other night?"

"We had the nicest time. I thought that at first he was going to stand me up because he was an hour late, but once he got there he was very nice to me," Jane gushed.

*An hour late and she sat there. Shit, I would have hauled ass long before that.*

"Why was he so late?"

"He didn't say and I didn't think that it was my place to ask him. I mean, we're just friends after all."

"But friends don't keep friends waiting that long without a good explanation," Solange said quietly. "Demand respect from the beginning of the relationship instead of trying to regain it later."

Jane seemed to bristle at the unsolicited advice.

"He apologized," she said.

"I need you to let everyone know that I'm having a meeting a two o'clock in the cafeteria and everyone should be there. I have some good news for a change," Solange said, adroitly changing the subject.

"No problem. I'll spread the word."

After Jane left the room, Solange just shook her head in resignation.

As Solange stood in front of the employees waiting expectantly for her announcement, she surveyed the room and noticed the pockets of little cliques. She basically knew who hung out with whom after work and the empty chairs between some of the groups reinforced in her mind that a Christmas party was exactly what they needed. "May I have your attention, please?"

Jane tried to hand Solange a mike, but she refused it, knowing that the crowd would settle down in a minute.

She cleared her throat once the room was quiet. "I wanted to let everyone know about something that happened. The elevator got caught between floors and trapped me." An interested hush fell across the room and looks of sympathy were reflected on many of the faces of her employees.

"First thing this morning I called the contracting company that fixes it and they'll be out later today. But remember," she warned, "the elevator is old, so you might want to take the stairs when leaving for the day. But if you do, make sure that you walk with a partner in the stairwell. It's never good practice to be alone in a dark stairwell, so take heed. Security around here isn't what it used to be, and with the recession there are a lot of displaced people around. You need to be proactive when it comes to your personal safety."

Her eyes met people in the crowd nodding their heads agreeably, and, buoyed that they seemed to be taking her seriously, she gave a comforting smile. "Now for the good part. I would like to thank all of you for your hard dedication to this plant and to your jobs. I know that things haven't exactly been easy lately. Losing coworkers and friends that you're used to seeing every day can make the atmosphere at a workplace depressing."

There were nods of agreement and whispers from the crowd. "You know you right," a voice in the crowd said.

"But I wanted to let you know that I spoke to Seth Dickerson this morning and he informed me that we're one of the few divisions that are working in the black and our branch is relatively strong, especially in this weak economy."

Solange's statement was met with a small spattering of applause. The applause grew louder as the reality of her statement sank in to people who thought that the meeting was to announce that their plant was being shut down and they would be losing their jobs. "As a gesture of appreciation of good will for all the hard work and for us to get ready for the new year, we'll be having a Christmas party on December nineteenth right before shutting down for a week."

Immediately a more enthusiastic round of applause filled the room and people smiled and looked relieved. "You do not have to attend, yet I really hope everyone will. I'm ordering a catered buffet and I'm sure that that we'll all have a good time."

"How about liquor?" Randy O'Connell shouted from the back of the room.

Solange gave a negative shake of her head. "No alcohol. We work on government contracts here, and alcohol is strictly prohibited."

"How about family members?" Arnold Benedict shouted, and an uncomfortable hush fell over the room.

"I'm afraid not," she said, feeling the hostility of his gaze. "This is just a small get-together for us to hang out and enjoy each other's company. The only thing I need you to do is sign your name on the sheet that Jane will hang on the bulletin board. That way I'll have an approximate number to give the caterer. That's all I have today."

As Solange watched the group file out, she was met with mostly smiles and thank yous. There was also some grumbling. "'Instead of forcing me to eat with people I don't like, she should have given me a gift card, something I can use," Solange heard someone whisper.

Upon hearing those words, Solange stiffened.

Ali sat at his desk and drew in a sigh of complete boredom as he completed the last stack of papers that needed to be filed. For the last couple of weeks, he'd been working as a clerk in Vice. He was chomping at the bit with cabin fever, ready to get back on the street. He was eager to try to really make a difference instead of creating a paper trail on women and men who'd given up on life.

"You look happy."

Ali looked up to see Randolph standing at his desk. The wry expression on his face showed Ali how much his partner commiserated about their desk duty.

"How would you like to go and get some lunch?" Randolph asked.

"Sure, what did you have in mind?"

"The regular greasy spoon fare we used to eat when we were real cops."

Once they hit the street, the cold blast of the November wind made Ali pull his collar up around his ears. Neither spoke during their short walk to the corner diner. Once there, Randolph pointed to a booth in the back of the room.

A pretty young waitress immediately came over to the table.

"I'll have the cheeseburger and fries, and a diet coke." Randolph said without looking at the menu. He shrugged his shoulders and looked at Ali. "My wife is on me about losing some weight. You have to save calories somewhere."

"I'll have the same, but instead of the soda, a glass of water will be fine."

"Sure thing." She smiled before walking back over to the short-order cook behind the counter.

"Has Internal Affairs talked to you yet?"

Ali gave a start of surprise. "No. Have they talked to you?"

"This morning," he said bitterly. "I was cleared of any wrongdoing, yet I've been denied my promotion because I didn't follow protocol."

"My God! How about the fact that you saved a fellow officer's life?"

Resentment flared in Randolph's dark eyes. "Their contention is that Davis would have taken care of things, and I disobeyed a direct order from Heath by leaving the patrol car. I'm relieved of desk duty and can resume my place on the beat, but I'm losing my promotion. Because I already passed my test, they said in six months they'll revisit the situation and I'll probably be moved up then."

"I think that the department is using this as an excuse to keep a brother down and not give you your money. I mean, what else could it be?"

For the first time since Randolph had been in his company, amusement was evident on his face. " 'Keep a brother down'? Where did you get that from?"

"That's what my dad would say every time he was denied a promotion. Every time he went up for a pay raise he'd have to accomplish more than some of his coworkers and I'd hear him tell my mom, 'They're trying to keep a brother down, but I won't let them,' " Ali said with a grimace.

"Well, I won't let them, either," Randolph said with a hard tone to his voice. "In six months, I'll get my position. And there's nothing anyone can do to stop me. I wanted to warn you because I'm sure Internal Affairs will be calling you next."

"I'm sure they will," Ali agreed with a worried look on his face. "Thanks for the heads-up. I just hope that they call me before Tuesday. I want this settled one way or the other. Wednesday Solange and I are leaving for Maryland to spend Thanksgiving with her family. I'm going to ask her father for her hand in marriage."

"Really?" Randolph asked with raised eyebrows. "I'm surprised that you feel the need to be so formal. I mean, after all, Solange is thirty-two and she is independent."

"I know that, but it doesn't hurt to be respectful."

"You're right," Randolph answered. "But wouldn't it be some kind of funny if he said no. I mean, you said that when she first introduced you to her parents you got a lukewarm reception."

"That's true, but we've been together for almost two years now, so I think they've pretty much accepted me." Ali gave a cynical shrug. "I showed them a picture of my dad in his police uniform, and that seemed to ease their fear that I'm a terrorist that somehow slipped into the country."

Randolph gave a negative shake of his head, and when he spoke his voice was laced with sarcasm. "It's amazing how some people react when you tell them that you're a cop. Sometimes they get a look of awe on their faces because they know that we're trying to make society better and protect them. Then others . . . they get a look of mistrust because something happened to either them or someone in their family and they mistrust policemen in general."

Ali nodded his head in agreement and said quietly, "I want Mr. Montgomery's permission to marry Solange. My dad told me when I was a little boy that no matter what the circumstances to ask my future wife's father for her hand before I married her. He said it would be better in the long run. Once I got older and knew the story, I realized that he felt responsible for my mother's family disowning her and the part that he played."

Randolph gave Ali a quizzical look. "What would you say if Mr. Montgomery said that he doesn't want you to marry her?"

"I would tell him that I'm sorry that he feels this way, but if Solange is willing, I am going to marry her anyhow."

Just then the waitress came to the table with a tray full of food. She put the plates on the table and batted her eyelashes. "Is there anything else I can get either of you?"

"I don't need anything else, thank you," Ali replied in an even tone.

"Then how about you?" She turned to Randolph and really turned on the charm, ignoring the wedding ring on his hand.

"I think I already have all I need at home."

"Ya'll are some good men," she said gracefully before leaving.

"The way I've been feeling lately, I needed to hear that."

"So did I," Ali agreed before digging into his plate of food.

When Ali arrived back at the precinct, there was a new pile of folders on the clear desk he'd left before he went to lunch. Disgusted, he sank into his chair. Feeling he was being watched, he looked over his shoulder and encountered the scrutiny of Cpt. Lyle Pritchard. When their eyes locked, Pritchard gave Ali a curt nod of acknowledgement before he strode off.

Solange snuggled up to Ali as they sat on his mother's couch.

Amira Marks observed the look of supreme happiness on her son's face and her heart filled with joy for him.

"Mom, tomorrow Solange and I are going to her parents' house for Thanksgiving and we wanted to tell you before we left that we're getting married."

"Oh, my God." Amira clutched her hands to her chest. "I've prayed for this day to come. I'm so happy for you."

Solange gazed at her future mother-in-law, a woman to whom she'd grown very close since she and Ali had been together.

Amira focused on Solange and said, "When is the wedding?"

"We're going to get married Saturday, July fifth. We want an intimate wedding with only close friends and family," Solange said with a smile.

Amira looked at Solange's bare hand. "Where is your engagement ring?" Then she turned stern eyes on Ali and said, "Son, don't tell me you haven't bought her an engagement ring. I thought that I raised you better than that!"

Solange smothered her laughter at the look of consternation Ali's face got after his mother's scolding.

"The jeweler that I use closes his shop down for a couple of months every year while he goes to Europe. Once he gets back, Solange and I are going to pay him a visit," he lied.

"I don't want to help pick out my engagement ring. I want you to give me the ring that you want me to have," she added shyly.

Ali scrutinized Solange's face intensely. "Are you sure you trust me?"

"Of course I trust you. I'll be happy with whatever you choose. I've trusted you in making decisions in our relationship so far, and look at the way things have turned out," she said and chuckled.

Ali leaned over and gave Solange a warm kiss. When he withdrew his lips from hers, she had to remind herself that they were not alone in the room.

Amira's eyes misted at the sight of them. Then she said quietly, "Ali, your father would be so happy for you, as am I." Then she captured Solange's gaze. "When are you going to give me grandchildren?"

"Let us have our honeymoon first, Mom. We're living our life one page at a time."

Amira was a little annoyed that she didn't get the answer she wanted, but she was interrupted from saying the response that came to her lips because Solange had picked up a picture that she hadn't seen before. It was a photo of Ali standing next to what appeared to be an Arabian horse. He was holding a trophy that was inscribed with the words FIRST PLACE. Examining it closely, Solange couldn't help but see the pride that was reflected from Ali's eyes as he stared at the camera. "You never told me that you ride," she said.

"I used to ride all the time." His voice sounded wistful. "Then life got in the way."

"Ali's father was a good horseman. We started Ali on lessons when he was a young boy. It takes most people years to get a good seat on a horse, but my son was a natural from the beginning. He could have been a jockey, but he was too tall. But he rode with the boys in the teen class by the time he was eight. His father was so proud of him the day he won that award," Amira said, beaming with pride.

"I thought that Ali was a teenager in this picture."

"No," Amira said proudly, "he shot up quickly. I used to call him my little big man."

Ali gave his mother an indulgent look. "I can do no wrong in her eyes, can I?"

"You don't do any wrong in mine, either." A look of intimacy passed between them and was only broken by the sound of Amira's voice.

"After you called and said that you were coming over I made baklava, and I want you to try it and see if you like it."

"Baklava?" Ali said with his eyebrows raised in surprise as they followed her into the kitchen and sat down. "What made you decide to make that?"

"I'm practicing. I received another letter from Anah. They are trying to get visas in order to bring Farrah over for a visit at the college. It takes a long time and much preparation to make such a trip."

Solange saw the look of annoyance that stole across Ali's face and then recognized his effort to try and mask his feelings about his relatives' impending visit from his mother. Busying herself by picking up her fork, she delved into the dessert that Amira had proudly set before her. "This so good, Ms. Marks," Solange said, biting into the fluffy pastry made with honey and pistachios that was layered in a flaky crust.

"You like it?" Amira beamed as she took her place at the table.

"I like it very much," Solange replied and watched Ali as he took a mouthful.

"It is very good, Mother," he admitted grudgingly, digging his fork into the pastry for another bite. "Mother, what do you plan to do for Thanksgiving on Thursday?"

"I have been invited to eat with Susanna from my bridge club."

"Are you sure that you want to do that? You know that you're more than welcome to go with us to my parents' house. Besides, I think that it's high time that all of you met," Solange said.

"I would go, dear, but you know I get car sick. I just don't want to spend my Thanksgiving holiday feeling unwell."

"Solange and I haven't decided if we're going to have the wedding in Fox Run or Lake City, where she's spent a lot of time with her best friend. But wherever we do have it, we'll fly you there."

Amira gave her son a grateful look.

"You don't get air sick, do you?" Solange asked.

"Not at all. I love the feeling of a plane taking off. I feel closer to the heavens," Amira replied.

# CHAPTER 5

"Why aren't you packed?" Ali asked curtly when he looked at the disarray of the open suitcase in the den.

"I am packed, Grouchy," Solange countered smoothly. "I just need you to close that case. I stuffed everything into it because I didn't want to bring more than one."

Without speaking, Ali crouched down and folded the remaining blouses that were on top of the heap. Pressing down hard on the case, he slid the zipper closed.

Solange rolled her eyes from behind him, and then plastered a smile on her face. "I guess Internal Affairs didn't call you in yet."

"No, they didn't," he answered. "It must not be good news. Randolph goes back on active duty after Thanksgiving and I want to be his partner."

"I understand that you feel a certain closeness with him, and you should. However, you'll have to get used to losing him as a partner in six months when he leaves for another department."

"That's different. That's good news for him, so I'm happy. This isn't the same thing."

"Honey," she leaned over and planted a kiss on his mouth and said with assurance, "I have a premonition that good news is right around the corner for you. Just you wait and see. Now try and put this out of your mind until you get back to work on Monday. There's nothing you can do but be patient and wait."

"All right," Ali said quietly.

"These people are bogarting me in this car. We should have driven my SUV," Ali complained.

"I thought we agreed to drive my car because it's easier to navigate in heavy traffic. I expected a mess on the turnpike, but once we get off of it I expect things to lighten up."

"I know," he said as he reached over and patted her knee comfortingly. "I'm sorry to be such a grouch."

"In the daytime, you have been a bit much to take lately," she teased, "but you more than make up for it at night."

"My nights are a pleasure, but my days are a bit of a chore."

Before Solange could respond, Ali breathed a sigh of annoyance as he peered out at the dark landscape only lit by yellow warning signs and red flares on the road. "There's a detour up ahead," Ali said. He looked at the GPS navigation system attached to the front window. "The GPS isn't working properly. It should have warned us."

"Let me see," she said. She touched the screen several times before she said in a frustrated voice, "The voice-activated part isn't working, but the road map is. I guess that's better than nothing."

"This traffic isn't moving. I think it's time for a bathroom break."

Solange breathed a sigh of relief. "Thank God. I need some air."

After crawling along for over another ten minutes, Ali veered off the interstate and pulled into the nearest gas station. When Solange left the warmness of the car, she braced herself against the frigid temperature, and without waiting for Ali to join her, she ran into the station and headed towards the ladies' room.

Once she relieved herself, she stood in front of the dirty sink and washed her hands after gingerly turning the knobs.

When she reentered the store area, she found Ali talking to the cashier. Solange sidled up to him and slid her arm into the crook of his. Looking down at her, he gently touched her on her cheek before saying with a look of consternation, "There's been a huge oil spill on the main road. A gasoline truck slid on the ice and they're rerouting people around the area."

"I hope the driver's okay," Solange said, including the clerk in their conversation.

"I don't know, ma'am." The clerk offered, "The news hasn't said."

"Gee, I'm sorry to hear that." Then she turned to Ali. "We should be okay with our GPS. We'll just follow the map."

"Is there anything you want to snack on? It looks like it's going to be a grueling ride to Fox Run. Thanksgiving is the busiest travel time in the year. This three-and-a-half hour drive has turned into five already. We probably should have flown."

"Probably should have," she agreed before she grabbed some chips and a honey bun off the shelf.

As their car inched along and followed a queue of cars, Solange succumbed to tiredness. She drifted in and out of sleep and was roused by the feeling of brakes being slammed. Alarmed, she sat up just in time to see their car sliding towards a high embankment of the side of the road. She turned her head away in fear as the embankment drew closer. As she turned towards Ali, she caught sight of the grim expression of powerful concentration on his face. Once the car slid to a halt, silence filled the interior of the car.

"Are you okay?" Ali shot a questioning look at Solange as she sat frozen in her seat.

"Yes," she replied. "Just a little shaken. How about you?"

"I'm just pissed. I hope that there isn't too much damage to your car." With barely controlled anger, Ali unbuckled his seat belt and, after grabbing a flashlight out of the glove compartment, he ordered tersely, "Sit tight."

Solange watched Ali walk gingerly around the periphery of the car, shining the flashlight up and down the car body. Then he walked back to the driver's side. He stomped his feet on the ground outside, shaking off the snow, and climbed back into the cab of the car. "I don't see much damage. It looks like the bumper on the back side where it collided has a dent, but everything else looks all right." Looking deeply into her eyes he said, "I'm sorry, Solange. I'll pay the insurance deductible to have your car fixed."

"This isn't your fault, Ali. It's just circumstances." Then looking around in the darkness she exclaimed, "Where are we? And why are no other cars around?"

"We finished the detour and I turned off I-95 to merge onto exit 74."

"That was the right way," she said. "But I've never seen this terrain before."

"I headed toward Fallston and then right to Hess," Ali said.

Solange gave Ali a look of exasperation. "You weren't supposed to take a right." She pointed to the map and said, "It shows you right here, Ali, You should have taken a left. That would have led you right to Fox Run. Can't you read a map?"

Ali bristled. "Yes, I can read a map. Maybe if I had a little help instead of a sleeping partner, I wouldn't have gotten turned around," he said, his tone laced with sarcasm.

"Well excuse me, Ali, but we've driven to my parents' house enough times that I didn't think you'd need my constant supervision to get us there. We'll have to double back to Fallston." Looking at his tired eyes, she felt some of her anger diffuse. "Do you want me to drive?"

"No, I prefer to arrive alive," he said sardonically.

Huffilly, Solange turned her head to stare out the window at the bleak darkness.

Ali turned the key in the ignition and put the car in reverse. The spinning of the tires as it hugged the embankment enraged him.

"If you keep doing that, you're going to flood it and we'll be stranded for sure," she said after the third try.

"Get in the driver's seat. I need to give us a push. Put the car in neutral and when I tell you, give it a little gas," Ali said shortly.

Staring into Ali's angry eyes that looked like crimson flames she mutely shook her head in agreement. As she took her place behind the wheel, neither spoke.

Solange let down her window so she could hear Ali's instructions. She cranked the car and put it in neutral. Then steadily she eased onto the gas. The car lurched forward, fishtailed and she gave it more gas spewing up pieces of snow and ice. She looked into the rearview mirror and saw a flurry of snow and ice spewing from under her tires and then she saw Ali go down. Frightened, Solange hurriedly put the car into park. She bounded out of the car and ran towards Ali. "Are you okay?"

"Yes," he grunted as he picked himself off the ground.

All of a sudden, Solange couldn't contain her laughter. Ali had patches of snow on his cheeks, forehead, and nose from when he'd hit the ground.

He glared at her while she laughed and then suddenly she sobered and lovingly wiped his face with her gloved hands. "I'm sorry I was cross with you, Ali."

"And I'm sorry I got us lost, Solange. Now let's get going before your family sends out a search party for us."

"I'll text message them and tell them that we should be there within the next hour."

"Good," he said quietly.

The minute Ali shut the car engine off, the front door of her parents' house was flung open. Light from inside the house cast a glow over her mother as she stood in the open doorway. A lump rose in Solange's throat when she saw that her mother's lips were pursed in concern. She knew that her mother had been on pins and needles waiting for their arrival.

"Go and greet your mother. I'll get our stuff," Ali softly ordered.

Solange opened her door and strode purposefully up the front walk. When she reached Claire Montgomery, she wrapped her arms around her and gave her a warm hug. Her mother's arms automatically went around her, and they held each other close. Then Solange felt her mother kiss the top of her head. Brushing away tears, Solange stepped back. "I'm so happy to see you, Mom."

"Me, too. Your dad and I have been looking for you and Ali since morning."

"But I told you that we wouldn't be getting here until this evening. Ali had to work half a day."

"I know, but it's after eleven o'clock. It's only a three-hour drive at the most. What took you so long?"

Solange hesitated. "The traffic was horrible, and we had to take a detour off the main road. Where's Dad?"

"I'm right here." Solange grinned at the sight of her dad dressed in a plaid nightshirt that had obviously been a gift from her mother. That had to be the only reason why he wore it, she mused.

"I had to put another log on the fireplace before my fire went out. I'll have to wait to give you a hug because I'm going to help Ali get your belongings out of the car."

As Frank Montgomery passed her, with a smile he pinched his daughter's cheek.

"I see Daddy hasn't changed at all."

Claire gave Solange a soft smile. "No, he's still the same. He's a man of few words. He lets his actions speak for him." She looked at Ali as he closed the trunk of her car. "So I see you and Ali are still going strong. Is everything going okay?" Claire watched her daughter closely.

"More than okay," she whispered. "We're getting married, but don't say anything to anyone. I think that Ali wants us to make an announcement or something."

"Oh, my God! I didn't think you'd ever get married," Claire whispered in response.

"He's everything that I want in a man. I am truly happy," Solange replied with satisfaction.

"What are you two whispering about?" Frank asked when he reached them.

Winking at her mother Solange grinned. "Oh, I'm just telling Mom how ridiculous you look in that nightshirt."

Frank blustered as he walked past them into the house. "I think you have a lot of nerve, young lady. Your mother bought this for me. I only hope that if you ever get married," then he slid Ali a backwards look, "you take as good care of him as your mother does me."

"I could only try," she whispered and watched Ali as he followed her dad into the house.

Solange had just left the shower, and after wrapping the towel around her, emerged from the bathroom. She was startled to see her mother sitting on the bed. "Mom! You scared me."

Claire's eyes twinkled. "I know you weren't expecting Ali, were you?"

"Of course not," Solange scoffed. "You and Dad won't let us stay in the same bedroom because we're not married. I know it's cold outside, but I don't think that it's cold enough for hell to freeze over."

"Well, it won't be long now before the two of you can share the same room."

"Where did you put Ali?"

"Outside in our make-believe barn," Clair teased. "No, I put him in the guest room at the foot of the stairs. He'll be bunking with your cousin Rufus tomorrow night."

Solange rolled her eyes. "Oh joy. You invited Rufus. You know how much he gets on my nerves."

Claire corrected her. "He invited himself. Now don't go acting funny about him. With the way the two of you used to play together as children, you should be used to him by now."

"Well, we're not children anymore. And every time I see him he says something really inappropriate. What happened to his wife, Lucy? I take is that she isn't coming since he's rooming with Ali."

"No, she flew to California to be with her family. Rufus had to work today so he's coming tomorrow."

"If he gets on my nerves I'm going to let him have it," Solange said and gave her mother a meaningful look.

"Be nice," Claire said. "This is still your home, and you know how you're supposed to treat company."

Solange's answered her mother with another eye roll.

Claire continued as if she hadn't seen it. "You cousin Rosemary and her family will be here in the morning."

At that news Solange's expression brightened. "That's great. I haven't seen Rosemary in ages. Is she still living outside of D.C.?"

"Yes, but she said she wants to move to a more rural place. She doesn't want to raise her children in the city."

"Then she should move back here to Fox Run. It's less than an hour drive from D.C. so you can still get all the culture, but you're in a suburban environment. I think it's a good place to raise children."

"How about White Plains? Are you and Ali going to stay there?"

A bemused sort of look crossed Solange's face at the thought of having Ali's children.

"I don't know. I haven't really thought about it."

"Well, you better start thinking about it." Her mother's face grew pensive. "There's no need to rush and get married unless you plan on having children. You're still young, have a career, and could travel the world. The only real reason for giving that up is the thought of bringing a human being into the world that might be the blessing that you have been to me and your father. Your presence saved our marriage. We wanted to keep the family together and we worked through our difficulties in order to give you the kind of home life that neither of us had."

"Ali and I aren't like that. We don't need anyone else to hold us together. We're best friends and share everything. We enjoy doing the same things, so that means we don't need anyone else to bring into our fold." She gave her mother a gentle look, hoping she understood what she was saying. "One day I'm sure we'll have a child. But that would be an appendage, not a lifeline."

He mother nodded her head understandingly and patted Solange's hand. "I hope that things remain that way. Time has a way of changing people." Then without saying any more she rose from the bed and walked to the door. Once she got there, she turned and blew Solange a kiss before leaving.

Solange snuggled under the covers, warding off the somewhat chilly air. *I know Ali and he knows me. What you see is what you get with us.*

The next morning, Solange entered the kitchen to see her dad turning sausage in a pan while her mother stood at the counter stuffing a turkey. "Good morning." She leaned over and planted a big kiss on his cheek and then her mother's.

"Good morning, sleepyhead." Her dad smiled and the lines of age made his eyes crinkle.

"Look who's talking about being a sleepyhead. Last night after you dropped my stuff off in the room, you took out of there like the devil was on your heels."

Frank nodded his head in agreement. "I know, but I was more than ready for bed. I'd been up since three-thirty yesterday morning."

"Why?" Solange asked as she poured herself a cup of coffee and stared out the kitchen window. Sometime during the night a fresh snow had fallen and there were icicles hanging from trees and her car was covered with snow.

"I had a load to deliver from my truck and I figured the sooner I left and got it done, the sooner I could get back home."

"Are you off for a couple of days?"

"Yes, I'm not going back until Monday."

"I thought that you were going to ease your workload this year."

Frank sighed resignation. "I didn't have to purposefully do it. With the price of gas the way it is, it's practically crippling all truck drivers. I only make local runs now, but I did yesterday's run for a friend of mine. He had to go out of town for a funeral and he really couldn't afford to lose the money. I took it so that he could go and be with his wife's family in their time of need."

"You're a good man, Daddy."

"I try to be." He put a plate of grits, bacon, sausage and eggs in front of her. "Eat up, you're too thin," he said in a gruff tone.

She laughed, picked up a piece of bacon and bit off of a piece. "Thin is in. Didn't you know that?"

"Well I think too thin is a sin and I won't have my daughter wasting away. I hope Ali isn't encouraging you to diet. Do Arab men like anorexic-looking females? If that's the case, you ought to leave him."

Solange's and her mother's eyes met across the expanse of the kitchen. "Ali likes me just the way I am, Daddy."

Just then Ali walked into the room. "I sure do," he said and bent over and kissed Solange lightly on the mouth. "I missed the lead in to that conversation. What'd I miss?"

"Nothing, dear," Claire hurriedly said. "Would you like a cup of coffee?"

"Sure, Mrs. Montgomery. But I can get it."

"No, I'll fix it for you. How do you like it?"

"Black."

"Just how he likes his women, right," Solange said with a teasing lilt to her voice.

"That's right," Ali said.

Just as they were all finishing breakfast, the sound of the doorbell ringing roused Solange from her seat. "I hope that's Rosemary."

Next Ali, Claire and Frank heard her scream, "It is!"

"I'll wait until they make it in here," Claire Montgomery said dryly. "Maybe the high-pitched screams will have died down."

Less than a minute later, Ali watched Solange reenter the kitchen with a baby girl in her arms, followed by a twenty-something woman.

Crossing over to her surrogate parents, Rosemary held her arms wide and flashed a bright smile. "Hi, Aunt Claire and Uncle Frank. It's so nice to see you."

They had a group hug and after a moment they broke apart. "Your baby is absolutely beautiful," Claire said.

"I know I'm supposed to say, 'Really?' but I can't. My Tiana *is* absolutely beautiful," Rosemary replied.

"Didn't you bring your husband with you?"

"No, he had to work today. You know Federal Express never really closes. At least not for managers."

"Oh, that's too bad. I haven't seen Willie since the wedding."

"I know," Rosemary said, sinking down onto a chair. Then she looked at Ali. "You're new."

Everyone in the room broke into laughter and the baby started mimicking them by also laughing. Once the antics had stopped, Solange sobered enough to respond to her cousin, "Ali's not new. You're old. Girl, I've been going with him for years."

"Well, blow me down," Rosemary said as she shrugged out of her coat. "You know there's an elephant in the room." She looked at her aunt and uncle and gave them a stern look. "Why didn't you tell me that Solange is going with an Arab?"

"Rosemary, you are too crazy, girl," Solange said.

Rosemary stared at Ali's honey-brown skin, coal black eyes, straight nose, and black shiny hair. "Do you have a brother?" Then she added, "Just kidding. Sometimes America treats Arabs worse than black people. My life is hard enough as it is."

Solange said brusquely, "Don't start trying to bring up controversial topics. It's Thanksgiving, remember, celebration of that first time when American Indians and Pilgrims sat down and had a meal together."

"Yeah, and look what happened. I don't think I should eat at the table with your man, Ali. He might take my house and give me some glass beads for it."

A look of anger crossed Ali's face. Just as he opened his mouth to say something, Solange said, "That's enough fooling around, Rosemary."

Rosemary said, "I'm just yanking ya, man. I think you're absolutely dreamy." She gave him a suggestive wink.

Ali stared at Rosemary with deep concentration.

She'd seen that look on his face other times when he was meeting someone for the first time, and she knew that he was trying to figure out what Rosemary really thought of him.

"Mom, I blame all this on you for inviting Rosemary in the first place," Solange said to ease the tension that had suddenly filled the room.

"Where else did you think I was supposed to eat? It is Thanksgiving, after all," Rosemary drawled. Then she turned to Ali and said, "Where's your family?"

"I'm an only child," Ali replied with a hard inflection. "My mother is in Brooklyn and my dad died when I was a teenager."

Now all teasing was wiped off Rosemary's face and she spoke with deep sincerity. "I know how hard it is to lose a parent. Mine were killed when I was young, and thank God for my aunt and uncle here," she said. "They took me in and treated me like I was their own."

"They treated you better than they did me," Solange joked. "You didn't have to do chores the first three months that you lived here. I was beginning to feel like Cinderella."

"You are always bringing that up, Solange. We were just giving Rosemary a chance to get acclimated," Claire said.

"Humph, acclimated?" Solange said as she jostled Tiana on her hip. "She'd be on the phone talking to her friends and when either you or Daddy would drive up she'd hang up, turn the television off and stare vacantly into space."

Rosemary laughed and looked at her aunt. "She's right. I did do that. I was a real stinker."

"I think you still are," Ali said decisively.

Taken aback, at first Rosemary said nothing, but then she broke into a grin. "I like him. He's a quick thinker. Now I'm hungry, and I think Tiana's hungry, too." She looked at Solange as she went and grabbed a plate out of the cabinet to make herself some breakfast. Rosemary said, gesturing at her baby bag, "Her baby bottle is all ready for you to give it to her, Solange."

Shooting her mother an *I told you so* look, Solange reached down into the bag and pulled out a baby bottle.

# *CHAPTER 6*

"Mom, is there anything else that I can do to help?" Solange swung her head around and surveyed the dining room. She'd set the table and they were waiting for the food in the oven to finish cooking so they could eat and relax after a busy day.

"No," Claire Montgomery said. "I think that's about it. You and Rosemary have been a big help to me. Even though I had prepared a lot of the dishes last night and put them in the refrigerator, it's still hard to get them all cooked and synchronized so that everything is hot."

"Where is Rosemary?" she said. "She was here a minute ago."

"I think she went to put Tiana down for her nap."

"That baby is too spoiled," Solange said, clucking her tongue. "Someone has to hold her all the time or she hollers."

"Yours will probably be the same way, so hush your mouth. Mothers are always like that with their first. And if that first is the only one that they have, Good Lordy!" she teased.

"All right, all right, Mom. I get the message."

"Where in the world are Ali and Dad?"

"I think they went to clean up after they shoveled the driveway and cleaned the snow off our cars."

Solange turned to her mother with an earnest look on her face. "You like him, don't you, Mom?"

"I absolutely adore him." Claire Montgomery's face grew pensive. "I didn't know if you were ever going to get married." Then she looked a little shamefaced. "I know that your father and I went through a really rough patch when you were growing up and I thought that maybe I should leave, for your sake, if not mine. But I stuck it out because I knew that the problems that we were having could be overcome. Your dad lost his job, and it made him feel less than a man. The fact that he had to go to the employment office, well, it was very humiliating for him."

"I don't know why people are embarrassed to go to the employment office. That's what it's there for."

"I know. Our lowest point was when we had to apply for food stamps. That made things worse, and he took that really hard. He'd worked steadily for years and put money in the system, so the money that he was getting from the government was only a fraction of what he'd paid out.

"Then his only brother, Trenton, was killed in a street fight. Your dad started drinking heavily and things got worse. He was supposed to pick you up after school because the bus didn't come this way. This one day when he didn't show, you got tired of waiting and began to walk home.

"I got home from work, and it was after dark, and he was on his way out to look for you. We went everywhere and couldn't find you so we finally gave up and came home to call the police station, but when we got home, you were here. Your dad tried to apologize to you, yet you said nothing. You just stared at him for a very long minute and then went to your room. That's the last day he had a drink. That's why I always say that you saved our marriage, because I was at my wits' end and ready to throw in the towel," Claire said quietly.

"I respect the fact that he was able to quit like that. Some people never get it together," Solange said slowly.

"He's a strong man. Your dad got a break and got a job and things started getting back to normal. Once we were caught up on our bills, I insisted on two things from him. That we go to church as a family, instead of him staying home on Sundays to watch a football or basketball game, and that also we get couples therapy. That was a big thing back then. When your dad's friends found out that we were going, they tried to make him feel like it was a joke. Some of those same men are divorced today and not laughing."

"I hear you. People always laugh at what they don't understand," Solange said. She walked over to her mother and laid her head on her shoulder. "I'm glad that you stuck it out. I hardly remember the bad times because so many good times erased them."

All of a sudden the large thud sound of a snowball hitting the window made them go to the door. Rosemary was standing in knee high snow laughing with another snowball in her hand.

"You better not break my window, Rosemary," Claire warned. "I'm going to make you pay for it if you do."

"Oh, Aunt Claire. Stop being such a spoilsport. Come outside and play."

"If I do that, who's going to rub my aching limbs next week?"

"Uncle Frank, of course," Rosemary said and chuckled.

"He has enough to do without me adding one more thing."

"Come on, Solange. Let's make snow angels," Rosemary whined.

"Rosemary's the only person I know that can make me do something like this at my age," Solange said as she grabbed her coat.

Once Solange got outside, she pulled the hood of her parka over her head. As she was doing so, Rosemary hit her with a snowball and then ran to the bottom of the driveway.

Solange bent down and grabbed a huge ball of snow and, after molding it into the facsimile of a baseball, ran after Rosemary, cornered her by the snow-covered hedges that flanked the driveway and hit her upside the head with the snowball. After that they began to wrestle. Falling to the ground, winded, they just stared up at the crisp blue sky.

"You know, Rosemary," Solange gasped, "I'm really out of shape. I can't believe I'm tired from that."

"You're not out of shape," Rosemary replied vehemently. "When you greeted me at the door this morning that's the first thing I noticed. I said to myself, cuz still has that flat stomach and big-ass booty."

"Thanks, I guess," Solange retorted dryly. Then Solange spread her arms out and moved her hands and feet in the snow until there was an imprint of a snow angel. Then she sat up and said, "What do you think of Ali?"

Rosemary's expression became contemplative and Solange could see that she was choosing her next words wisely. "I like him. And I do think that he's drop-dead gorgeous. I'm really surprised that you hooked up with him. You've always been about the brothers."

"I know," Solange said, sitting up. "It wasn't intended or anything. I mean I didn't go on Match.com or eHarmony and fill out a form that I wanted to date an Arab."

"I'm sure that you didn't," Rosemary declared emphatically. "I'm just surprised that when he asked you out, and I know that's the way that it happened, that you accepted."

"I was on the train going to New York. I had been living in White Plains for three months and not one man had approached me or asked me out on a date."

"That's because you're so intimidating. You're beautiful and they probably already figured that you had someone. Remember when we'd go out to parties before you went away to school, no guy would ask you to dance?"

"I know," Solange replied resentfully. "That's pretty much why I quit going."

"The reason they didn't ask you was because they thought it was a waste of time. You look like too much work. Instead they'd go for the easier conquest."

"I should take that as a compliment, but I don't. Ali really had to work to get a date with me, and I appreciated the effort. For months we just hung out as friends. He showed me around Manhattan and we did tourist things and all the time I was getting to know him. The more time I spent with him, the better I liked him. And then we just sort of gravitated into a sexual relationship."

Rosemary laughed. "You didn't sort of gravitate. He'd planned that from the moment he saw you."

"I'm sure that he did," Solange acknowledged with a smile. "But I still value the fact that he gave me the time that I needed to feel comfortable with him."

"It's obvious that you two are really in love and I'm happy for you. But since," she slid her eyes away from her, "you know, since the war with Iraq, hatred of Arabs and Muslims in general is on the rise."

"I think not so much since Obama became president, but I do know what you mean. Sometimes when he and I are on the subway in New York, I catch people staring at him as if he's something to be feared. And the crazy part is you should see how those people look. I really do fear sitting near them."

"That makes sense. People don't always see themselves as others see them. I just hope that you know what you're doing." Rosemary screwed up her face. "I mean, even in our own family, I'm sure that there will be comments."

"I better not hear it," Solange said in a menacing tone. "If I hear one negative word about my man, I'm going to get them straight. Now let's go into the house, my big ass is cold."

The tinkling sound of Rosemary's laugh followed Solange up the driveway.

The flames licked logs in the fireplace and cast a warm glow in the room. Frank and Ali sat sipping brandy companionably sat in overstuffed chairs that flanked a large brown wooden coffee table. Deliberately putting his glass on a coaster, Ali looked directly at his future father-in-law. "I want you to know that I'm very much in love with your daughter," he said quietly.

Frank said nothing. He just sat and waited for Ali's next words.

"I am asking you for her hand in marriage."

Frank gave Ali a penetrating look. "Solange is an adult. She can do whatever she wants without my permission," he said.

Ali nodded his head in agreement. "But we want your blessing."

Frank Montgomery cleared his throat. "Marriage is hard. And in today's time, I think it's even harder to stay married because it's so easy to get out of. Back in the day, people worked things out because they thought they had to and sometimes that was the best thing to do," Frank said. "How about children?"

"We're in no rush. But we want them."

"How would they be raised?"

"What do you mean?"

"Christian or Muslim?"

"I've attended church services with Solange and have no problem with our children being raised in whatever religion she feels is best for our children."

Frank drained his glass of brandy and set it down on the end table. "If you marry my daughter, I have expectations of you. I don't want you cheating on her or taking her for granted."

Ali nodded his head in agreement. "Obviously I don't think that will be a problem."

"In the beginning of a marriage, no one ever does," Frank retorted in a forthright manner. "Also, if you are going to be the head of household, that includes making decisions about the unpleasant things as well as the easy ones."

"I agree," Ali responded.

"Ali, if you don't think that you can enhance her life, then don't marry her. But if you think that you can be there for her and make her happy, then you have my blessing."

Ali stared Frank squarely in the face. "I wouldn't marry her if I didn't think that I could do that."

Frank took a long look at Ali. He eyes started at the tip of his head and slowly moved down to his feet. Then he looked at him and said quietly, "Then you have my blessing. You may marry my daughter."

Ali and Frank entered the kitchen just as Rosemary and Solange were hanging their coats on the rack next to the door. Solange looked questioning at Ali and he gave an imperceptible nod of agreement. A slow smile of immense happiness crossed Solange's face and Rosemary intercepted it.

"What? What happened? What's going on?"

Solange walked over to Ali and slid her arm around his waist and he put his arm around her shoulder.

"I asked Mr. Montgomery if I can marry Solange and he said yes," Ali announced.

Claire smiled. "Welcome to the family, Ali. But I don't think you need to call us Mr. and Mrs. Montgomery now, since you're going to be family."

"How about Mom and Dad?"

"That works for me," Frank replied evenly.

"I want to be matron of honor," Rosemary said.

There was a taut silence in the room before Solange said, "I've already asked Grace to do it, but I have a premier spot for you to be my number one bridesmaid."

"Okay," Rosemary said, dragging out the words. "If that's the best you can do for me, I'll guess I'll have to accept that." Then before anyone could comment she looked around pointedly and asked, "Where the hell is Rufus? I'm starving. We don't have to wait for that slowpoke, do we? I mean, that's what microwaves are for."

"I guess we should sit down and eat. It's getting to be late afternoon," Claire said.

"I'm going to go and check on Tiana and then I'll be right back." As Rosemary left the room, the telephone rang.

Frank answered it. Solange and her mother were placing portions of their dinner in bowls and taking them into the dining room, but Claire stopped when she saw the furrow of irritation settle on her husband's brow.

"I'll be right there," he said sharply before hanging up the phone.

"What's wrong?" Solange asked her dad while Ali stood waiting to hear what was going on.

"Rufus is in jail. He was arrested for having an open container and driving with a suspended license. I need to go down there and see what's going on."

"See, Mom," Solange said testily. "I told you that you shouldn't have invited him."

"Oh, dear," Claire exclaimed, clearly agitated.

"I'll go with you," Ali said.

Frank gave Ali a pensive look. "Rufus said that they're going to keep him overnight."

"Maybe yes, maybe no," Ali responded in a non-committal tone. Then he looked at Claire. "Don't wait on us for dinner. You guys have worked hard all morning, so enjoy your meal. We'll be back as soon as we can."

Rosemary had rejoined them just at the end of the conversation, jostling Tiana on her hip. "I guess Ali might be useful to have around after all," she said, trying to lighten the atmosphere as she watched Frank and Ali's retreating backs.

The women were cleaning up the kitchen when they heard three car doors close. Looking out the window, Solange drew in a sigh of relief when she spotted her fiancée, father, and Rufus stomping up the driveway. "I'll fix a plate for Ali and Mom you can fix one for Daddy. Lucky Rosemary, you get Rufus's if we decide to let him eat," she added sarcastically.

"Be nice," Claire instructed as she opened the back door and let them in out of the cold.

Before anyone could say anything Rosemary asked, "What happened?"

Ignoring her, Rufus gave his aunt a guilty look and then a big bear hug. Then he did the same for Solange and Rosemary. "Sorry to mess up the family dinner, but at least I got to meet my future cousin-in-law. He sure came in handy down there."

"You got lucky today, boy," Frank said tersely as he washed his hands. "But you won't always be able to count on that. Why don't you just try not breaking the law?"

"Come on, uncle. I already explained to you and Ali at the police station what happened."

Solange watched Ali as he took his turn at the sink and gave him a grateful smile. "Thank you for going with Daddy."

"If it wasn't for him, Rufus would still be locked up," her dad said before digging into the plate of turkey, stuffing, green beans and mashed potatoes set before him.

"This is my family. I aim to please," Ali said before touching the tip of Solange's nose with his forefinger and sitting down in the chair next to Solange's father.

"We still don't know what happened," Rosemary demanded in a frustrated tone.

Ali didn't answer. He just dug into the plate of food Solange placed in front of him.

Rufus leaned against the counter watching Rosemary fix his plate. "I was driving with a group of cars. All of a sudden this state trooper comes out of nowhere and pulls me over. I asked him why he'd pulled me over and no one else and he said I was speeding." Rufus held his finger up. "Now mind you, I wasn't in the front or the back of the group. This cop practically crashes into other cars trying to get to me."

"I believe you, man," Rosemary piped in. "That's racism. And it happens all the time. Cops are always picking on black people." Then she gave Ali an awkward look. "I'm sorry, but it's true."

Before Ali could respond, Rufus said, "Ali, you know what I'm saying is right, don't you? I mean after all, you're an Arab. Normally, I wouldn't be gung-ho about cuz here marrying a foreigner, but in today's world we need an edge and we minorities need to stick together."

"Ali is not a foreigner. He's Arab-American, dumbass," she said frostily.

"Not to them, he isn't. He's just a plain old Arab like I'm a plain old black man that they decided to lock up. But because he's a cop he was able to pull some strings to get me out of there. If it wasn't for Ali, I'd have to spend the night in jail with common criminals." Before he sat down at the table he looked at Rosemary. "Give me more stuffing than that, please," he said.

Ali spoke in a measured tone. "I don't think that it's the state trooper's fault that you had an open container of beer and a suspended license."

Rufus pointed his index finger at his chest. "But my point is if he hadn't stopped me in the first place, he wouldn't have even known that. It's a clear-cut case of racial profiling."

"Why is your license suspended?" Claire asked in a scolding tone.

Rufus shrugged his shoulders. "I had a ticket I forgot to pay. Then they added all these fees to it and I just hadn't gotten around to taking care of it." He added defensively, "I work long hours and by the time I get off everything's closed. You know those city employees go home at six o'clock on the dot. They don't mess around."

"If you knew you were driving with a suspended license, why in the world would you speed and attract attention to yourself?" Solange asked.

Rufus spoke to Solange as if she was a young child. "I already told you that I was moving with the traffic."

She retorted in the same manner. "How about drinking and driving?"

"I wanted to stop and have a drink, but knew that I had to hurry up and get here because everyone would be waiting for me. Besides, I only had one beer and passed the DUI test."

"Oh, my God! Rufus, you've haven't changed since we were children."

"Neither have you," he charged. "You always have been too judgmental. Are you sure that you want to marry her?"

"I'm positive," Ali said without hesitation.

"I mean, Solange is a little overbearing and it's always been her way or the highway. Be careful or she'll be wearing the pants."

Ali replied sternly, not caring for the reference to his manhood. "That's the last thing I'm worried about."

"That's right," she said, ticked off by Rufus's statement that she was overbearing. "Rufus, why don't you hit the highway? Oh, that's right, you can't because you don't have a driver's license. And I'm pretty sure that they impounded your car. Oh, no, wait a minute, let me pull up your pants leg and see if they have an ankle bracelet on you."

Rosemary broke into laughter following that exchange. "You guys bicker the same way you did when you were growing up. I hate to miss any of this, but I hear Tiana crying." Grabbing a bottle out of the refrigerator she shook it. "I bet she's hungry."

A long silence filled the kitchen and then Solange and Rufus's eyes locked and simultaneously they broke into laughter, too.

After Solange and Ali said goodbye to her parents, Ali drove the Cadillac down the street. After about twenty minutes, he sat at a four-way intersection and studied the map on the GPS. "Take a left," she said mildly.

Turning left, Ali slid a look at Solange. "Well, that was an interesting couple of days."

"It was. My family likes you," she stated with satisfaction.

"Ahh, they tolerate me," Ali corrected her.

"After they get to know you better, they'll love you just as much as I do," she said dropping her hand down between his legs. She cupped his manhood and found that it was rock hard.

Ali gave Solange a look filled with sexual yearning, "I can't wait to get you home."

"That makes two of us," she replied. "I noticed you and Rufus seemed to be doing a little male bonding today. Why don't you ask him to be one of your groomsmen? Now that Rosemary's going to be in the wedding, we need another male to even things up."

"Let's not and say we did," Ali quickly answered. When he saw the sharp look Solange gave him, he explained. "I mean, I was thinking the same thing, but I want to ask Randolph to be Rosemary's partner."

"I hadn't thought of him, but that's a really good idea," she answered sleepily before she drifted off.

# *CHAPTER 7*

Ali Marks sat in the waiting room of Internal Affairs. He sneaked a look at his watch, hoping the receptionist didn't see his impatience. Ali fumed but determined not to lose his discomfiture, he channeled his thoughts of something more pleasant. An image of Solange emerging from the shower floated to his consciousness and he didn't realize it, but the receptionist saw the sly smile that formed on his lips.

Suddenly, the office door opened and in walked Franklin Petty. His crisp white shirt was starched to perfection and his navy blue slacks and tie made him appear as if he was more concerned with appearances than product.

Petty walked over to the receptionist and after Ali heard her murmur something unintelligible, Franklin looked over at where Ali sat and crossed over to him with his hand extended.

Ali rose to his feet. Towering over Petty, he easily shook his hand.

Franklin released Ali's hand and stepped back, putting some distance between them. He cleared his throat. "I'm sorry to keep you waiting, but something came up and I had to attend to it right away."

"No problem." Ali's response was short and businesslike.

"Let's step into my office," Petty said as he led the way through a door past the receptionist's desk.

As Ali strode past the pretty blonde, he saw her give him a quick once-over. His lips twitched in amusement.

Once inside Petty gestured to the chair that was positioned in front of his desk. Ali eased his long frame into it gingerly, barely fitting the narrow chair.

Franklin Petty picked up a folder from his desk, turned it around and opened it. "You've been cleared of all charges. I need you to write your name and then sign below it."

Ali gave a start of surprise.

"Because your partner and another policeman were in danger, you had no recourse but to take the action that you did." Petty's tone was undecipherable, but his nostrils flared in annoyance.

Ali slowly took the folder from him and scanned the contents. He felt a sudden relief flood throughout his body and weeks of worry melted away. Without looking up, he withdrew a pen from inside the jacket that he wore and sealed the deal with a flourish. Handing the folder back to Petty, Ali gave him a look of awareness. Yet his expression belied any knowledge that he realized that this was not Petty's doing, but someone else that had a higher pay grade than him. "When may I resume my duties?"

"Monday you'll be back with Vernon," Petty replied brusquely. "I heard that you're on the list to take the test to become a detective in January."

"Yes, sir," Ali replied briefly.

"Try not to do anything daring until then, you'll be better off." Then Petty picked up his telephone receiver and started punching numbers.

Ali knew he was dismissed and, striding past the receptionist without looking at her, he left. Ali was silent until he got into the empty elevator. On his way down to the ground floor he said loudly and clearly, "Thank God!"

"Solange Montgomery here."

"What time are you getting off work?"

Solange smiled into the receiver. She hadn't heard this lilt in Ali's voice for too long a time. "When do you want me to get off from work?"

"I made eight o'clock reservations for us to have dinner at Nobu on Hudson Street."

"Wow! De Niro's Japanese Restaurant?"

"Sure. We can stay at my place tonight since neither of us has to work tomorrow."

"That sounds like a plan. Ali, that's some mighty fine dining you're treating me to," Solange breathed excitedly. "What's the occasion?"

"Well, we never really celebrated our engagement the way we should have. I always thought that when I got engaged, it would be something that I'd planned, instead of something that just sort of happened."

"So I guess you wanted to do the asking instead of being asked. I'm sorry if you think I took away your perfect engagement dream from you."

"No," Ali said, "that's not it. Your proposal was the biggest high of my life. Besides, you gave me an out." Ali chuckled. "After we're married if I ever mess up or something I can say, that's why I didn't propose, I'm such a loser."

"You could never be a loser, Ali. You're everything I've ever wanted in a man," she murmured into the receiver.

"And you're everything I ever wanted in a woman. It's just that you still don't have your ring or anything, and I want to do something special for you."

"You are something special, Ali. Don't you know that?"

"I know you make me feel that way. No woman in my life other than my mother has been able to make me feel as wanted as you do. Also, I have some other news."

"What is it?" Solange crossed her fingers, waiting for the news she'd been secretly praying about for the last several weeks.

"Internal Affairs has cleared me of all charges and on Monday I get to go back on patrol with Randolph."

"I knew that everything would be okay, honey. All you had to do was be patient and wait."

"Well, you had more faith in the system than I did," Ali admitted.

"I didn't have the faith in the system. My faith was in you. You saved two lives. They ought to give you a medal."

"Now that's a bit of a stretch, isn't it?"

"Not to me," Solange responded with feeling.

"Can you be in the city by seven o'clock?"

"Can you pick me up at the station at seven-thirty?"
"Sure can," Ali said.

Solange stood naked in front of her full-length mirror and assessed her body. She had buffed and oiled herself from head to toe and, after grabbing a bottle of Clean by Provence, she sprayed her neck, pulse area, stomach, and the inside of her thighs. Then she grabbed a lace thong, quickly slid it on and donned a matching black bra. Crossing over to the closet, she eyed its contents critically.

Reaching her hand way into the back of her closet, she withdrew a black cashmere knit dress that fell below her knees. Pulling it over her head, Solange was barely able to fit into the dress. As she stood again in front of the mirror and looked at herself from every angle, she shrugged her shoulders.

Solange quickly added moisturizer to her face and, after lightly applying her makeup, she grabbed her pocketbook and coat to embark on her ride to the parking garage near the train station.

As the train ground to a halt, Solange took her gloved hand and wiped it across the frosted mirror, peering into the darkness. Her heart did a flip-flop when she spied Ali standing in the light under a lamp post. He wore a long wool black overcoat with a red muffler tied around his neck. His black hair glistened in the light and she was overcome with a sense of love as she watched him anxiously survey the train windows, hoping to lock in the location of where she was seated. Once the motion of the train car ended, through the glass their eyes locked.

Quickly Solange stood and reached into the unoccupied seat next to her, she grabbed her overnight case. Following the queue of people who were completely silent, she gingerly descended the train steps to be folded into her fiancé's warm embrace.

After Ali released her, he took his hands and turned up the lapels of her coat around her neck. "You should have worn a hat," Ali chided her. "It's freezing out here."

"I know," she replied with a whimsical smile, "but I didn't want to mess my hair up for our big date."

Ali took her overnight case from her and grabbing her hand. "Let me hurry up and get you out of the cold. I don't want my baby getting sick."

Solange held Ali's hand tightly and almost had to skip to keep up with his long strides. Looking back and seeing her struggle, he slowed his gait to match hers.

Once seated in Ali's warm SUV, Solange looked at her watch and said, "How long do you think it will take us to get to the restaurant?"

"It's about a twenty-minute ride."

"Good, I'm starving."

"Me, too," Ali said suggestively and let his eyes drop down to the rise and fall of Solange's breast underneath her overcoat.

Traffic was unusually sparse for a Friday evening and required little concentration on Ali's part as he navigated the SUV through the New York City streets.

Placing her hand on Ali's thigh, Solange said, "Every time I ride the train, I reminisce about how we first met."

"Is that a good memory?"

"Of course it is, silly. That's the night my world changed."

Ali grinned. "Let's just say, you warmed up to me. In the beginning I didn't think that I had a chance."

"In the beginning, you didn't," Solange agreed.

"I'd been trying to catch your eye the whole trip into the city, but you didn't even notice me."

"I felt you staring," Solange disagreed. "But just because a man is looking at you, I don't think that it means that he wants to ask you out."

"I had been sitting there trying to figure out how to get your attention. Even though I checked out your ring finger and saw that it was bare, I still figured out you had someone."

"I hadn't even had a date since I had moved from Atlanta. But I wasn't interested in dating at all. My plate was quite full with my new job."

"You were so into your novel, I had to wait until you got off the train and pretend as if that was my stop, too."

"I remember what I was reading, too, because I loved it so much. It was *Never Say Never* by Michele Cameron. It's based on an interracial love story. Maybe that's why I was open to being approached by a man outside my race. That book had me all primed. The main character is black and her love interest is white."

"Then why did you scream when I touched your arm after we got off the train?"

"Hello," she held her hands out, palms up. "I don't like being stalked. A friend of mine went through that in college and even after the culprit was arrested, she felt traumatized for a long time."

"I'm not a mad stalker, Solange. I just stalked you."

"And it's not my practice to pick men up on a train."

"It'd better not be your practice."

"Ali, not that we ever would break up, but just for the sake of argument, say we did. I would never give another man I met on a train my phone number. I mean, what's the point? What are the chances of a man and woman meeting on a train, falling in love and getting married? I mean, lightning never strikes twice in the same place, does it?"

"Not that I know of."

They were seated at a traffic light and their attention was drawn to a commotion on a street corner. There were five cop cars flashing their strobe lights. On the sidewalk stood two black men standing handcuffed, staring at the ground, and another, also black, was handcuffed and face down on the ground. At the sight, a knot of fury curled inside Solange's stomach. "Does it take ten cops to subdue three men? I mean to me, that seems a little over the top."

Ali replied shortly, "We don't know the circumstances. Some are probably just for backup to protect their partners."

"I guess those men are the only ones in New York committing crimes tonight," Solange said in a harsh tone. Then she turned her head to glare out the window.

Ali didn't respond but an undercurrent of tenseness that wasn't there before filled the car.

Once they reached Nobu, Ali parked the car. After he cut the engine off, he stared at the profile that had been turned from him the last ten minutes of their ride. "Are you going to let that spoil our night?"

His remark was met with silence. He said, "That scenario has nothing to do with us and what we are to each other." Then abruptly Ali unbuckled his seat belt and climbed out of the car.

A feeling of contrition now battled with the one she had of anger. After her car door was held open for her, she climbed out of the SUV. Once she stood next to Ali, she slid her hand in his and held it tightly as they walked the short way to the restaurant.

Once inside the restaurant, her attention was immediately drawn to the elegant and rustic décor of the David Rockwell-designed interior. A beautiful young Japanese woman was standing behind a maple walnut counter to the right of the foyer. Behind her was an array of expensive coats. Suddenly Solange's heavy wool overcoat seemed to pale in comparison once in the same room as every style of mink imaginable. Then she mentally shook herself.

Ali motioned for her to turn around so he could help her out of her coat. As she did so she caught a glimpse of the owner walking down the corridor.

Turning excitedly to Ali she gasped. "I just saw De Niro walk by," she said.

He gave her a quizzical lift with his brow and replied in amusement. "He is co-owner of this restaurant, you know." Turning to the coat check girl he handed her their coats. "We're just on time for our reservations." He surveyed couples on standby for a table that flanked the chairs lined up against the wall and others that were sitting in a waiting area bar to the left. "I'm starving," he said.

"So am I," she murmured.

"Then let's go eat." Ali stepped aside for Solange to walk in front of him on their short journey to the next attending clerk, and as she strutted, she felt Ali's eyes on her derriere.

Solange stopped at the next podium. "I believe we have a reservation for Ali Marks."

Another beautiful woman, this time African-American, spoke with an English accent. "Your table is ready and waiting. Enjoy your meal," she said.

Once seated, Solange was glad to see that they had a corner table. "I like our seats," she complimented Ali. "How did you manage to cop one of these?"

"One of the waiters had a son that ended up in the precinct when I was on desk duty. He gave me a card and said if I ever needed a favor he could help me out."

A waiter appeared at their table and, after handing them menus, said, "My name is Jacques and I am your waiter for the evening. Would you like me to bring you anything to drink while you look at your menus?"

Ali looked at him and said without hesitation, "A bottle of your best white wine, please."

"You always know what I want." Solange smiled at Ali after the waiter Jacques left.

"I don't know what to order. I think I'll play it safe and get sushi," Solange said.

"I've heard that if you don't know what to get, they have a sample tray and that way you're sure to get something that you like."

Suddenly, Jacques reappeared at their table and asked, "Might I make a suggestion?"

"Please do," Solange said handing him the menu.

"We have what is called the *omakese.* The chef chooses your meal and he makes sure that there is something that will satisfy the novice eater of Japanese food or the veteran." Jacques pointed out a side of the menu to Ali. "These are the price ranges for the *omakeses.*"

"Money is no object," Ali said.

To this Solange raised her eyebrows.

Handing Jacques the menu he'd not even looked at, he said after a nod of agreement from Solange he said decisively, "We'll have that."

"Have you gotten a promotion that I don't know about?"

"If I had gotten a promotion, you'd be the first to know," he replied dryly. "I just wanted to do something special for you. I mean for us. While I was waiting for news from Internal Affairs, I wasn't in the best of moods and you were very supportive."

She held his gaze with hers. "I know how important your career is to you. Being under pressure at work can be a horrible thing. We work hard to get the job that we want and then it's even harder sometimes to keep it." She added almost musingly, "Then it can be yanked from you without a moment's notice." Solange added in a soul-searching tone, "I don't know what I would do if my career was suddenly taken for me. I hope I'm not shallow in thinking that I would feel incomplete without it."

"No, you're just being honest. You're a smart woman and there's nothing wrong with wanting to be a successful one at home and at work. People aren't one-dimensional, and most of the time it takes a combination of things to make a person really happy. Much as I love you, if I had been demoted, or even worse, lost my job, I would have a huge void in my life."

"But you don't have to worry about that, and now you're all set to take the next step."

An expression of apprehension crossed Ali's face.

"What is it? You're not worried about the test, are you?"

Ali started to say something, but then he stopped and only shrugged his shoulders nonchalantly.

"Ali," Solange said confidently. "You have nothing to worry about. I've met some of those detectives that you work with and if they can past the test, I know that you can."

"I'm not a good test taker," Ali said. "I've always had problems in that area. Vernon said that the test is really hard and he barely passed it."

"Then I'll prep you. What's the date of the test?"

"January second, the day after New Year's."

"For New Year's we'll stay home. That way you'll be fully rested for your test," Solange said decisively.

Ali took his hand and covered Solange's. "You're going to make a good wife."

"I'll do my best," she promised.

As seemed to be his manner, Jacques appeared out of nowhere. He took an array of dishes off a huge tray and the aroma of succulent juices floated to their nostrils. In the subdued lighting of the restaurant and because of the unfamiliarity of the dishes, Solange didn't know exactly what to try first.

"What you have before you are some of our house specials. Tiradito, white fish marinated in yuzu, with lemon juice and cilantro, our house sushi, and steamed vegetables. I will be back to check on you and if you do not like any of the dishes, I will replace it with something else," the waiter said.

Tentatively at first, Solange dug her fork into the whitefish. The smooth taste of the boneless fish as it dissolved in her mouth and practically slid down her throat made her eagerly reach for more. She nodded at Ali, who had been waiting for the verdict before trying anything. He then followed suit and rolled his eyes and murmured, "Umm. This is some good-tasting fish." When Jacques reappeared, Ali waved him away. "This fish tastes as good as sex," Ali teased.

"It'd better not," Solange warned. "And don't get too full or I'll get jealous. I really need you to want more fish tonight."

Ali broke into a raucous laughter, attracting the attention of couples in their vicinity.

"This is a four-star restaurant. You're supposed to be demur," she said to Ali.

"Any man in here would have reacted the same way if he knew what was in store for me later tonight."

They were finishing up the last of their bottle of wine and had declined dessert when suddenly the lights were dimmed and a spotlight was centered on a couple in the middle of the room. A hush fell as the people in the restaurant felt as if they were part of some drama unfolding. Everyone watched as the young man reached into his pocket and took a royal blue velvet box out of his coat jacket.

Guessing what it was, the woman clasped her hands excitedly and he spoke clearly enough for everyone to hear, "Ava, I love you more than words can say. Will you marry me?"

Tears were streaming down Ava's face and she held her hand out for him to place the ring on her finger. "Yes, Danforth. I will marry you." Then soft music floated in the air and they heard a haunting melody that sounded like the musical score from the movie *An Affair to Remember.*

The spotlight was taken off the couple and the people in the restaurant were allowed to resume whatever they were doing.

Jacques appeared with Ali's credit card, and, looking bored, he said, "I'm sorry about the wait, but we were asked to remain stationary until they were finished." He rolled his eyes and said, "That little drama is going to be a segment on another one of those tacky reality shows. They get a $100,000 wedding and they hardly even know each other."

Solange shook her head. "Really, how gauche."

"They need to save it for the divorce," Ali commented dryly.

Then Jacques lowered his voice. "Mr. De Niro had no idea until tonight that this was agreed to, and I think that heads are going to roll. He wants this place to remain upscale. This is his private project away from Hollywood and all the glitz."

"Then I'd hate to be the person that okayed it," Solange said with feeling.

They were on their way out of the restaurant when Solange paused. "I want to use the ladies' room before we hit the road."

"Okay, he said. "I'll wait for you in the foyer."

When Solange emerged from the cubicle and was at the counter washing her hands, she heard her name being called from behind. "Solange Montgomery. I can't believe it!"

Whipping around, Solange broke into a grin when she saw her college friend from Spellman, Isabel Collins. "Oh, my God, Isabel," she exclaimed and let herself be engulfed in a big bear hug. Finally breaking their embrace she asked, "Whatever are you doing here?"

"I'm throwing a function at the restaurant. I'm in the party planning business. Anything you want planned, I do it. Weddings, bat mitzvahs, funerals."

Grinning at her, Solange asked, "Do you live in New York now?"

Isabel made a snorting sound. "I sure do. I moved from Atlanta over a year ago. I couldn't believe how a city a large as Atlanta was that I kept running into my ex every time I turned around."

Solange's eyes opened wide. "Your ex? Do you mean you and Gerald broke up? I thought you two would be together forever."

"So did I. Every time I think about how faithful I was to him our whole time when I was at Spellman and there were all of those good men to choose from, I get pissed all over again. Well, you know what they say, hindsight is always better than foresight. I'll never date the same man for three years again without a ring. What's the point?" Then she looked speculatively at Solange. After a cursory look she asked, "What's going on with you?" Looking pointedly at her hand she said, "I see you're still single also."

Solange answered hesitantly because she didn't want to rub it in. "Actually I'm not. I recently got engaged. My fiancé brought me here as sort of a kind of engagement celebration."

A flash of jealousy crossed Isabel's face before her expression changed to one of obvious sincerity. "Congratulations, Solange. I wish you the best. I'm a little surprised, though, because in college you acted like you never would get married. You never even dated the same guy long enough to fall in love."

"Yeah, I was really gun-shy about the whole commitment thing, but Ali has changed that for me."

Sticking her hands under the water faucet and vigorously washing them, she asked, "What does he do?"

"He's a New York City policeman," Solange answered proudly. "Would you like to meet Ali? He's in the foyer waiting for me."

"Sure. Does he have a brother?" Isabel asked hopefully.

Solange grimaced. "I'm afraid not. He's an only child."

"You're lucky." Isabel added derisively, "One of the reasons Gerald and I broke up was because of his interfering, naggin'-ass family."

Solange's tinkling laughter floated through the air. "I am lucky. Ali's only family is his mother, and I absolutely adore her."

Once Solange spied Ali leaning on the wall in the foyer and crossed over him, she slid her hand in his, pulling him towards her. "Ali, this is a good friend of mine from college. Isabel, this is my fiancé, Ali."

Solange immediately realized that Isabel was taken aback by Ali. Recovering quickly, Isabel stuck out her hand. "It's so nice to meet you, Ali."

"Likewise," he answered smoothly, returning her handshake.

Solange proudly noted that Isabel's attention was arrested by Ali's carriage and intonation.

"Congratulations on your engagement," she murmured.

"Thank you. I'm a lucky man."

Isabel watched Ali slide Solange a look, and when their eyes connected she felt as if she was intruding on a very intimate moment.

Blinking, she turned to Solange, whipped a card out of her wallet and handed it to her. "We're in the banquet room in the back, which is probably why we didn't see each other at dinner. Call me soon and we'll do lunch."

Solange took the card and slid it into her coat pocket. "I will," she promised. After they hugged briefly, she watched Isabel scurry back into the restaurant. Turning to Ali she whispered, "Isabel's such a nice person. I hope one day she finds the happiness that I've been blessed with."

"It'll probably happen when she least expects it. I know that it did for me. We'd better get going because it's getting late."

On the way home in the car, Ali shot Solange a look in the dark recess of the car and made a reference to the antics at dinner. "I know that you wouldn't have wanted to be proposed to the way that couple did it, but don't you kind of wish that there had been more of a fanfare than what we had?"

"Well," she drawled, "I do kind of wish that you had proposed to me instead of the other way around. But just as long as we don't tell our children, it's okay with me."

# CHAPTER 8

When they entered Ali's apartment, Solange gave a slight shiver from the frosty air that enveloped the place.

"I've been on my landlord for weeks to check the heater and he hasn't done it yet." Ali stomped over to the thermostat against the wall and turned the knob. "I raised the temperature up to eighty-five. It ought to feel better in here soon."

"Eighty-five," she said, aghast. "That's way too hot."

Holding out his hand for her coat, he took it and hung it up next to his in the hallway closet.

"Not really. It will only feel like seventy regardless of where the dial is. I already have an electric blanket on the bed, so I'll go and turn that on, too."

While Ali walked the short distance to the bedroom, Solange surveyed the room. His apartment walls were stark with few paintings, but she noted as she walked into the kitchen area that everything was spotlessly clean. Opening the refrigerator, she spied an unopened package of bacon, sausage and a carton of eggs. She smiled wryly because she figured that he'd probably purchased those items that afternoon when they'd finalized plans to stay at his place for the night.

"It's warming up in here already," Ali murmured in her ear.

"I didn't know you were behind me," she breathed. "You walk as stealthily as a cat," she murmured, turning around to face him.

He took his hands and slid them down the long length of her body. "I love what you're wearing. When you took your coat off in the restaurant, I could have easily forgone dinner, brought you home and had my way with you."

Solange's heart did a flip-flop. "Well, you have me at your mercy now. Do with me what you will."

Ali gave Solange a look of intense passion and scooped her up into his strong arms. Turning towards the bedroom, he swiftly strode down the hallway, cradling her.

Solange buried her face in his chest, and the smell of Ali's signature cologne, Cool Water, wafted to her nostrils. She drew in a deep breath, loving the smell of him, and a fire of anticipation ignited in her abdomen. Once they reached his bedroom, Solange's eyes fell on the small candle that illuminated the room.

Ali lay her gently down on the bed and she sank into the mattress. Ali reached his hand down and slowly lifted her dress.

Solange leaned forward, lifting her arms, impatient, ready and eager to be naked.

Once Ali divested her of her dress, he bent down and slid down the zipper of first one boot and then the other, ridding her of those encumbrances. Then he took one finger and slid it under the side of her underwear. Solange moved sinuously against his touch as he found her center. Gently, he inserted his finger into her and arched it up towards her clitoris. With eyes closed, Solange spread her legs wider, welcoming his intrusion into the sensitivity of her womanhood.

Ali's finger played with her, and she lifted her hips up towards him. The slickness of her made a squishing sound as she drenched him. Ali withdrew his finger from her, and feeling the loss of him, she opened her eyes just in time to see him licking the finger that he'd used to pleasure her.

Ali held her eyes captive with his as he shrugged out of his clothing. He settled in the bed alongside her, pulling the heated blanket over the two of them. The warmness of the blanket wasn't any hotter than the fire in her loins and, in unison, they turned towards each other and silently held each other close for an eternity. Solange closed her eyes as Ali moved across the top of her and lowered his lips to her. Gently, his mouth touched hers and his lips descended onto hers. "Tell me how you want it." His voice had a deep, raspy sound to it.

Without speaking, Solange moved from beneath Ali and turned around on her knees facing the headboard. Ali positioned himself behind her, clasped her waist with his hands, and entered her.

Solange screamed in pleasure and Ali began to thrust. They were long, slow thrusts, and it seemed as if each time he pulled back, he would fall out of her, but Solange held onto him by gripping the insides of her vagina. After what seemed like an eternity, Solange exploded. Then and only then did Ali release into her.

Spent, Solange collapsed on the bed and Ali settled on top of her. His breathing was ragged, and once it steadied, he moved off of her, dragging her along to lay on her side in his arms and buried his face in her hair. "Promise to always love me, Solange."

"I promise to always love you, Ali," she murmured before they both fell into a deep sleep.

Ali sat in a swivel chair at the snack bar and watched Solange as she stood at the stove and carefully flipped an omelet.

"I'm going shopping for Grace's family's Christmas presents today while I'm here in the city."

"I'll go with you, if you want."

"I thought that you wanted to spend the day studying for your exam."

"I do," he admitted grudgingly.

"Then I think that you should do that. I can handle the shopping for the two of us."

"Do you know what you want to give them?"

"For Grace, a spa package over in Florence, since that's the closest city. I can buy it online, and a day at the spa is like a vacation without having to go too far. That's always a hit."

"I'll remember that. How about everyone else?"

"I want to get Livingston an Around Town Baby Driver that I saw advertised on television." She slid the omelet on the empty place in front of him.

"What's that?"

"It looks like a steering wheel and it teaches learning through sounds and melodies. It lights up and children get used to learning letters and colors."

Ali asked, as he dug into his omelet, "Isn't he too young for that?"

"You're never too young to start learning. And Ebony is getting a Hannah Montana game for her Wii."

"And what's that?"

"Boy, you better start paying attention to this computer stuff or our children are going to be smarter than we are. Wii is an interactive video game system. You buy disks and load it. People are transported from their living room. She gets to dance with the controller that's loaded with Hannah Montana songs and Ebony will be a pop star touring Europe."

"Whatever will they come up with next? How about Jet?"

"I don't know. It's so hard to buy for a man that has everything he wants. What do you think?"

"How about tickets to a pro game or something?"

"They don't have a pro anything in Lake City, South Carolina. It's so rural."

"No, but the Hornets in Charlotte aren't that far away, so if you gave them tickets, it could easily turn into a nice getaway weekend for the two of them."

"I don't know," Solange said doubtfully. "Grace never wants to leave the kids with a babysitter."

"Then that's just what they need. An impetus to make sure that they spoil themselves."

"Okay. I guess if you put it like that."

"I'll go on the internet and purchase the tickets myself," Ali offered. "That way I'll feel as if I'm doing my part and contributing to the cause."

"Cool. Do you promise after we have children to make sure that we have date night?"

"I promise to try and make every night feel as if it's date night."

Solange entered her townhome and dropped her packages with a huge sigh of relief. She'd have to make sure and tell Ali that he'd really lucked out by not going with her because of the huge chaos that she had to wade through in the mall. However, she managed to get a lot accomplished and had even gotten something for herself. She'd browsed in a jewelry store and saw a pair of yellow coin-drop earrings and had fallen in love with them and bought a pair.

Once she'd secured her first job after graduating from Spellman she'd made it a habit to purchase something special for herself at Christmas and her birthday. The worst part of her day had been the toy store, but sticking it out in line she'd finally secured Ebony and Livingston's gifts. Hours later, as Solange lay wearily on the couch the ringing of the telephone was the only thing that could propel her into action. "Hello," she said, tiredness evident in her voice.

"Hey, honey. How'd your day go?"

Ali's voice sounded warm and mellow and her heart melted the way it always did when he spoke.

"Not too shabby. I got the kids' stuff."

"How about your parents?"

"I ordered their stuff online weeks ago. I bought Mom a George Foreman grill. After I saw her broiling the bacon in the oven at Thanksgiving morning I got the idea, and for Daddy, a leaf blower. Raking a yard full of leaves every autumn has got to be monotonous. Since we're going to be in South Carolina, Amazon is going to ship their gifts fully wrapped for me so they'll have them Christmas morning."

"You're a thoughtful daughter, Solange. They should enjoy those presents."

"What do you want for Christmas?"

"You," he replied simply.

"You already have that," Solange responded, and now a sexual quality entered her voice. "When are you coming home?"

"That's one of the reasons why I'm not there already. I called an air conditioner man and he's coming early in the morning, so I might as well stay in the city," Ali said regretfully.

"Well, that does make sense instead of you coming out here just to pretty much turn around again. Why do you have to do the calling? Shouldn't your landlord be handling that?"

"Yes," Ali replied dryly. "I've told him several times about the lack of heat in the winter and air-conditioning in the summer and he hasn't taken care of it. Once I get it fixed, I'll give him a copy of the bill and then deduct the amount that it takes for the service call and whatever else from my rent." Ali added, obviously annoyed, "It's always something in this place."

Solange mulled this situation over for a minute. "Why don't you move in with me?"

Ali exclaimed, "You said that you would never live with someone unless you were married to him."

"Things change. The reason why is because I've seen the havoc that it causes when people break up. There's the dividing of the things that they bought together and the heartache when they're packing to leave. In college, a couple of friends of mine lived with their boyfriends and then right before it was time for us to graduate, their boyfriends broke up with them. My girlfriends were devastated, and it ruined what was supposed to be one of the happiest times in their lives."

"You never told me why you felt the way that you did," Ali murmured.

"But you and I are engaged, and I'm not letting you get away, so if you don't mind, Mr. Ali Marks, will you move in with me?"

"As soon as possible."

Later that night, Solange lay on one side of the bed as if Ali was in his usual position on the other. Turning over, her eyes fluttered open and she lay still in the darkness. Blinking, she tried to fathom what had stirred her from her slumber. The room was completely black and silent. Solange's eyes were drawn to the window facing her that was covered by curtains. A shiver ran down her spine, and paralyzed she was unable to move or investigate why she felt a sudden jolt of fear. Then suddenly the feeling left her and her fear lessened. Only then did she stealthily climb out of bed and part the blinds to peer into the darkness. She saw nothing.

Solange made her last check mark on her things to do list. She'd ordered and double-checked via internet that everything she'd ordered for the Christmas party would be arriving at around three o'clock. She'd be glad when it was over. In the beginning, she'd been uplifted at the thought of the camaraderie that she was sure would ensue once everyone attending the party got a bellyful of food and drink, but she hadn't anticipated how much energy it would take to get the whole thing together. Even though the party was being catered, getting an accurate amount so that there was enough food but not a wasteful amount had been a time-consuming affair, as people waffled indecisively as to whether or not to attend.

Solange lifted her head to see Jane standing there. She did a swift perusal of her attire. Jane wore a red knit dress with a black sash tied on the side, and on her feet were four-inch black patent leather pumps. *Gee, she is really dressed up for an office party.* Then she thought wryly, *I know her feet are killing her.*

"I wanted to let you know that the caterers have arrived. The cafeteria door is locked, so they can't get in."

Then Jane hesitated before saying, "They're acting kind of impatient."

"Oh," Solange said, opening her desk drawer. After rifling through it, she pulled out a key ring with an assortment of keys. "I'll have to take care of it because the security code sequence is on it."

"Oh," Jane said, "I understand. I also need the Harrington-Granger file before you leave. The secretary called a little while ago wanting an update on shipping."

Solange hesitated for a minute and then handed Jane her key ring with the key to her filing cabinet and office. "That file is in the top left-hand drawer. After you remove the file, make sure to relock it. I'll get it from you when I see you."

"Will do," Jane said and smiled as she took the key ring from Solange.

When she entered the long narrow hallway that led to the back of the building, Solange was immediately met with the aroma of Italian meatballs and chicken wings. Her appetite was immediately roused and she sniffed the air appreciatively. Solange stepped aside and greeted three men in white chef's jackets and hats. "I'm sorry to have kept you waiting out here in the freezing cold."

"No problem," the tallest of all the men affably responded. "We actually only arrived a few minutes ago and were still pulling trays out of the back of the van."

Solange punched the security code and then unlocked the door for them.

An hour later the party was in full swing. Solange scanned the room and was pleased with what she saw.

There were groups of people chatting, and others had separated themselves but sat in groups eating and drinking juice. Solange spied Celeste Manning as she sat alone, balancing a plate of food on her lap. Walking over to her, Solange slid into the empty chair next to her. "Are you enjoying yourself?"

Celeste swallowed a mouthful of food and, after shyly returning Solange's smile, she said, "I sure am. I really appreciate you throwing us this party, Mrs. Montgomery."

"No need to thank me," Solange denied. "I think that all of you deserve a little fun. It's been quite a grueling year."

Celeste gave her a perceptive look and said, "It must have been very hard for you also. I mean," she stammered, "having to let so many people go. Some bosses it might not bother, but you're not made like that."

Solange gave a start of surprise and Celeste gave her another small smile. "When I'm cleaning the offices, I have a lot of opportunity to observe people. I also hear the tail end of a lot of telephone conversations." She gave a self-conscious shrug. "I mean, no one pays any attention to the maid."

"You're not a maid," Solange emphatically denied.

"No, but I'm a custodian for right now." Then she added in a prideful tone, "I have one more semester and then I'll have my degree."

"I didn't know that you're in college."

"Yes, ma'am. I'm a single mother so I'm able to go to school using a Pell Grant," Celeste added in a somber tone. "I have a five-year-old and I hate leaving her with my sister three nights a week because she's my responsibility, but once I graduate, I'll be able to get a job doing something that I'm proud of and I can make a nice home for my daughter."

Solange looked at Celeste with admiration. "What will you be getting your degree in?"

"I'm going to be a school psychologist," she replied with conviction. "I want to help young people not make the mistakes that I have. Besides, I'm real interested in what makes people tick." Then she gave a sort of shamefaced look and added, "My sister said that I'm just plain old nosy and have figured out a way to get paid for it."

Solange grinned. "At least you'll be doing something that you enjoy. I don't always enjoy my job."

"I'm sure you don't." Then, with averted eyes, she murmured, "People get mad at the wrong person when times are tough. Hard times make strange bedfellows."

Solange looked at Celeste and was just about to ask her what she meant, but she was distracted by a commotion on the other side of the room.

A red-faced Arnold Benedict was pointing his finger at Robert Cherry, who was a lot shorter than Arnold but not backing down.

Solange rose to her feet and quickly walked over towards them, but before she was abreast of them, another employee, Sullivan Granger, had pulled Arnold away and after he waved his hand disgustedly at Robert, Arnold stormed out the side door, slamming it.

Solange gave Robert a stern look and asked, "What was going on?"

"Oh, I'm tired of that loud-mouthed Arnold. I have to hear him bitch all the time." Robert apologized before he continued saying, "No matter what Obama does Arnold turns it into something negative. I don't feel like hearing that shit at a Christmas party, too. Sorry again."

"I agree," Solange said, and patted his arm in a consoling manner. "Don't worry about it and try to enjoy the rest of your time here."

Robert swung his head around and observed the crowd that was lessening. "I think that everyone's getting ready to leave anyhow. I guess we sort of cleared the room," he said with a look of apology.

Solange looked and she realized that people were indeed gathering their belongings and throwing paper plates away in the huge garbage can. "It's okay, Robert."

The caterers were wheeling empty trays. As people walked by, their goodbyes were a mixture of "thank you" and "good party." Solange caught some not-so-friendly looks at Robert Cherry as he stood by her side.

"Would you like me to stay and help you clean everything up?"

Solange looked in Robert Cherry's eyes, and, for the first time since he'd been employed as a computer technician at Microsystems Computers, she realized just how good-looking he was. He stood about five-feet, eight-inches tall, which was shorter than she usually liked her men, but his coloring was a smooth mahogany brown and his wavy black hair cut close to his head. He was dressed casually in a light blue polo shirt and a pair of khakis.

Solange had heard from Jane that he'd recently separated from his wife and had moved into an apartment closer to work. Seeing the mirror of interest in his quizzical eyes she felt an immediate denial form on her lips. "Thank you, Robert, but I don't need any help. A cleaning crew is coming in the morning in order to get everything ready for the start of the new year."

"Okay, Miss Montgomery. Just since you have everything covered."

A firm smile was Solange's answer and then her attention was drawn to Jane as she hurried towards them. Pieces of her hair were sticking up on top of her head as if she'd been in the wind and she wore a harried expression. Once she reached her and Robert, Jane thrust out her hand and in her palm was the set of keys Solange had loaned her hours ago. "I'm sorry about just giving these to you," she apologized, "but I totally forgot that I had them."

Solange replied frostily, "I told you that I needed them back right away, Jane. Every time I remembered that you had them and tried to find them, you weren't in the room."

Robert was obviously embarrassed by their confrontation and felt he'd better excuse himself. "I think that I'd better be going. You ladies enjoy your two weeks off during the holiday."

Jane turned cold eyes on Robert but didn't answer.

Robert returned her stare and then pointedly turned to Solange. "Goodnight, Miss Montgomery."

With another smile at Solange, Robert nodded his head and walked out of the room.

"I didn't want to say in front of Robert, but my time of the month came on me suddenly and I had to go back to the office and get some stuff for it."

"Oh." Solange nodded her head in understanding as she took the keys. "I understand. I hate when I get caught off guard."

"Yeah, and now I'm ready to go home, take a shower and relax. So if you don't need anything . . ."

"No, I'm good. All I have to do is turn the alarm system on and then I'm out of here myself."

"Okay," Jane said. Then suddenly Jane reached over and hugged Solange. When she stepped back, an indiscernible expression crossed her face and then it was gone. "Have a good holiday, ma'am."

Solange now wished she hadn't been so testy with her at the outset of their conversation. "You do the same, Jane."

Solange threw a paper plate that was left on the table in the huge garbage can, and after cutting off the stereo system, she keyed in the security code. Once she heard three beeps, she hurriedly left, the door closing behind her with a decisive click. Clutching her pocketbook close to her side, she swiftly walked through the garage to the stairwell.

Solange looked over her shoulder to make sure no one was behind her and once inside the stairwell quickly descended it. Her heels made a clicking sound on the hard concrete floor and then she realized that she heard another set of footsteps coming from the direction she was heading.

Solange halted her steps and began to back away, when all of a sudden the image of large person ascending the stairs was outlined by the yellow bulbs that illuminated the stairwell. Breathing deeply, Solange began to turn in order to run back into the direction she'd just left when her apprehensive gaze settled on Ali as he reached the landing. "Ali, what are you doing here?"

"I came to escort you home since I knew that you'd probably be leaving later than expected." He glared at her with censure and said, "What are you doing alone in this stairwell? I thought we already had this conversation."

She returned his look of censure with one of her own. "What are you doing scaring me half to death? Why didn't you call and tell me you were coming?"

"Check your cell. I did call. Several times, in fact."

"I don't need to check," Solange replied testily. "If you say you did, then you did. You have no reason to lie about it. I just probably didn't hear it ring over the din of music and partying people."

Taking his arm, Ali let it rest around her shoulders and propelled her back into the direction she'd just started to bolt from. "I'm parked next to your car in the garage. Let's get out of here and start our vacation."

"Yes, let's," she agreed, and, her nerves beginning to calm, she let him guide her to safety.

# CHAPTER 9

The drive to Lake City was peaceful in contrast to the harried one they had experienced when going to visit Solange's family during Thanksgiving. The comforting voice of the new GPS Ali had purchased kept them abreast of any roadblocks or difficulties that there might be on the highway before they reached it.

"I need to use the restroom before we get off the main highway."

"Me, too," Ali agreed. "Our turn is only a short stretch, and we should be in Lake City within thirty minutes once we leave I-95."

Solange gave a long stretch. "My bones ache."

"I'm kind of stiff after driving eight hours," Ali said.

"I told you that I would help."

"Once we get off the main highway, you can take over. You know these small towns better than I do."

"I sure do. I've visited Grace enough times."

"I'm glad that you have someone that you feel so close to. Besides you and my mom, I have no one."

"You have Randolph."

"Yes, I have him, but I met him at work. I mean I don't have someone that's been a constant friend of mine through the years."

"Grace and I became so close when we were in college, it was like she was my sister. We lived in the same suite but we weren't roommates. Neither of us were getting along with our roommates so we switched."

"How did the other girls make out? Did they become lasting friends?"

Solange gave a derogatory snort. "No, those heifers couldn't get along with anyone."

"That's women for you."

Solange gave Ali a look of surprise. "That's a sexist remark."

"You think so? I've observed that beautiful women don't really hang together. At work, the good-looking women hang with either the men or women that aren't as attractive."

"Well, I disagree. Grace is absolutely gorgeous and I've been told," she slid him a look, "that I'm easy on the eye. And she and I are as close as sisters."

"But you're unusual, Solange. I've noticed when other women enter the room, I never see you looking other women up and down for some flaw. I *have* seen that look on other women's faces."

"But I have no reason to look for flaws in other people. I have everything I want. A man who loves and wants to marry me. A career that I enjoy, and family that only wants the best for me. Maybe that's why I'm able to be so generous. You have helped me become the satisfied adult that I am."

"Ditto. I think that you were put in my life for a specific purpose. You make me want to be the kind of man that women write romance novels about."

Solange blushed at his compliment and, letting her hand drop between his legs, she cupped him.

"Don't do that when I'm driving because you know that I can't do anything about it right now."

"Yes, sir," Solange answered demurely and settled back against the leather interior of her seat.

When Ali pulled off the interstate, he looked to his left and then his right as he tried to make a decision as to which service station he wanted to use. Solange pointed to a combination gas station and grocery store. "Go to that one. I want to buy a couple of pecan log rolls and they usually have fresh ones."

"I don't know how you eat those things," Ali said in mild disgust. "They're so sugary sweet."

"What are you trying to say? Do you think that I need to go on a diet or something?"

"Of course not." He shot her a look as he pulled into the gas station and parked by a pump. "As a matter of fact, I don't think that you've put on any weight since I met you."

"I've always had to watch my weight, but the minute I take that wedding dress off, I'm going to eat any and everything that I want. Once I get that ring on you, why deny myself?" Solange laughed. "People are going to ask you where you got that plump wife from."

"I like my women a little on the meaty side. In some cultures, the fatter the wife, the more of a status symbol it is for the man."

"Then maybe we ought to move to one of those places," she said before she reached into the back seat and picked up her pocketbook. Grabbing her overcoat from around her bucket seat, she shrugged into it before she opened the door in the below thirty-degree weather. With a grimace, she turned to Ali. "See you inside." Solange's boots crunched on the frosty ground and she gingerly skipped to keep from falling on the icy pavement.

Once inside, she made a dash to the restroom. Straddling over the toilet, she aimed and hit her mark. *It's times like these I wish I was a man.* Once she relieved herself, she stood at the sink and smoothed her hair in front of the smeared window. Gingerly touching the faucet handles, she rinsed her hands and then hit the automatic hand dryer with her elbow. Helping her hands to dry quickly, she shook them. She grabbed her oversized purse from the hook of the bathroom door and made a hasty escape.

As Solange strolled up and down the aisles, she picked up a package of chips, checked the expiration date and replaced it on the shelf. Then she saw an end cap of only pecan rolls. Satisfied with the expiration date, she put one under her arm and then picked up another.

Her attention was diverted to the large mirror that hung cater-cornered above the display. Though it was dusty, she saw that the clerk was leaning over trying to see what she was doing. Then she saw Ali walk in, nod at him and go straight to the head. Walking up to the cash register, Solange put her items on the counter.

The clerk quickly tallied up the total and spoke with an accent that sounded like a male version of Ali's mother. "That will be eleven dollars and thirty-four cents, ma'am."

Solange pulled a $100 bill out of her purse, and instead of handing it to him, placed it on the counter.

The clerk then picked it up, shone a light on it, and then placed it in a money bag. He opened the drawer and quickly counted her change out, placing it on the counter. "Thank you," he said.

Picking the money up, Solange's only response was to grunt at him. Then she grabbed her bag and walked back down the aisle, picked up a magazine, pretended to peruse it and waited.

Ali exited the restroom and, once he spied Solange, gave her a smile and started walking up and down the aisle. She knew that he was looking for something healthy to eat and, instead of watching him, she watched the clerk.

He hadn't given Ali a second look as he strolled around and instead he had his back turned towards him and counted cartons of cigarette stacks that were behind the counter.

Solange inwardly fumed.

Once Ali went to the counter, he had to attract the clerk's attention by clearing his throat. The clerk turned around, gave Ali a gracious smile and reached for the package of sun-dried fruit Ali wanted to purchase.

She stormed out of the store, hitting the door with a bang as she left.

Ali had moved the car in front of the store and Solange fished her set of car keys out of her pocketbook and once inside, threw her belongings once again in the back seat.

Ali had a quizzical look on his face as he approached the car. "What's ticked you off?"

"That damn clerk was watching me to see if I was going to steal anything," she blustered.

"Oh, God," Ali muttered. "Here we go again."

"What do you mean by that?" Solange demanded.

Ali drew in a deep sigh of annoyance and said, "Every time we leave the house you find racism somehow, somewhere."

"I don't find racism. It finds me. Don't blame me because I'm astute."

"I think that you're way too sensitive," Ali retorted in a nonchalant manner.

Now Solange's voice raised several decibels higher. "That clerk watched me the whole time that I was in there, yet he didn't give you a second look."

"He gave me a second look," Ali replied calmly.

"But when I slapped that hundred-dollar bill on the counter, I guess I showed him," Solange said with a touch of smugness.

"Maybe that's why he didn't watch me too hard. He figured that we were together so whatever I couldn't afford to pay for, you'd have my back."

Solange became ticked off by Ali refusing to validate her feelings. "We didn't come in there together. What would make him think that we would even know each other?"

Now Ali lost his patience with the argument and said in a disgruntled voice, "Then let's just say that I just don't look suspicious."

Solange's eyes opened wide from anger. "Are you saying that I do?"

"No," he replied soothingly, "I'm just trying to tell you to lighten up."

Solange held the palm of her left hand out for emphasis. "I hate it when you pretend there's no racism in this country."

"I know that there's racism in the world, Solange. I just don't see why we're having an argument about someone that doesn't mean shit to us."

"Well go ahead and bury your head in the sand to reality, Ali."

"I'm not burying my head in the sand as to some of the ugliness that exists," Ali said. "I've had to deal with racism ever since I started school. But I refuse to ruin my days worried about other people's preconceived notions."

"Well, your countryman . . ."

Ali interrupted her by saying, "Excuse me? My countryman?"

"You know what I mean," Solange argued heatedly.

"You mean the United States of America, I take it. Now anyone listening to you, if they didn't know you, might think that you're a racist."

Solange clammed up after that and after turning the key in the ignition, she gunned the gas pedal and backed up. "I can't wait to get to Grace and Jet's house. This car seems mighty small all of a sudden."

Ali's answer was to not answer.

After Solange exited I-95, she followed the signs to Lake City. The clear blue sky made light reflect off the mounds of fresh snow that flanked both sides of the two-way thoroughfare. Huge elm trees were bowed from icicles and for the first time since she'd left New York, a sense of peace consumed her.

Solange carefully drove through small town after town. Finally, once she'd reached the outskirts of Lake City, she halted at a four-way intersection that was her landmark for the country road that led out to the last leg of their journey. She shot Ali a look. When she saw his stern profile, a small curl of apprehension settled in her stomach. "We're almost at my family's house. I hope you're not going to let them know that we had a disagreement. I'd hate to ruin everyone's evening and make them uncomfortable."

His tone was clipped. "You started the argument, Solange. I'm just along for the ride."

Now a feeling of remorse flooded through her and she pulled the car over to the side of the road. Turning to Ali she admitted contritely, "I'm sorry, Ali. I took my anger out on you."

Obviously still annoyed, he responded without looking her way, "Yes, you did, and it's not the first time. We need to find more important things to fight about, or at least argue about something that can be fixed."

"You're right," she agreed. "I thank God that you're more forgiving than I am. If you had lashed out at me like that . . . I get angry too quickly."

Ali stared at Solange and he held her gaze with his. "Yes, you do, and you need to work on that. Make it your New Year's resolution. Don't get pissed every time Ali doesn't agree with you about something."

Shamed, Solange hung her head. "I'll try."

Ali took his hand and lifted Solange's chin. He leaned over and pressed a warm loving kiss on her mouth and Solange melted inside and out.

"Now hurry up and get me to my future sister's house. I need a damn drink."

When Solange turned into her best friend's driveway, she spied Jet supposedly helping Ebony build a snowman. She smiled because it appeared as if Jet was doing most of the work, while Ebony ran around in circles doing absolutely nothing to help the cause. Solange looked at Ali and she recognized that there was a look of jealousy on his face as he watched Jet playing with his daughter. She nodded her head at them and after putting the car into park and shutting it off, she patted his knee. "One day, that'll be you," she said.

Ebony had stopped her antics and stood watching them. Solange knew that Ebony couldn't see them through the tint of the windows, so Solange teasingly let her window down just enough to show the top of her head. Ebony continued to stare and not move towards them. Jet had stopped making the snowman, and with a half-crooked smile, watched Ebony. Then Solange let the window down a little more, revealing her and Ali's heads.

Ebony screamed in excitement, "Daddy, it's my godparents!" She ran as fast as her short, eight-year-old legs would carry her to the car.

Solange and Ali climbed out of the car and Solange ignored the stiffness in her joints and held her arms out for Ebony. Ebony hit her with such force that she almost lost her balance and toppled over onto the ice-covered driveway. "Goodness, girl. You're getting so strong," Solange teased.

"Mommy feeds me and Daddy a lot," Ebony replied in her high, squeaky voice.

"So I see," Solange replied and shot Jet a look. It was true. When Solange had first met Jet a couple of years ago he'd been a reed. Now he was a little thicker, but still fine as wine with just a little hint of a gut. Over six feet tall, with smooth, light-brown skin, he had the looks that made women stop and stare. Yet she'd never sensed an inkling of vanity from him.

As he strode towards them, he clapped snow from his gloves before he enveloped her in his arms, and then gave Ali, who had come to stand by her side, a manly hug. Solange smiled inwardly at the haste with which the men broke their embrace. She knew that they were real men's men and if it wasn't for the fact that they liked each other so much, they wouldn't have hugged at all.

Jet turned to Solange and said, "Ever since you called and told Grace that you'd just left the interstate, she's been inside cooking up a storm."

"Good, because I'm starving and tired of gas station snacks and fast food."

"Well, you won't find anything like that here. If I remember correctly, I saw Grace with a bag of pinto beans and ham hocks."

"One of my favorites," Solange beamed. She looked down at Ebony. "I'm going in the house. Do you want to come with me?"

"Yeah, because I'm tired."

"From what?" Jet interjected.

"Daddy, I helped you in the beginning," she said, looking at the half-made snowman.

"You sure did, honey. Go in the door through the garage so you don't trample snow in the foyer. Not you, Solange. The front door's open."

"I'll go through the side door, too. I don't want to make any more housework than necessary for Grace."

"I help, too," Jet added and pretended to be hurt by Solange's thinly veiled insinuation that he didn't help around the house.

She lifted an eyebrow and answered, "When do you do that, Councilman Jethro Newman? According to Grace you usually arrive home after ten o'clock most nights. After you sign more papers to help urban development in Lake City, or maybe after you stop by the free health clinic that you started and still help run?"

"I guess Grace has been talking to you," Jet answered a little sheepishly. "Maybe we should get a nanny or a housekeeper to help out."

Ali gave Solange a chiding look. "Mind your own business, Solange," Ali said.

Solange returned Ali's chiding look before saying to Jet, "I'm really just kidding. And you don't know your wife at all if you think that she would let a nanny take care of her kids. And as for the housework, Grace is such a neat freak I can see her cleaning up behind the housekeeper, so you'd be paying her for nothing." Then she gave Jet a real earnest look. "Grace hasn't been complaining about your schedule. She has a lot of deep respect and admiration for what you're doing. She says that when they made you, they broke the mold."

Jet dipped his head, probably to keep Solange and Ali from seeing him blush from the compliment that Solange repeated from his wife.

"I think my job is done. Let's go, Ebony."

Ebony put her mittened hand in Solange's and began pulling her through the open garage door towards the entrance of the house.

As Jet and Ali watched Ebony and Solange walk into the garage, Jet said to Ali, "They broke the mold when they came up with Solange, too, Ali."

"I know. She picks on you every time she sees you. That's how you know she really cares about you."

"I know," Jet agreed amiably. "I'm glad that the two of you are getting married. It makes life a lot simpler since we wanted both of you to be godparents. Neither Grace nor I have any real family. You guys are it."

"All my childhood I wanted a brother. Then when I lost my father, I knew that my mother would never marry again and I felt that was it for our family tree. Then once Solange entered my life, I knew from the first moment I saw her that she was the one. Yet I didn't stop to think about the extended family. Thank God we all like each other," Ali said earnestly.

"You're right. Getting a family together isn't always the process that you think that it's going to be, but any way you're blessed with it, thank God for it."

Ali slid Jet a look. "Have you done the formal adoption papers for Ebony?"

"Yes, we took care of that a while ago. We had to wait a year after the tragic death of her mother in New York, but no one knew who her father was and no one ever stepped forward, so the adoption was uncontested." Jet gave a lopsided grin. "She's ours, lock, stock, and barrel."

"I'm sorry that her mother's life ended the way it did. Being hit by a car must be a horrible way to go. But you and Grace have given her a steady home, love and everything that she could ever want something she might not have had if it wasn't for you guys."

"Well, we don't give her everything she wants because we'd be buying stuff every day. We want her to understand the value of a dollar and it's so hard today when her classmates go to school every day bragging about the latest craze toy that their parents bought them."

"Then you might not be too pleased with Solange. You should see what she bought her for Christmas."

"That's okay. Christmas doesn't count. I'm not a Grinch or anything."

"It's some Hannah Montana dance thing. It has a music DVD and sing-along mike and everything."

Jet chuckled. "Remind me to strangle Solange later. It's not about the gift. It's about the noise. Livingston is a light sleeper."

"Funny, I thought that once babies were eight months old they slept through the night."

"He does that. But once he wakes up in the morning, he's nonstop," Jet said. "I really should get Grace some help."

"She would kill you."

"The nanny deal is out. She'd never go for it, but if I get her a housekeeper as a Mother's Day gift, she'd have to accept it. A gift's a gift."

"You're right. Speaking of gifts, is mine all set up?"

"Yes, tonight around five we'll say that we have to go to the store for something. If we waited any later, the girls would know that it's a lie because it's Christmas Eve and everything will close earlier than usual. I'll come back alone and put them off when Solange starts demanding to know where you are. But hurry, because you know how she is."

"How far is it?"

"Just about five miles down the road. I even arranged for them to have the thermos of hot toddy that you asked for."

Reaching in his back pocket for his wallet Ali asked, "Did I send you enough money to cover everything?"

Jet held his hand out, motioning for Ali to put his wallet away. "More than enough. As a matter of fact, I think that I owe you some money."

"Keep it," Ali ordered. "I couldn't have done this without you. I hate the way Solange and I got engaged, and I want to fix it once and for all."

Jet gave Ali a matter-of-fact look. "By the way, Grace knows but I made her promise not to tell Solange. She's almost as excited as if it was herself getting proposed to tonight." All of a sudden, Ali and Jet heard their names being called.

Solange stood in the driveway at the garage door. "What are you two still doing out here in the cold?"

"Getting all this stuff out of the car that you brought," Ali hedged.

"Okay. Now's a good time to bring in the gifts because Ebony is asleep."

Once they entered the house laden with gifts, the smell of pot roast made Ali's stomach grumble.

Grace turned from the stove where she was stirring a pot and gave Ali a knowing look.

He smiled and gave her a conspiratorial wink. "Where do I put these presents?"

"The tree is set up in the living room. Ebony already knows there's no Santa Claus, so I don't feel the need to hide her stuff."

"Yeah," Solange said. "We just don't want her bugging us to open them up tonight, so it's better to sneak them in."

"I'll put these in your bedroom," Jet said and walked down the long hallway to the last room on the left with the suitcases.

# CHAPTER 10

"Can I have some more pot roast?" Ali said.

Grace smiled, showing her perfect white teeth. "You sure can, Ali," she said, and she started to get up from the table.

"I'll get it," Solange said. "You take care of your man, and I'll take care of mine."

"I can't believe how domesticated you've become since you got with Ali. During college you were the Pop-Tart queen," Grace said to Solange with a snicker.

Looking up from the pot at the stove she was digging into, Solange said, "I didn't feel the need to be domesticated. To be honest, I really don't like to cook, but for Ali, I don't seem to mind so much."

"That's how you can tell if your woman really loves you," Jet said to Ali as he cleaned his own plate of food. "When people do things for you and try to make life easier for you, that means that they're looking out for your best interests. No matter what time I get home at night, there's something waiting for me on the stove. And trust me, at eleven o'clock at night a plate of food with aluminum foil over it is a welcome sight."

Putting Ali's refilled plate down in front of him, Solange eased back into her chair and said, "That's what I'm going to have to do for you if you do get changed to nights."

"Why would you be getting changed to nights?" Grace asked.

"I take my test to be a detective next week. If I pass, I'll get a promotion."

"Ali has been studying religiously for months. He sits at the kitchen table and pores over the questions in the book. Sometimes I quiz him and he knows the answer before I even ask the question. So now I change it up and try to trick him and he still can gets them all right," Solange bragged. "My baby is going to score a 100, and soon we'll be calling him Detective Marks."

"But I'll be at the bottom of the totem pole when it comes to seniority. That automatically means that I'll be switched to nights," Ali said.

Solange groaned, giving Grace and Jet a look. "I hate the thought of it. Yet I know how badly my baby wants this, so I'll just have to work with him on it. That's some of the reason why Ali's moving in. Otherwise we wouldn't get to see each other enough."

Grace raised her eyebrows in surprise. "Ali's moving in? You didn't mention to me that the two of you were going to live together before you got married. Forget about her cooking. Solange has always said that she wouldn't live with any man before she married him."

"That's how I felt, because I've seen what happens to so many women. They live with the man in order to make him see how great it would be if they were to get married, but men are so unrealistic," Solange said and shot the men at the table a look. "Sorry, guys but you are. They think people should never argue and life should be a bed of roses. Then when reality sinks in and they see it for what it is, they head for the hills."

"I'm an unusual man then, because I know life with you will never be a bed full of roses. But I like a little, I mean a lot, of spice. It keeps me from being bored," Ali said.

"Same here, dude," Jet said.

"You two are really funny," Grace said, coming to her feet. "I'm going to check on the kids. I can't believe that Ebony is still asleep. You wore her out."

"She didn't even do anything. She wore herself out," Jet protested.

After Jet watched Grace's retreating back, he turned to Solange. "So the wedding is in July. Have you decided on a location yet? As best man I think that I have a right to know."

"Yeah, I talked to my mom just before we left and she wants it to be in Maryland because of her church cronies." She drew in a sigh that was a mixture of irritation and resignation. "She knows that they'd never come here and she says that she's been to wedding after wedding after wedding supporting their children and giving them gifts. I think that she just wants to show me off, and I am her only child. I just wanted something small, but it seems this wedding is going to be bigger than I expected. I don't even know those people."

"Will it hurt you to give her what she wants?" Jet asked.

"I guess not," Solange answered slowly.

"Then give her what she wants," he advised.

"That's what I told her," Ali added quietly. "Besides, my mom will be thrilled, too."

Grace reentered the room with a worried look on her face as she juggled Livingston on her hip. "Ebony said that her legs hurt. I'm going to rub some alcohol on them," she said as she handed Livingston to Jet.

"Give him to me while the two of you tend to Ebony," Solange suggested.

Once Solange and Ali were alone with Livingston, she settled him into his high chair. He stared at them for a moment and then burst into tears. "Shush, Livingston. I'm your godmother. You're supposed to like me," she told the infant.

Ali smothered a laugh at the look of consternation on Solange's face as Livingston started to cry louder. He got up from his chair and found an empty space on a wall. "Look, Livingston. Look what your godfather can do."

Ali crouched down and then very slowly lifted himself on his hands to stand on them using the wall as a backdrop of support.

All of a sudden Livingston stopped howling. Even though his tears coursed down his chubby cheeks and gathered under his chin, Ali held his rapt attention.

"Hurry up and feed him," Ali grunted from his upside-down position.

Quickly, Solange grabbed the bowl of potatoes, shredded pot roast, and beans that Grace had pureed earlier. Holding a spoonful of the concoction in front of Livingston, he opened his mouth and allowed Solange to feed him. All the while he watched Ali, whose face was now beginning to turn red from his exertion.

Once Livingston had swallowed the food, he took his hand and hit the high chair table. "You can climb down now, honey. The taste of the food has kicked in. We should be okay now," Solange said as she spooned more food into Livingston.

Ali gingerly unraveled himself out of his position. Lying flat on his back on the hardwood floor, he gasped deep breaths. "Good, because I don't think that I could have held on much longer. We better hurry up and have our kids because I'm too old for these antics."

Solange sent Ali a look of longing that she'd been bestowing on Livingston. "Maybe we'll have a honeymoon baby," she said.

Once she'd finished feeding Livingston, Ali wiped his mouth with a washcloth he'd taken out of the linen closet and wiped his face and hands that he'd managed to stick into the bowl of food. "I'm going to go and see what's going on with Ebony," Solange said.

Before she could rise from her chair, Grace and Jet came in with a look of confusion. "I don't know what happened," Jet said.

"You know how Ebony is." Grace sank wearily into the couch and observed Livingston now sitting contentedly on Ali's lap chattering in a language that no one but he understood. "She just overdid it being excited about Christmas and all."

"Is she feeling any better?" Ali asked.

"I think so. Jet massaged her legs and I gave her a children's aspirin. If she's not feeling any better on Monday, I'll take her to the doctor. Everything's closed until then and I want her to see her pediatrician, Dr. Jesse."

Ali said with concern, "I hope that she's feeling better tomorrow. It would suck to feel sick on Christmas, and her baptism is the next day."

"I know," Grace responded, worry very much evident in her tone.

"Where are you going?" Jet asked as she started to get up.

"To do the dishes," Grace answered.

"I got them," Jet said.

"I'll dry," Ali offered.

"Sit down," Jet ordered. "I'm stacking the dishwasher and I don't need any help wiping down a few kitchen counters."

After Jet cleaned up the kitchen, he went into the garage and threw the damp dishcloth in the washing machine. He returned a few minutes later. "I need to go to the store and get some film. Ali, do you want to ride?"

"I sure do," Ali said immediately, getting up from an easy chair positioned in front of the television set.

"Where are you going to get film from this time of day?" Solange asked.

"From Walgreen's, of course," Jet answered succinctly.

Grace and Solange sat companionably on the sofa enjoying the solitude as they were alone for the first time that day. Johnny Mathis's Christmas album was playing softly in the background. Solange turned the album cover over and looked at Johnny Mathis pictured in a red sweater standing in the snow. Putting it down, she smiled gently at her best friend. "I see that you still have that record player."

"Every time it breaks I have it fixed. I only use it to play my mother's old record albums."

Solange gave Grace a look of intense scrutiny and said with relief, "I see that you've finally come to terms with your past."

"It took a lot of work. Counseling helped. And Jet of course. Now when I think of my mother, I don't feel the burning anger or resentment," Grace said.

"And the death of your ex-fiancé, Livingston, who also happened to be Jet's best friend?" Solange carefully scrutinized Grace's face. "Have you finally come to terms with that?"

"The day that I almost lost Jet for good, I stopped living in the past." Grace screwed her face up, remembering her past mistakes. "I can't believe how I almost blew it with him because of guilt."

"Don't be too hard on yourself. Your fiancé was killed the night before your wedding. You were allowed to make mistakes." Solange shuddered at the memory. "There are a lot of people that couldn't have ever recovered from such an ordeal."

"I was afraid that Jet would end up dying, too, because everyone I ever loved did."

"I haven't died," Solange interjected.

"No, you've been a stable part of my life for over a decade and I thank God for that. But in some kind of crazy mixed-up way, I felt that Jet would come to some big misfortune if we married and that I would be paid back for not being true to Livingston's memory. But Jet is some kind of man."

"He sure is." Solange looked at the sleeping infant on the other end of the couch. "He was man enough to name his son after the first love of your life. That's a strong man."

Grace said in a somber tone, "But Jet loved him, too, and he wanted us to always remember that if it wasn't for Livingston, we would have never fallen in love. I let all the guilt of finding true happiness and the resentment that I had from my childhood dissolve as Jet chipped away at it bit by bit. In hindsight, the only real failing that my mother had was that of being an alcoholic. My counselor even made me find a silver lining in that cloud."

"What is it?"

"Alcohol abuse is a disease and it runs in my family. I shouldn't drink too much. But I'm not the only person in the room who has changed. You vowed that you'd never get married and you've come full circle."

"That's because of who the man is. I'm not too certain that I've totally come to terms with my childhood, but I haven't had to face those demons. With Ali, I don't have to be everything and do everything in order to have him."

Solange nodded her head in understanding and said softly, "The way your mother did for your dad."

"Yes. I mean she handled everything. She wrote out the bills, did the shopping, managed me and then even took on the added burden of Rosemary, and never once did I hear her complain."

"She probably did behind closed doors," Grace said.

"Maybe," Solange admitted. "I've downplayed to my mother how I feel about all that, but why marry someone if they don't pull their own share? She gave so much."

"But in the end it was worth it. She kept her family together and now all of you have a very close relationship."

"Yes, we do," Solange softly agreed.

"I think women back in the day were made of stronger stuff. Maybe it's because they were closer generations to slavery or something. I mean, compared to them I'm what you would call soft. There are days that after the kids go to sleep, I almost pass out from exhaustion and I'm a stay-at-home mom," Grace mused.

"But you keep an immaculate house. You cook almost every day and volunteer at Ebony's school. Every time I call you you're busy. You're not sitting in front of the television watching soap operas."

"Soap operas?" Grace asked in mock curiosity. "What in the world is a soap opera?"

"Did I ever tell you that my mother went to college?"

Grace asked, surprise evident in her face and expression, "She did?"

"She wanted to get a degree in business administration and be a bank manager. That's how the bills got paid at our house because she was so good at juggling things.

Knowing how to rob Peter to pay Paul is a great asset when times are hard." Now there entered a stiff inflection in Solange's voice as she continued, "But then going to school got to be too hard, so she dropped out her after her junior year. She never went back."

"That's very unfortunate."

"I know," Solange said quietly. "She would have been an awesome bank manager."

"You're a strong woman, Solange. You could handle everything if you had to."

"But I don't want to." They heard the sound of the garage door opening. "The boys are back."

Grace made no reply. "I'm going to go and check on Ebony," she said after darting a quick look over to the slumbering Livingston.

When Jet came into the room, Solange looked questioningly behind him. "Where's Ali?"

"He told me to tell you to get on your coat, hat, scarf and mittens and come outside."

Solange protested, "Hell, no. It's cold out there and I'm not in any mood to finish off the half-assed snowman you had out there in the yard."

"Just do it," Jet ordered softly.

As Solange stood at the hallway closet and started layering her body against the onslaught of cold that she knew awaited her outside, she thought, *I must be crazy in love to go out there in that weather.*

Just as she was buttoning the last button on her coat, the doorbell rang. She looked at Jet. "For goodness sakes, why is Ali ringing the doorbell?"

Jet simply shrugged his shoulders and after glancing at the still-sleeping Livingston, walked past her to go to Ebony's room.

Once Solange opened her door, Ali stood there with a whip in his hand. In amazement, she stared past him and saw stationed in front of the house, a red carriage with four horses. She marveled at the long, flowing hair that stopped just above their hooves. "Oh, my God!" Throwing her arms around her neck she buried her face deep into his chest muttering, "Ali, I love you so much."

"Ditto," he choked out emotionally. "If it's not too cold, would you like to go for a ride?"

"Too cold? My body feels as if its temperature is ninety degrees," she breathed.

Ali took his arm, and putting it around her shoulders he guided her to the open carriage. The horses were taking turns snorting, and every time they did a puff of cold air rose from their noses. They were dancing lightly, shifting their legs as they impatiently waited for their commands. Once she reached them, Solange took her hand and gingerly patted the ones that stood in the front. A huge beautiful chestnut brown one turned his head and nuzzled her shoulder. Tears formed in Solange's eyes from the fine-looking sight of nature that one so rarely saw in New York.

Smiling at the look of pure amazement on Solange's face, Ali climbed into the cab and then, turning, he hoisted her up with his hand. Reaching for a warm blanket, he pulled it around her, making it a snug fit before he gently propelled her to her seat. Then he reached down on the floor and lifted a straw picnic basket. Opening it, he reached for a thermos. Once he unscrewed the top a steaming liquid smell of brandy wafted to her nostrils.

"What is it?"

"It's a hot toddy." He smiled.

"What's in it?"

"Brandy, lemon, cinnamon. Everything you need to make you feel all warm and fuzzy inside." Ali poured some in a huge mug.

"We'll share," she said, snuggling next to him. As Ali sat down on the bench that served as the driver's seat, Solange took a long sip, draining quite a bit of the drink. "I'll pour while you drive," she offered.

Ali placed the small leather whip on the floorboard and, picking up the reins, made a clucking sound with his tongue.

The horses neighed and immediately broke into a trot. Since Jet and Grace's house was so far out into the country, Ali didn't have to look to see if any cars or obstructions were in the vicinity, yet he looked over his shoulder as if he was driving a car.

The horses took up a large part of the lane as they ambled and then broke into a trot. The adrenaline of the ride, and the proximity of Ali as he guided the horses, made desire ooze between Solange's legs. She loved the feel of the wind as it whipped her face, and when Ali took his eyes off the horses for a second to check to see if she was all right, she smiled at him. No words were needed or spoken as they each enjoyed the majestic beauty of the horses and the countryside as they rode by it. After about thirty minutes, Ali began to slow the horses by slowly pulling the reins towards him. They had approached a clearing that Solange knew led to a small pond where Grace and Jet picnicked during the spring and summer.

Once the horses stopped, Ali dropped his reins. He turned to Solange and she handed him a cup of hot toddy she'd poured once she'd seen that he was stopping. Taking the glass, he drained it and handed it back to her. She obligingly filled it up. "This is the best Christmas present I've ever had, Ali. You never cease to amaze me with how thoughtful you are."

"I aim to please, ma'am," he answered quietly.

"And you do," she said, leaning over to plant a kiss on his cheek. It was cold and icy, but the fire in his eyes made her melt.

Ali stuck his hand inside his coat pocket, fumbled around, and then withdrew a black velvet box and opened it.

Solange gasped at the size and shape of the ring before hurriedly taking off her glove and sticking her hand out, grinning like a Cheshire cat.

Ali slid off his chair to his knees and, in the small expanse of the area between the horses and the bench, he said, trying to hold back laughter, "Solange Montgomery, I love you. Will you marry me?"

"Ali Marks, I will marry you."

In the dusk of the evening light the dazzling princess-cut diamond twinkled at her. The brightness of the ring would compete with any stars that might emerge later that evening.

Ali slid the ring on her finger, and tears of joy cascaded down her face. Getting up from his reclining position, Ali took his hand and wiped her tears. "You're going to get icicles if you keep this up."

"I love icicles. But not as much as I love you," she whispered. "Take me back to the house so I can show you how much."

Ali picked up the reins and once again after making a clucking noise, the horses took off.

Once they arrived back at the house and Ali slowed the horses, Solange saw two men she'd never seen before standing at the end of the driveway. She cast a questioning look at Ali, who said, "They're right on time to collect their property."

"You certainly took care of it for them. You never used the whip once."

"I don't like them. If you know how to handle a horse, you really don't need them." He gave her a look as he reached for his wallet. "I'll be in shortly," he said.

"I'm going to wait for you to bathe. But first I want to show off my ring."

Throwing off the blanket, Solange nimbly climbed out of the carriage and walked as quickly as she could without falling on the ice up the driveway into the house. "Grace," she shouted once she got inside.

"Stop yelling. I'm right here," Grace said as she and Jet sat close on the couch.

"Look," Solange said, thrusting her hand out. "I'm officially engaged."

Jet made a low whistle. "That must have set him back a few pay checks."

"Don't be crass, Jet," Grace said. She picked up Solange's hand and eyed the ring. After she let Solange's hand fall, she turned to Jet. "That *must* have set Ali back a few pay checks." She and Jet broke into laughter.

Ali entered, hearing the tail end of their conversation. "It set me back more than a few." He took his hand and ruffled Solange's hair. "But she's worth it." Then he turned to Grace and Jet and asked, "How is Ebony?"

"Grace's face brightened. "She feels better. I'm sure that she's going to wake everyone up early tomorrow morning in order to open presents. But I still think that I'll take her to the doctor next week for a check-up."

"Good," Ali said with satisfaction. "I'm glad to know my goddaughter is feeling better." He breathed a long sound of weariness. "Now I need to take a shower. I smell like the horses and don't want to sit on your furniture until I bathe," he said.

"I need a shower, too. And I'm tired from that long drive, so I think that I'm going to take a nap," Solange said, following Ali so closely she almost stepped on his heels.

Grace and Jet gave each other looks that let each other know that they were ready to take a nap themselves.

Once they went to the bedroom, they walked straight to the dark bathroom and started shedding their clothes.

Solange found what looked like a new shower cap on the hook on the inside of the bathroom door and, while Ali turned the faucet on, she stuffed her hair underneath it. Through the shadows of the room, Solange saw Ali step into the shower and with lightning speed she followed him.

The stinging heat of the shower pelted their bodies, and Solange reached for a loofah hanging on a string. After squeezing a generous amount of shower gel on it she motioned for Ali to turn around. He did her bidding and bowed his head. Solange methodically soaped Ali from the back of his neck, down his shoulders, across his buttocks, down the back of his thighs and his legs, and then, turning him around, rinsed him. Then she started on his front. She took a small quantity of soap in the palm of her hand and gently kneaded it on his face, making sure she didn't get any in his closed eyes. Then she added more soap on the loofah and began to wash his neck and shoulders.

When her hands massaged his pecs, she felt them flex, but her real thrill was the feel of his six-pack. Then she felt his manhood close the distance between them and she grasped him, pulling his penis towards her, then away from her and then towards her again. Ali bent his head and watched her movements. His breathing became ragged and she felt the sweetness of his breath as it fanned her. Becoming more aggressive, she sped up her tempo and her hand gripped and pumped him. He flung his head back under the spray of water that spewed from the nozzle and then suddenly he burst, releasing all of his love into her hand. Turning around spent, he braced himself for support with his hands on the shower wall.

Stepping close to him, Solange placed her hands around his middle and buried her face in his shoulder blades. "Go to bed," she murmured. "I'll be in soon." Nodding his head silently, Ali stepped out of the shower and Solange saw him reach for a towel just as she reclosed the shower curtain.

Humming her favorite song she thoroughly washed herself. Once she left the shower, she grabbed a fluffy towel that was folded on the counter. She briskly dried her body and then reached inside her overnight case that had been left in the bathroom earlier that evening. She rubbed oil on her skin from head to toe and then sprayed a light scent of honeysuckle on her neck, wrists, and on the area of the inside of her thighs. Refreshed and naked, she strutted into the bedroom. Solange stopped short, peering into the darkness when her eyes settled on Ali on his back, legs spread-eagled, snoring lightly. His chest rose and fell from deep breaths of slumber and his member was flaccid as it lay to one side.

With a look of indulgence on her face, Solange crept over to the closet and withdrew a blanket. Practically tiptoeing on the hardwood floor she took the blanket and gently tucked it around Ali's body in the same manner he'd done for her earlier that evening. Then gently easing herself onto the bed, she slid under the blanket, turned on her side and, after sliding her arm over where his waist lay, she fell into a sleep full of contentment.

# *CHAPTER 11*

Solange was awakened to the sound of three little taps on her bedroom door. She grinned and, getting up out of bed, pulled her housecoat around her. Solange eyed the sleeping form of Ali. Somehow during the night, he'd manage to rid himself of the blanket she'd covered him with and he lay on his stomach with his face buried in a pillow. The rise and fall of his taut naked buttocks made Solange hasten to the door before Ebony, impatient and tired of waiting, opened it and saw Ali in all of his naked glory.

Opening the door a mere crack, she smiled indulgently at Ebony as she stood outside the door with her arms folded in front of her. She was dressed in red pajamas with the feet attached to them. Solange's eyes danced with delight as she observed Ebony's stance. She was standing in the exact pose Grace had when she was tired of waiting for something or someone. Putting a pretend look of irritation on her face, Solange growled, "What do you want?"

"Get up," Ebony said, not at all put off by Solange's fierce look. "Mommy cooked breakfast and I want to open my presents."

"It's too early," Solange said, continuing to rib Ebony.

"No, it isn't. It's after eight o'clock. Where's my goddaddy?" She pushed on the door in an effort to get into the room.

"Sweetheart, go and wait for me in the den. We'll be out soon," Solange said hastily.

"Promise," Ebony said, not moving.

"Promise," Solange agreed.

With these words, Ebony turned around and, sliding in pajama socks, sped down the hallway, disappearing out of sight.

Solange turned to see Ali getting out of bed. "Good morning, and I heard," Ali said.

Solange said with mock trepidation, "We'd better hurry before she comes back and gives us a spanking."

When Solange and Ali entered the living room, the vision that they saw could have been a Christmas commercial. There were loads of presents under the tree and Jet sat with Livingston, his mirror image, sitting on his lap. Livingston was also dressed in red pajamas and appeared to be fascinated by what Ebony was doing. She was on the floor next to the tree and was picking up the presents one by one. Looking at the labels on them, she'd started separating them according to who they belonged to.

Grace entered the room and plopped down on the loveseat next to Jet. Impressed by Ebony's systematic approach, Solange gave Grace an inquiring look.

"Her daddy told her that if she could read the names on the gifts and separate them once she was done, we'd start opening them. I'm surprised you're up this early. I thought that you two would be sleeping in. I know that you must have been exhausted from your trip."

"I was asleep until an impish elf paid me a visit," Solange said and smiled.

"I told her not to bother you. When she disappeared like that, I thought that she was in the bathroom or something," Grace said.

"I'm glad she did come. I can sleep anytime I want, but I can't see my family in Lake City anytime I want. Every minute we spend together is precious to me and Ali. Right, honey?"

"Right," Ali agreed.

Then Solange held her hands out, and Jet obligingly handed Livingston to her. Solange held him close, and the smell of baby powder made her feel a tug in her innards.

Grace said, "Breakfast is done, by the way. Jet and I already fed the children. Ours is being kept hot in a warming tray."

"Thanks, but I don't eat this early. It's only eight o'clock in the morning, and my stomach isn't even awake yet," Solange replied.

"How about you, Ali?" Jet asked. "I know you're ready for some food."

"I sure am. On my job I've already eaten breakfast and I'm trying to decide what I'm going to do about lunch. But I want to wait until Ebony has her fun." He looked at Ebony, who was deep in concentration as she fulfilled her bargain. Amused, all the adults watched and listened as she read the names on the gifts. Once she was done, she looked up excitedly.

"Go ahead," Jet instructed tolerantly.

Everyone watched as Ebony sat on the floor surrounded by presents.

The first box she opened held a pair of white ice skates. "Daddy, I love them!" She rushed over to Jet and threw her arms around his middle.

"You notice she said Daddy and not Mommy," Grace whispered softly to Solange and Ali. "She gives him credit for everything. She thinks her daddy can fix any problem in the world, and he loves that feeling."

Jet's eyes looked wet as if he was going to cry. "Go ahead and see what else Santa Claus bought you," Jet said.

"You're Santa Claus, Daddy."

"Your mother and I are, pumpkin."

Ebony went back over to her spoils, clothes, boots and a portable CD player.

"So she can listen to that mess in her room," Grace said, rolling her eyes. "I swear that child could listen to music all day long if I let her."

"You don't let her listen to that dirty rap, do you?" Solange asked.

"Of course not."

"I hear you." Solange grimaced. "When I was young, I didn't even bat an eye, but I just can't tolerate all that mess anymore."

Just then Ebony opened up a gift and started screaming. "Hannah Montana. Mommy, you got it!"

"Not me. Your godparents must have gotten that for you." She mouthed "I'm going to kill you" to Solange.

Solange grinned and gave her a thumbs-up.

Ebony started opening the box and started ripping pieces out of its Styrofoam packing. Then she grabbed a microphone dashed out of the room to her bedroom.

"Now maybe we can see what the rest of us got," Jet said.

"I got mine already." Solange thrust her hand out, showing off her engagement ring, and Livingston, fascinated by its brightness, tried to eat it.

"Here's something small to go along with it," Ali said and handed her a small box.

With a smile, she handed a sleepy-looking Livingston to Grace. "He can play with his gift later."

Grace rose and disappeared down the hall with him.

When Grace returned, she had a pleased look on her face. "He's down for the count. He's been up since four this morning," Grace said.

Jet handed Grace a box and she, in turn, gave him a large one.

They all looked at each other and Solange said, "Let's unwrap them on the count of three, and that way we can see what everyone else has."

"One, two, three," Solange counted.

There were tearing sounds as each of them tore into their presents.

When Grace opened hers, she found a large gift set of her favorite Dolce & Gabbana perfume. She looked up to thank Ali and noticed that he was staring at his present with a peculiar look on his face. It was a black attaché case with his initials monogrammed on it. "That's for you and your new job," she said excitedly.

Ali continued to stare at the briefcase for a long minute, saying nothing.

"Don't you like it?" Solange asked with some trepidation.

"I love it," Ali responded quietly. "I'll just be glad when the test is over and I get my results stating that I made it."

"You will," Solange said confidently. "I have complete faith in you."

Then their attention was drawn to Jet, who was staring at a large ten-by-twelve-inch picture. When he turned it around to face them, they saw it was him as a toddler sitting on his mother's lap. He was dressed in his Sunday best and had a look of contentment as he stared into the camera.

"I had it restored and blown up," Grace said softly. "I thought that we could hang it in the foyer."

"This is a wonderful present, Grace," he said. "Thank you for taking the time to have that done for me."

"Well, it's actually for us. I loved her, too," Grace said quietly.

She dangled a gold bracelet that held two charms and showed it to Solange and Ali. "Look what my husband got me. There's a charm with each of our children's birthstones. An emerald for Ebony and a diamond for Livingston. I absolutely love it."

Jet carefully leaned his gift against the sofa, took the bracelet from Grace and fastened it on her wrist. Then he leaned over and planted a firm kiss on her mouth.

"Let's see what this is," Solange said, opening a card. Inside were two tickets to the Alvin Ailey Dance Theatre of Harlem show. "Thank you guys so much. Look, Ali, the tickets are for the start of their summer season in July."

Sitting down next to Solange, Ali put his arm around her shoulder. "Cool. I've never been," he said.

"They are awesome," Solange explained. "It's amazing the way they tell the history of African Americans through song and dance. I haven't seen their show in years, though."

"I remember you telling me that last year you didn't get a chance to go, and I thought it was a shame with you being right there in New York and all."

She shrugged self-consciously. "Sometimes you forget everything that the city has to offer with being so busy and all. With the recession the arts are really struggling. People need to make a concerted effort to attend at least one event a year, or we may lose them."

Jet was in the process of opening a card labeled to him and Grace. "Wow," he said, showing them to Grace. "Check it out. Front row seats to see the Charlotte Hornets when they play the Knicks. I can't wait to see their point guard Sexton Johnson in action."

"I thought you would. They say he's the next Michael Jordan," Ali said.

Jet said admiringly, "He certainly has the potential." He turned back to Grace and added, "We'll make a weekend of it."

"I don't know about leaving the children for a whole weekend. Livingston will be teething soon," Grace said.

"Your godmother Liza will be able to handle that."

"I never met your godmother, Grace," Ali said. "I didn't even know you had one."

She made a hunching movement with her shoulders. "We're not close. She's a little too nosy for me. And I think that she's getting senile, but I let her babysit occasionally because she's actually Ebony's maternal grandmother."

"Oh?" Ali said with raised eyebrows.

"When Ebony's mother passed, she couldn't take her because of her health and she already had a few nieces and nephews that she was keeping."

Later that afternoon, Grace and Solange had separated themselves from the men because they had gotten bored with seeing them stare transfixed at the television watching a basketball game.

They sat at the kitchen table sipping hot chocolate. "Have you started working on the details for the wedding?"

"No, because Ali has been so tied up with studying for his test, he hasn't had the time. He said that he wants to be involved with the planning."

"July isn't that far away," Grace warned.

"It was going to be something simple, but then my mother got involved," Solange said wistfully. "Through the years, I've enjoyed the sermons that Pastor Greene has delivered and I really wanted to do something small at your church. And after the wedding, I figured that I would treat my parents to a vacation at Myrtle Beach, but Mom wants something fancy done at her church."

"It's your wedding, Solange. You should have it done the way you want it," Grace said.

"But she asks for so little. The bottom line is I'm marrying the man I love, so I guess the location of it isn't that big a deal."

"I know. Lake City is so meshed with the history of this country."

"I know. It's hard to imagine that such a small town has played such a large role. Being the birthplace of the astronaut Ronald McNair is something to be proud of."

"I know," Solange replied in a somber tone. "When the space shuttle *Challenger* went down, it seemed as if space travel took two steps back."

"It was a real blow to the people in Lake City. They still talk about it as if it just happened yesterday."

"There seems to be have been a lot of history made in Lake City through the years."

"Yeah, don't forget that in the fifties they burned Rev. DeLaine's house down in Summerton. Then he moved here to Lake City and they burned his church down. Once the *Brown vs. Board of Education* ruling came through they terrorized his family, because he's one of the people that had the guts to start petitioning the school district for a school bus. As principal he fought for his students and brought national attention to how difficult it was for our children to get an education. Thank God Rev. DeLaine was posthumously cleared in 2000 of attempted murder charges," Grace said.

"Too many years too late," Solange added derisively. "He died a wanted man, when all he was trying to do was stop people from harming his family."

"By the way, Solange, have you seen the movie *Proud* starring Ossie Davis?"

"No," she replied. "Is it any good?"

"It's awesome. The movie is based on the true story of the *USS Mason* that fought in WWII. You know the navy was still segregated and this was the first and only African-American ship that was allowed out to sea to engage in battle. There was a terrible storm and it served as a convoy and helped lead other ships to safety, saving the lives of men from the United States and Europe."

"Really?" Solange said, eyes wide with interest. "I'm going to have to rent it from Blockbuster."

"Yeah. The radio operator on the ship that warned the captain and other ships of Germans location in the water is James Graham. He was born and raised right here in Lake City."

"Get out of here."

"No kidding. I love movies like that, because sometimes we forget the struggle and need to be reminded. I mean, if it wasn't for people that forged the way for me decades ago, there's no way in the world I would be a manager at Microsystems Computers and in charge of over eighty employees," Solange said.

The next morning, Solange stared in admiration at her fiancé. Ali was dressed in a black pinstripe suit with black and white spectator shoes. He looked like a model out of *GQ* and she felt her heart surge with pride. She had donned a winter white cashmere suit and wore black pumps as a contrast, and she'd even pinned her hair into a chignon. She came to stand next to them and stared at the striking picture they made. "I think that we look like fit adults to be godparents to those adorable children."

"Yeah," Ali agreed, slapping her lightly on her butt. "I think that we'll pass the test. Come on. We better hurry or we'll be keeping everyone waiting."

When they entered the foyer, Solange gave a low whistle at the sight of Grace and her family. Grace and Jet were dressed in black. Grace had also dressed the children in matching colors. Ebony looked adorable in a white organza dress with a red sash on it, and Livingston, as he cuddled in Jet's arms, was decked out in a white double-breasted suit.

Grace smiled at them approvingly. "You two look great!"

Solange slid her hand into the crook of Ali's arm. "I know my man is fine. I better hold tight onto him until we are safely away from the church. I don't want any hungry females getting the idea that he's available."

"You don't have to worry about that," Grace said. "I already told Pastor Greene when I went over the particulars of the ceremony that even though the two of you have different last names, it wouldn't be that way for long because you're engaged."

"Good," Solange said. "I hope he passed the word."

"He probably did. Nothing's a secret at Deep River Holiness Pentecostal Church."

In the foyer, there was a load of presents that Solange knew were presents for the children at church. "I think that Ali and I will follow you in my car."

"That's a good idea. Then Ebony won't bombard you with questions all the way there."

Jet walked over to the hall closet and returned with a mink coat that he put around Grace's shoulders.

Ali lifted an eyebrow and asked with a touch of humor, "Animal fur? Aren't you afraid that some animal rights activist will throw some red ink on it?"

"They'd better not," Jet warned with a hard glint in his eyes. "My wife has a right to wear anything she wants. The same way they have a right not to wear it."

Grace gave Ali a look. "I wouldn't buy a mink coat, but this has a special place in my heart. It was Jet's mother's. Besides, no one in Lake City would dare to say anything or question me wearing it. They eat squirrel, raccoons, and possum. Their priority is keeping a hot meal on the table and a roof over their heads."

Solange listened to the low, deep, melodic voice of Pastor Greene as he preached from the Book of Job. They were seated in the pew behind the deacons and Solange looked around the crowded church and smiled when she saw faces that were familiar to her from past visits. Every time the door opened, Liza Taylor peered into the back of the church to see if she knew who was coming in.

Solange sat beside Grace and she suddenly felt her stiffen.

"What's wrong?"

"I forgot my camera and I want to have pictures of the christening."

"Uh-oh. Are you going to send Jet back to the house to get it?"

"I can't. He can't leave because he's one of the deacons. I'll have to go."

"You can't go," Solange said. "If you took the kids, it would cause too much of a disruption and you can't leave them. What if one of them needs you? Do you want me to send Ali?"

"No. It's tucked in my nightstand in my goody drawer."

"Then I'll go," Solange whispered.

Suddenly a sound for them to hush was emitted from someone sitting behind them.

Simultaneously, Grace and Solange looked over their shoulders with apologetic looks.

Solange whispered, "I'll be back as soon as I can."

She gave Ali a look that spoke volumes. "I'll be right back," she whispered as an answer to his questioning stare. She climbed over him and the last three people sitting at the end of the pew. Once she was in the aisle, she held up her index finger, and as quickly as possible with head bent, practically tiptoed down the aisle and out the church. Once she was in the vestibule her attention was drawn to a man staring through a windowpane on the side of the door that let people see inside the church. Smiling a brief hello to him, she hurried out the door.

Once outside Solange breathed a sigh of relief. That was as difficult as getting out of solitary confinement in prison. Drawing her overcoat tighter around her, she found her car in the church parking lot and quickly backed out and headed towards Grace's house.

Once she hit the outskirts of town, she slowed when she saw a queue of cars stopped. A police car with two officers was conducting a checkpoint. As she sat and waited in line, her thoughts were buoyed by the fact that they seemed to be moving quickly. Grace left a large expanse of area between her and the truck in front of her because it would obstruct her view as to what was going on if she got too close. It was an eighteen-wheeler that had tree logs that were hanging out the back.

Once the truck reached the checkpoint, an officer walked up to the driver, tipped his hat at him and then waved him along. Then he held his palm out to Grace to stop.

Grace inched her Cadillac up and rolled her window down. "Yes, officer?" she said politely.

"Driver's license and registration, please."

The officer was chewing profusely on something and when he spoke by the brown stain on his teeth Solange knew that it was snuff. *He didn't ask homeboy that was in front of me for his license and registration. His truck is a safety hazard with all that crap hanging out the back of it.* Instead of voicing her thoughts, she reached into the glove compartment and took her registration out and handed it to him. Then she reached into her wallet and took out her license and insurance card. He took them and went to his patrol car, slid inside and began calling in her information.

Solange looked at the other officer, who watched her with an unblinking stare. "Pull over to the side of the road, ma'am." He spoke slowly, with a slow Southern drawl.

As Solange navigated her car to the shoulder, she felt her temper begin to rise. She looked in her rearview mirror at the large number of cars that had formed while she'd talked with the officer and her temper boiled when she saw him waving other cars through the checkpoint without checking their credentials.

He spit some tobacco out onto the ground. "I see you're from out of state. What brings you to our neck of the woods?"

*None of your damn business.*

The officer looked at Solange's stoic expression and silence and then began to walk the periphery of her car. He disappeared through the back and remained motionless for a moment. Then he came back and said, "One of your taillights is out."

"What?" Solange asked in surprise.

"I said," he said, his voice holding a tinge of triumph, "your right tail light is out. We'll have to give you a ticket. That's dangerous for someone who's driving behind you. They might not realize that you're trying to stop and ram right into you."

"Not if they're not following me too closely," she answered hotly.

"Well we can't take a chance on that can we?"

Then he went over to the patrol car, said a few words to his partner and then came to stand in the street, taking down the yellow cones that had signaled that a checkpoint was in progress.

Solange got out of her car and stomped to the back of it. She stared at her taillights and saw a piece of the red signal light that had been damaged when she and Ali had gone to her parent's house at Thanksgiving. *They still work. But I will not give him the satisfaction of arguing. I won't win, and it would only give him his jollies.*

The first officer strode back over to her car and handed her a ticket while the other stood off to the side watching her reaction. "Here you go, ma'am," he said.

Solange grabbed it and got back into her car. Then she took it and without looking at it stuffed it in the console between the two front seats.

"Have a good day," he said suavely.

*If it wasn't Sunday and people weren't waiting for me at church, I'd take a chance of going to jail and curse him out.*

Instead, she gave him a haughty stare and eased her car back onto the road. Once she looked into her rearview mirror and saw that she was out of sight from the policemen, she stepped on the gas. Soon she was pulling into her sister's house. Letting herself in with her key, Solange stormed into the house, stalked to the bedroom and after opening the drawer of the nightstand, withdrew the digital camera. After backing down the driveway, she tore off to the church.

Solange didn't realize that she had a ferocious look on her face when she plopped down on the seat between Grace and Ali. Pastor Greene was in the process of praying for an old woman in the front of the church. "What's the matter? What took you so long?" Ali whispered.

Solange remembered Ali's previous words: 'You find racism everywhere you go.'

"Nothing," she muttered. "Everything's just peachy."

Once Pastor Greene stopped praying and took his hand off the forehead of the woman in front of the church, she ambled back to her seat, leaning on the arm of the man who obviously was her son. Then he nodded at Jet and Grace. "We're on," Grace whispered.

As they stood in front of Pastor Greene, a quiet feeling of seriousness had descended on everyone inside the church. Pastor Greene held his hands out and gathered Livingston close to his chest. The members of the deacon board were lined up on his left and the deaconess board was on the right. As Solange and Ali faced the pastor, the enormity of the responsibility that she and Ali were taking on suddenly enveloped her and she made a silent vow that she would do everything she could to be a good role model for her godchildren. Ebony stood directly in front of her and Ali, and she seemed to understand how important the ceremony was, because she had a pensive look on her face and was completely still.

Pastor Greene spoke in his soothing manner. "We are here to christen the children of Grace and Jethro Newman." Then he took some blessing oil from the bottle that was handed to him by the church mother. "I christen and dedicate this child, Livingston Newman, to our Lord Jesus Christ." He took a dab and rubbed it into Livingston's forehead.

Livingston didn't squirm but instead stared unblinkingly at Pastor Greene.

Then Pastor Greene took the same amount of oil and placed his hand on Ebony's forehead. "I dedicate this child, Ebony Newman, to our Lord Jesus Christ.

"We are also formally inducting Solange Montgomery and Ali Marks as their godparents. This is a responsibility not to be taken lightly. By agreeing to be their godparents, God forbid if something were to happen to their parents, you are expected to raise and love these children as if they were your own." He gave them a stern look. "Do you agree to do this?"

"We do," Solange and Grace answered in unison. Then they smiled at each other.

"You are to make sure they get a college education. High school is not enough anymore."

"Yes, sir," Grace said, and her voice trembled.

"You are to give sound advice to the parents when needed."

"Yes, sir," Ali answered for them.

Pastor Greene bent down and spoke to Ebony, but everyone in the church could hear what he was saying. "You are to listen to them. Being a godchild does not mean that you are to always expect them to buy you things. If your parents are not around, you are to do what they tell you. Do you understand?"

Ebony leaned her body on Grace. Then she nodded yes.

Pastor Greene looked at Livingston, and, smiling, said, "Do you understand?"

Livingston stared at him and then let out a yell. Everyone in the church chuckled.

"Then I, Pastor Edward Greene of Deep River Holiness Pentecostal Church of Lake City, declare Solange Montgomery and Ali Marks as the godparents of Livingston and Ebony Newman."

There was a spattering of applause that got louder as he handed Livingston back to Jet and Grace as they had stood to the side and watched the ceremony. Now that the ceremony was over, Liza Taylor ran to the front and began snapping pictures from every angle possible.

As they filed back into their pew, Solange's attention was drawn to the man that she'd encountered earlier when she'd left the church. He was seated in the last pew, and, as he stared at them, his eyes narrowed in a way that made a shiver run up and down Solange's spine. When their eyes locked, she turned hers away.

# CHAPTER 12

When they finally pulled up at the house, Solange was worn out. They had decided to eat at the Golden Corral so that everyone could get what they wanted, and the restaurant had been so crowded with the church crowd that Solange had developed a headache. She glanced at Ali. "I'm glad that we're going home in the morning. I miss my house," she said.

"I miss you," Ali said. "I'm tired of sharing your company with others."

"I feel the same way." She let her hand drop between Ali's legs and cup him. "What's that on the door?"

"I don't know," Ali answered. "It looks like a note or something."

They unbuckled their seat belts in order to leave the car and watched Jet go and pull the note off the door.

"I'm going to go and help Grace unload the kids," Solange said.

"Hand-delivered Christmas card?" Ali asked when he reached Jet.

"Sort of," Jet said, quickly folding the envelope and its contents in half and sticking it into his pants pocket. Then he said, "Tell Grace that I need to run an errand, and I'll be back as soon as I can."

"Sure. Do you want some company?"

"No," Jet said, averting his eyes. "This is business."

After Jet had jumped in his car and peeled out down the street, Grace and Solange looked at Ali questioningly.

He shrugged and said, "I don't know. He said some important business had cropped up."

"Someone probably is asking him to do a favor for them or something. He usually keeps that sort of thing to himself."

"Mommy, look what I can do." Ebony had the remote to her Wii and started belting out one of Hannah Montana's songs from the player.

Ebony stood in front of the sofa where Grace and Solange sat and started gyrating as if she was in concert.

"Oh, my goodness. Kill me now," Grace said.

Ebony screwed her face up in concentration as she belted out song after song. After a while she plopped down into a heap on the floor, her breathing erratic.

"Thank goodness," Grace said in relief.

"Mommy, my legs hurt again."

"I guess so," Solange muttered wryly.

"Does that mean that you're done for the day, or how about the year?"

"What?" Ebony said, not getting the meaning.

"Nothing, pumpkin. Why don't I fix you a warm bath and let you soak in it?"

"Okay, Mommy."

Ebony slowly got off the floor and walked towards the bathroom down the hall.

Jet parked his Yukon in the parking lot of the deserted Ford dealership. With barely controlled anger he viewed the beat-up looking Mustang that pulled up behind him. Opening his glove compartment he looked at the loaded .38, then closed the compartment door and climbed out.

The man halted in front of Jet and held out his hand. "How are you doing? I'm Sidney Mack."

Jet didn't take the proffered hand. His hands remained stuck in his pockets, clenched from anger. Instead he sized him up.

Sidney gave Jet a look of reproach. "I had hoped to be greeted a little more civilly," Mack said.

"Why would you think that? You come to my home and leave a note declaring that you are my daughter's father, basically threatening that if I didn't meet you that you would come back later and announce to everyone who you are. What kind of reception did you expect to get?"

"I would think that you would be happy for Ebony to learn who her real father is."

"I'm her father," Jet said through clenched teeth. "And where in the hell have you been all this time?"

"Overseas. I didn't even know about her until two years ago."

"Two years. Her mother was alive then. Did you contact her?"

"No, because Naomi and I ended on bad terms."

"So you let that keep you from the daughter that you now supposedly want in your life?"

Sidney looked away, then back at Jet. "Ebony's mother and I had a thing. I mean, we weren't boyfriend and girlfriend, so . . ."

"Then why do you want to be a part of her life now? How do you know that you're her father? Did you take a blood test? You're not listed on her birth certificate. It says father unknown."

"Well, I'm not really sure. I mean, like I said, we were together off and on. I would like you to bring Ebony in for a blood test and then we'll see."

"You're crazy as hell," Jet spat out. "Do you think that I would subject my daughter to this kind of ghetto mess?"

"Well, to be honest, Mr. Newman, I'm just trying to find myself. I've been unemployed for a while and I really don't have a way to take care of her. She seemed so happy today in church with all of you, and you seem to have the American dream. But if I stay in Lake City, I see no reason not to be a part of her life."

"If you stay in Lake City," Jet said slowly.

"Yes." Mack coughed. "I want to make a new start in L.A., but it's so expensive there. I need some money to help get started until I get some contacts. I want to be a rapper."

"At your age?" Jet scoffed derisively.

"It can happen," Mack replied in a surly voice. "But I need some spending money."

Jet's eyes had narrowed to slits. "What are you saying?"

"I don't want to hurt nobody. If I had $25,000, I'd be more than happy to leave the area."

"And not come back," Jet stated with a hard inflection.

"Sure. I have no family here. Of course maybe Ebony. Otherwise, I have no other reason to come here."

"I'll give you the money," Jet said through clenched teeth. "Not because you're blackmailing me. But any man that would sell his child would ruin her if he was allowed to be in her life. Come by my clinic tomorrow around three o'clock and I'll have your money. It's located at . . ."

"I know where you are. I've been in town for almost a week."

"Yet you choose now to show yourself," Jet said.

"I'll take cash," Mack said smoothly.

"Of course. But you will sign a paper giving up all legal rights of paternity."

"No problem," Mack said. "I don't know if she's mine anyhow."

Disgusted, Jet sat in his SUV and watched Mack rattle out of the parking lot.

Hours later, Grace and Solange sat on the sofa companionably drinking apple cider when they heard the garage door open. "It's about time," Grace said with relief. "I was getting ready to send out a search party for my husband."

"Maybe Ali will wake up now. He got bored with just the two of us chattering. He decided to take a nap."

"He needs it anyhow, with you guys leaving in the morning," Grace said regrettably.

"I hate to leave with Ebony feeling sick again. It's so unlike her."

"I know," Grace said pensively. "I can't wait until the doctor's office opens tomorrow."

Grace noticed the strained look on Jet's face.

"What's the matter?"

"Nothing," he said brusquely. "Where are my children?"

"They're asleep. Ebony's legs hurt again, so I rubbed them down with alcohol."

Without saying another word, Jet stalked down the hallway before quietly opening Ebony's door and going inside. He walked over to her bed and stood in the dark watching her.

Sensing his presence, her eyes opened. "Daddy," she whispered.

Jet sat down on the edge of the bed and gathered her into his arms. He held her so tightly, she began to wiggle.

"Daddy, you're hurting me."

Jet released her. "I'm sorry, pumpkin. I would never hurt you. Your mother said that your legs hurt."

"Not anymore," Ebony answered. "Mommy fixed them."

Jet smiled in the darkness. "Of course she did. Now go back to sleep."

"Yes, Daddy," Ebony whispered. Her eyelids immediately began to droop and only after he heard her light snores did Jet leave her side.

When Solange and Ali arrived back at home, they were so exhausted from their trip, they dropped their luggage in the foyer and staggered like blind people towards the bedroom.

Once Solange emerged from the shower, she looked at her freshly showered fiancé as he lay under the covers and said, "This week I need you to take my car to the shop. One of my tail lights is broken."

"Will do," he muttered sleepily. Once she slid into bed, he gathered her close and, after burying his face in her hair, fell into a deep slumber. She soon joined him.

When Solange got home from work a couple of days later, she smiled at the sight of Ali and Randolph dragging boxes out of a small U-Haul.

She walked over to them and kissed Ali lightly on the lips.

"Where's mine?" Randolph teased.

Ali shot him a dark look. "Dude, you're really trying me today," he said.

"Man, that's what you get for bothering me to help you with this little bit of stuff. Why'd you even rent a truck? It was a waste of money."

"When I rented the truck, I didn't know that Solange was going to make me get rid off all my stuff."

"That was your idea. I just said that we should put some of it in storage. You're the one who decided to sell it or give it to Goodwill," Solange said as she stood beside Ali with her arm around his waist.

"It was easier. There are so many broke people, once I put the flyer on the bulletin board my stuff went like hotcakes. In the aftermath of the recession people are still afraid to spend money."

"I know I am," Randolph said. "I really need my promotion."

"So do I," Ali echoed.

"Are you ready, man?"

"As ready as I'll ever be," Ali stated.

After Randolph left and they finished dinner, Ali grabbed his training manual.

"Would you like me to quiz you again?" Solange asked as she stacked the dishwasher.

"If you don't mind," Ali replied sheepishly.

Exhausted from the busy day she'd had at work, she grabbed the booklet and sank into a chair.

"What are the Miranda Rights?" Solange patiently asked Ali for the umpteenth time.

"It's the statement that a detective reads to a suspect before questioning that states that he has the opportunity to request a lawyer before making a statement."

"What is protocol if a suspect asks for a lawyer?"

"Pretend you didn't hear him."

Solange grinned at his answer.

"Just kidding," Ali said.

"Does a detective have to let a suspect call his lawyer before he is booked?"

"No, he does not. His first job is to secure the perpetrator for safety reasons and then the suspect is allowed one phone call."

Solange wearily passed the palm of her hand over her eyes. "Ali, you're ready. You've been ready for months. Don't over-study. It might be counterproductive."

"All right," he acquiesced. "Go ahead to bed and I'll be in shortly."

It wasn't until daybreak that Solange felt the mattress move from the weight of Ali's body as he lay down next to her.

When Ali entered the precinct, Randolph was waiting for him in the foyer. He hurriedly waved him over and when Ali reached him he said, "Cpt. Heath is looking for you."

"Why?" Ali asked, instantly worried.

"The word is that because of the budget cuts they're doing a lottery as to who can take the test. It's the luck of the draw."

"Shit," Ali spat angrily. "I've been studying for this test for months. How the hell are they going to pull the rug out from under us like this?"

"It's called a recession, man. You better get in there and at least give yourself a shot."

As Ali rode the elevator to the third floor and the testing site, he sent up a silent prayer that he'd secure a chance to test. Once he entered the room, he saw a group of fellow officers huddled in a group. He walked over to them. "Did you hear?" Dayle Hitter asked Ali.

"Sort of. I guess we're not going to all be able to take the test."

"Cpt. Heath was in here a minute ago. He said that the testing administrator drew names at random and he'd be back in a minute with the results," Eric Pritchard said.

"Then all we can do is wait," Ali said morosely. He went and sat down at a desk in the front of the room and soon the others followed suit.

Ten minutes later, Cpt. Heath entered the room followed by a man in uniform. Cpt. Heath stood at the podium and cleared his throat. He didn't need to ask for silence because he had all twenty men's full attention.

"I'm sure by now that everyone in here has heard the news. Because of the budget cuts we are held by the city to only have a certain number of promotions. I'm sure that each and every one of you can pass the test. So in order to cut down on the controversy as to who will actually get the promotions, when the test results come through, the department has decided to limit the amount of officers allowed to take the test at each session."

There were sounds of grumbling and Cpt. Heath patiently waited. "I agree," he said solemnly. "It sucks. But it is completely out of my hands and," he gave a pointed look at the man standing by his side, "and it isn't the fault of Cpt. Torres."

In spite of Cpt. Heath's announcement, dirty looks were shot at Cpt. Torres, who seemed unmoved.

Cpt. Heath opened his leather-bound ledger and withdrew a piece of white paper. "The following policemen will be allowed to take the test today. Ernest Snyder, Ali Marks, Jennifer Hastings, and Angel Cruz." Then he looked regretfully at the people whose names weren't called and said, "I deeply apologize to the rest of you."

Dayle Hitter stood to his feet in one violent movement and his chair clattered to the floor. Without looking at it or attempting to pick it up he stormed out of the room, slamming the door. For what seemed to be an interminable length of time, no one moved or spoke. Then in stony silence everyone whose name hadn't been called shuffled out of the room with a downcast countenance.

Ali tried to decipher question eighteen for the umpteenth time. His eyes focused on the question. *What is a adnariM thgiR?* Ali furiously unscrambled the letters to the words in the question and then filled his answer.

"That's time," Cpt. Torres announced in an unemotional tone.

Ali closed his test. He already knew, as always, that he was the last test-taker in the room. He took a final anxious look at the clock before nodding in resignation at Cpt. Torres, who came over and picked up his test.

Showing no emotion, Torres took Ali's test and, after checking that all his personal information was correct, he said, "Good luck."

Ali gave him a steady gaze. "Thank you," he said before leaving the room. When Ali opened the locker room, he could hear the strident voice of Dayle Hitter. "I'd like to know why the hell they didn't draw names in front of us."

Ali hesitated by the door, and recognized that the next voice as Eric Pritchard.

"That Cpt. Torres doesn't know any of us. He has no reason to show favoritism. We got a bum rap, but someone had to."

"Did you notice how only minorities got picked?" Dayle sneered. "They bend over backwards to accommodate everyone but white men."

"That's not true," Eric Pritchard retorted harshly. "Did you stop to think that more minorities put their name in the hat to get the opportunity to take the test? By the way, it wasn't all minorities, Jennifer got chosen and she's white."

"She's a woman and that, too, is a minority," Dayle countered.

Ali had heard enough and entered the locker room.

All of a sudden a hush fell on the two men. Eric looked at him and said sincerely, "How do you think you did?"

"I guess okay. We'll just have to wait and see."

"I hope you passed, otherwise you'll probably get to take the test next time, too, and take someone else's spot," Dayle said, and then he slammed his locker door shut and stormed out.

"Ignore him. It'll blow over," Eric said.

Ali shrugged his shoulders in an uncaring manner. "He has a right to be pissed." Then he grabbed his duffel bag out of his locker and said to him, "I'll see you tomorrow."

"Later, Ali," Eric Pritchard replied.

That night in bed, Ali tossed and turned.

Finally Solange shook him awake. "Whatever is the matter with you?"

"Nothing," he mumbled.

Perceptively she said, "You need to relax. There's nothing you can do but wait for the results. Now that the pressure is off and that test is over we can get started working on our wedding plans."

Immediately Ali's spirits lifted. "Have you decided whether or not you're going to let Isabel help plan the wedding?"

"Maybe a little. But I want the two of us to plan most of our wedding."

"Me, too," he answered, and now his voice had gotten drowsy from sleep.

Solange sat in Starbuck's with her latté and waited anxiously for Isabel. Finally, she saw Isabel enter the restaurant and waved her over.

Isabel plopped down into the seat, shrugged out of her coat and laid it on the bench. "I'm sorry I'm so late. I had a blind date that went real well."

Solange's eyes widened. "A blind date?"

"Well, not really a blind date. We've been communicating via e-mail for over a month and we finally met for breakfast. He is tall, dark, handsome, and available."

"Really?"

"Yeah," Isabel said. "He's a good catch."

"But how do you know that the people that you're talking to aren't misrepresenting themselves?"

"Why would I think that they are? I'm not. I'm single, black, educated and a good woman. That's what I put down when I fill out the questionnaire." Then Isabel thrust her lip out in annoyance. "What's the matter? You think that a woman would have to be desperate or something to meet men like this?"

"I didn't say that," Solange said. "I just want you to be careful. There are some real freaks out there."

"I don't think it's any scarier than picking a man up on a train," Isabel said with a catty tinge to her voice.

"Ali is a cop," Solange retorted.

"Yeah, and statistics label them as some of the most violent of all men."

Silence descended on the duo.

"Well, I'm just saying that you said that he came up to you out of the blue and started talking to you."

"Not quite," Solange corrected her. "He'd been seeing me on the train and he worried about my safety. A couple of women had been mugged recently."

"But how did you know he was for real?"

"How do you know that that man you met on the Internet is who he says he is? At least Ali had a badge number, and I did do a background check. Maybe you should do the same for mystery man."

"I might just do that. Now what did you want to see me about?" Isabel asked a little stiffly.

*A little of Isabel goes a long way. I think that I need to rethink whether or not I want to have her involved in planning the biggest day of my life.* "Nothing special," Solange lied. "When I ran into you at Nobu we had agreed to get together, and since I was in the city on business I thought that this would be a good time."

"Well, I'm really glad you called. Since I've been in the city I find people a bit cold. I mean, I meet them at work and everything but my business is so fleeting I never see the same people twice."

Solange gave her an understanding smile. "I felt the same way after I moved here from Atlanta. But," she cautioned, "don't feel too despondent that you don't have a crowd around you all the time. I've found that life is a lot easier if you keep a small circle of friends. That way you're not splitting your time up too much and being torn into all different directions."

"You can say that because you have someone," she said in a tiny voice. "Maybe if we could get together more often, I wouldn't feel so lonely."

Solange felt backed into a corner. "I'll try to make it a point to keep in touch better," she promised in a half-hearted voice. She looked at her watch and exclaimed, "I can't believe it's this late. I wanted while I was over here to check in on Ali's mother for him." She reached into her pocketbook and pulled out her wallet. Pulling out some bills, she placed them on the table under the check the waitress had left while they were still eating. "This time it's on me."

Isabel gave her a smile and said, "Don't you let the next time be a long time."

"I won't," Solange said standing to her feet. Looking at Isabel's sad expression, she leaned over and gave her a small peck on the cheek. "See you soon."

As she walked away, Solange didn't see the look of jealously Isabel didn't attempt to hide as she watched Solange happily strut away.

Solange parked her car in the one vacant spot in front of her future mother-in-law's house. After ringing the bell, she stood patiently waiting for Amira to come. Beginning to worry, Solange pressed the bell again, and when she saw through the sidelight Amira descending the staircase, she felt a deep sense of relief.

Amira flung open the door and Solange was immediately appalled by her red-rimmed eyes. "Whatever is the matter?"

"My mother died a couple of weeks ago." Amira stepped aside to allow Solange entrance.

Quietly she followed her to the kitchen and sat across from her at the kitchen table.

"I'd hoped that we'd get together in time to mend our fences. Now it is too late."

"Did you call Ali?"

"No," Amira replied softly. "When I speak of them, he says nothing and his eyes are distant. He wants nothing to do with his family."

"It's because of the way they treated you, not because he wants to deny his heritage."

Silence enveloped the room.

"How did you find out?"

"Anah thought that I should know. This has postponed their trip because my father has no one to look out for him in Baghdad but Anah and Yusef. He has many business affairs that need tending to."

"Why don't you ask him to come to New York when they do?"

She shook her head. "He won't. He's so stubborn."

"Maybe with the death of his wife he might be more open. No one knows how long they have on this earth."

"I'll write Anah and enclose a letter to him. Maybe he will finally read it. Thank you so much, Solange. You are a good daughter."

When Solange got home, she sat close to Ali on the couch. "Honey, your grandmother died," she told him.

Confused, he looked up from the basketball game. "Who?"

"Your mother's mother," Solange said in a solemn voice. "She died a couple of weeks ago. Anah wrote your mother and told her."

He focused his attention back on the television. "Am I supposed to cry or something?"

"No," she said slowly, "but your mother is."

"How can you mourn a relationship that's been dead for over thirty years?"

"She's mourning the relationship that they had before it ended. And she's mourning the fact that now she'll never be able to repair it."

It was like a light bulb went off inside his head and a look of understanding surfaced on his face. "I'll call her," he said quietly.

"You're mother feels as if you're trying to deny your heritage."

"What heritage is that?" He gave her a penetrating look. "I'm American."

Solange brushed aside his deliberate attempt to deflect their discussion from the real issue at hand. "She feels that you want nothing to do with them when they come to visit."

"She's right," he flatly agreed.

"I get it, Ali. But for Amira's sake you are going to pretend that you do care. You are going to do whatever it takes to help your mother mend fences with the relatives she has left. Do you understand?"

At first, Ali just gave Solange a stony stare. "You weren't there when I saw her weeping because they treated her like she didn't exist. They were adults and knew the hurt they were inflicting, so as far as I'm concerned they will reap what they sowed," he said in an emotional voice. Then he picked up the remote and turned the volume up.

Solange knew by his actions that for the time being, their discussion of the matter was over.

# *CHAPTER 13*

"Fuck!" Ali balled up the results of his exam and threw it in the garbage can. He fought down the desire to hit the wall as the nemesis of his childhood had once again taken control of his life.

He stormed into the locker room to get his duffle bag, and when he got in, he saw Jennifer excitedly chattering to Eric Pritchard. "I can't believe I passed. It was so hard I guessed on some of the answers."

Dayle Hitter stood off to the side watching some of the other officers as they congratulated Jennifer. "How'd you do?" he shouted over to Ali.

Ali ignored him and turned to leave.

Then he heard Hitter snicker. "I guess I know what that means."

*Six-year-old Ali Marks was sitting in the last seat of Miss Towers's English class. He wasn't allowed to go out to recess until he finished his five question fill-in-the-blank test. Ali's attention wandered and he stared outside at his fellow classmates playing basketball.*

*Then suddenly, Miss Towers appeared next to his desk. "If you want to go outside, Ali, go ahead. You can finish this when you get back from recess."*

*"Thank you, ma'am," Ali responded disconsolately. "But I think I'd rather stay and finish my paper."*

*"As you wish," she responded gently and went back to her seat, where she was grading papers.*

*Ali didn't make it outside to play that day or many others.*

Something came over Ali and before he'd had a chance to think, he grabbed Dayle Hitter by the collar and pinned him. Ali slammed his head two times against the concrete wall.

"Ow," Dayle Hitter screamed. "Let me go!"

"Ali, don't," Jennifer yelled.

The next thing Ali knew, Eric Pritchard was pulling him away from Dayle Hitter.

Ali grabbed his duffel bag that he'd dropped during the scuffle and stormed out of the locker room.

When Ali got home it was late. He'd driven around for hours dreading the fact that he was going to have to break the news to Solange that he'd failed his test. He knew she'd be as upset as he was and she wouldn't understand.

A worried-looking Solange greeted him at the door. "I called you on your cell phone. Why didn't you answer it? I've been worried sick."

"I'm sorry. I had it off at work and forgot to turn it on when I left."

Solange followed a despondent-looking Ali as he walked into the den and plopped down into the chair. He stared blankly at the television and started absently channel surfing.

Watching him, a sick feeling of anxiety filled her stomach. "Did you get your test results today?"

"Yes," Ali said, and now he bent his head and stared at a piece of lint on the carpet. "I failed."

There was a look of disbelief on Solange's face. "How on earth did you fail that test? You knew every one of those questions by heart."

"I don't know," he said resentfully. "I guess that I should've known the answers by heart instead of the questions."

"I think that there's been a mistake," she protested. "Grace said when she taught school that there were mistakes made all of the time when it came to standardized tests."

"There was no mistake," Ali mumbled. "Take it from me."

"I refuse to believe that you really failed that test." Solange sat down on the couch cushion next to him. "The computer could have malfunctioned. Ask them to hand-grade it. For months I've been grilling you on those answers and you could answer them before I even finished asking you the question."

"Solange. All my life I have failed test after test after test." The eyes he now showed her were a mixture of embarrassment and defeat. "I'm dyslexic."

A confused look appeared on Solange's face and she repeated the word, "Dyslexic?"

"I have a disability, and when I take tests I either freeze up or give up."

Solange was quiet for a while as she tried to digest this newfound disclosure. *How has he been able to hide this from me for so long?* She frowned at him. "How long have you known?"

"My teachers figured it out when I was in middle school. Then they started pulling me out and showing me how to deal with my disabilities."

"Why didn't you ever tell me this?"

"I never saw the need to talk about it. My disability only rears itself at the most inopportune time. Timed tests and I don't get along."

"But, Ali," she said soothingly, "you can pass the test. All they have to do is make accommodations for you."

"I didn't ask for special accommodations. I thought that I knew the test well enough that I wouldn't need the extra time."

"Ali," Solange said, choosing her next words very carefully, "only the weak don't ask for help when they need it."

Ali dropped his head.

"Promise me that you'll sign up to take the test again, and that this time you'll ask for extra time."

Silence was the only response that she received.

"I want you to be happy," she said. Now a warning tone crept into her voice. "You won't be happy remaining a street cop on a beat. You aspire to be greater. Don't blow it because you're embarrassed about something that isn't your fault."

"Okay, Solange. I'll sign up to retake the test and this time I'll ask for unlimited time."

The minute Ali left early for work the next morning Solange called Grace.

"Hello, Solange."

Solange knew that Grace's caller ID had alerted her that it was her. "Ali has dyslexia," she blurted out.

"What?" she exclaimed. "How do you know that?"

"He 'fessed up last night. He failed his test and had to give me a reason why."

"Oh, no. He must be devastated."

"He is. I've never seen him so down. He said that he's known since middle school. I feel like such an idiot. There were all kinds of signs."

"Don't feel like the Lone Ranger on that one. When I taught school, I had a student that had a tinge of dyslexia and I didn't figure it out for a while. People with that disability are quite adept at hiding it."

"Now I know why when we go on a trip, no matter how many times we go to the same place, he gets lost."

"That makes sense," Grace agreed in a compassionate voice. "People that have dyslexia have trouble reading road signs. Their brain scrambles the letters and signs."

"One of our Sunday breakfast rituals is that I read the first paragraph from the headlines. I always thought it was cute. I thought that he just likes the way I read."

"He probably does, Solange," Grace said soothingly. "Don't look for drama in every nuance that involves the two of you."

"Dyslexia is hereditary, isn't it? What are the chances of our children inheriting this?"

"Shame on you, Solange," Grace said in a chiding tone.

"I didn't really mean that," Solange said, feeling embarrassed that she'd actually voiced her fear aloud.

Grace spoke soothingly as if she hadn't heard her. "If you do have children with dyslexia, it's not the end of the world. Of course, they would need to be taught how to compensate for their disability. That means extra time for tests and oral instructions. But as long as you catch it at an early age they'll learn to cope and it won't seem like such a handicap to them. Ali should ask for the accommodation of having his test questions read to him. That gives him time to decipher and reassemble the words. If he does that, he'll be just fine."

"I'm glad to hear that, and I'll tell him. Not right now, though, because I don't think that he'd be happy to know that I shared this with you. Obviously this is a touchy subject for him," Solange said.

"Jet and I will never let on that we know."

"Jet?" Solange uttered in surprise. "He's not listening on the phone, is he?"

"Of course not," Grace drawled. "But you know that Jet and I tell each other everything."

When Ali entered the precinct, he spied Cpt. Heath and Lyle Pritchard engrossed in deep conversation.

Heath gave Ali a penetrating look.

Heath waved him over.

When Ali reached them, Lyle Pritchard spoke first. "I need to speak to you about an important matter. Instead of dragging you to my office, Cpt. Heath has said that I can use his."

"Certainly," Ali answered with composure.

Once Ali was seated across from Pritchard, he eyed him carefully.

Lyle Pritchard took a folder from a drawer and placed it on the desk in front of him. Then he clasped his hands.

"What happened yesterday between you and Hitter?"

"I lost my cool."

Pritchard studied Ali's face. He couldn't tell from his body language what he was thinking and his tone gave nothing away.

"Were you upset about something and then took it out on him?"

"I failed my test so I was angry. Hitter caught me at the wrong time and place. That's about it. Why all the questions? Is he pressing charges for assault?"

"No," Pritchard said. "He didn't say anything about it. I heard he was pretty shaken up, so he's probably too embarrassed to lodge a complaint. I heard about it through the grapevine. I was just curious to get your perspective of the situation. Do you think that there will be any more problems between the two of you?"

"Not on my part," Ali replied honestly. "I've pretty much stated my case, and once I'm done with something, then I let it go."

"I like the way you think. That's the kind of mentality that you should have in order to be a successful sniper."

"Sniper?" Ali retorted, totally caught off guard by the sudden turn of conversation.

"Yes," Pritchard said suavely. "I think that you would be a good candidate for sniper school. Have you ever thought about pursuing that field?"

"Yes, I have," Ali said in awe. "But I thought that you had to be a seasoned veteran of the force to even be able to apply."

"In the past there has been a lot of red tape, but the United States has a need to beef up our number of qualified snipers. Our military needs backup for certain domestic issues. The number of snipers we have available has lessened because we've been so stretched because of Afghanistan and Iraq."

A vision of Ali's father flashed in front of his eyes and the expression he had showed him bursting with pride.

"Are you interested?" Pritchard asked with a raised brow.

"Hell, yes," Ali answered.

"From all over the country trainees will convene in Florida. There's a training base in Orlando and you'll stay in the barracks."

"In Orlando, Florida?"

"Yes. We find the flat terrain and excruciating heat gives a pretty realistic picture of some of the terrain snipers are made to function in."

Ali's brain started working overtime. Pritchard said in a warning tone, "It will be a very rigorous training camp, and you only have one chance to make it. If you fail, you don't get a chance to go back."

"How long does that program take?"

"Six months to a year, depending on how well you do. You'll be on leave of absence from the department and once you complete your program, you'll be able to resume your position here until you get placed. Usually you have to be a member of SWAT to even be considered. This is a one-shot deal."

"There you will also be required to pass a written test. If you do, then you'll be sent to do field work with seasoned snipers for a short introductory period."

Ali's heart dropped. The old feeling of inadequacy consumed his belly. He swallowed the lump in his throat before he spoke. "There's a problem with me passing the written test. I'm dyslexic." Ali spoke these words impassively. "I can past the field test, but I would need accommodations for the written test."

Pritchard said dryly, "I know you can pass the field test. You showed sharpshooter ability when you saved my son and your partner's life a couple of months ago. So when I was asked for input in implementing this program, I immediately thought of you. As for the written test, that shouldn't be a problem. You won't be the first one, and I'm sure not the last, to need special accommodations." Pritchard held out the yellow folder that was on top of the desk. Ali's name was plastered on it. "Here's the paperwork. Would you like time to look it over and think about it?"

"No," Ali answered without vacillation, "my decision is made. I would feel privileged to enter the program.

Being a sniper was an unobtainable dream that has turned into a reachable goal."

"You need to be ready to leave in a week."

Ali took the folder that Lyle Pritchard offered and began signing on the dotted lines.

An exuberant Ali entered the house with a bottle of champagne and a bouquet of red roses. He put the champagne in the refrigerator and walked towards the bedroom, where he heard the shower water running. He sat patiently down on the side of the bed and waited.

When Grace walked out of the bathroom, Ali sat there grinning.

Tying the sash on her bathrobe, her mouth fell open in surprise at the exuberant look on Ali's face.

"Was I right? Was there a mistake on your test scores?" Solange breathed a sigh of relief. "It must be because when you left here this morning you looked like it was the end of the world. Now, look at my man. He's back to his old self."

For a split second, Ali's expression clouded, but then it cleared again. "No, I'm not even thinking about that," he said dismissively. "I have better news for us."

"What?" Solange asked obviously bewildered.

Ali's chest seemed to puff out. "Cpt. Pritchard asked me to go to sniper school. They're handpicking candidates for a special program."

"Oh, my God!" Solange screamed excitedly.

"Yes, ma'am. I should be a certified sniper in six months to a year." He handed her the flowers. "This is for you. Solange, you always stick by me through thick and thin. You're my life vest when the waters get rough."

Solange took the bouquet and bent her nose into the spray. She took a deep breath, and when she looked up tears of happiness glistened in her eyes. "That's because you're worth it." Then she sat on his lap and curled one arm around his neck and rested her head on his shoulder.

Ali's hand snaked around her waist and they held each other close for a long time, not speaking, content to only cuddle each other.

Finally, Solange stirred. "I want to put my flowers in a vase. Follow me into the kitchen. Dinner is all ready. I made pork chops," she said.

Ali walked behind Solange and watched her as she filled an empty vase with water. "Solange, we're going to have to get one of those credit cards with frequent flyer miles."

"Why?"

"For us to travel back and forth. We need to try and get something for all the shuttling we're going to be doing."

Solange turned to Ali with her flowers still in her hand. "What on earth are you talking about?"

"Hello! Flying back and forth to and from Orlando."

"What are you talking about?" she exclaimed.

"I told you the training center is in Orlando, Florida."

"No, the hell you did not." Solange had paused between each word.

"Yes, I did," he answered curtly.

"Ali Marks, your ass did not tell me that you would be moving to no damn Orlando, Florida," Solange said angrily.

A look of genuine contrition etched his fingers. "I'm sorry, honey. I'm just so excited I left that out."

"Left that out," she echoed his words. Then she said authoritatively, "You can't go."

"Excuse me?" His tone was clipped.

"We're getting married. I'm not moving to no damn Orlando. What about my job?"

"Solange." He drew in a sigh of relief. "Is that the problem? Neither one of us is moving to Orlando. I just have to take my training there. Then I'll be back and try to get a position in the tri-state area."

"How long will you be in Orlando?" she asked doubtfully.

"Six months to a year." Finally the full enormity of how long that time frame was struck him, and it seemed to be a much bigger problem than it was when he'd taken Lyle Pritchard up on his offer.

"Six months to a year!" Solange took the bouquet of flowers and hit Ali across the top of his head with them. They fell from her grasp and fluttered to the floor, where they looked like a pool of blood at their feet.

"Don't do that, Solange," Ali said.

"I know you didn't bring your happy ass in here and tell me that you agreed to move to Orlando for a year without running it by me. If you don't want to marry me, Ali, you don't have to move to Orlando. You can move your ass right around the damn corner and I'll leave you the hell alone."

Ali's color ran from his face and fear gripped him. "That's not what this is, Solange," he said quietly. "You know that."

Solange shouted, "I'm beginning to think that I don't know you at all. First of all you're dyslexic and kept it from me. Now you want to move to Florida and be a damn sniper. The next thing I know some ex-wife with a passel of brats will show up out of the blue."

"You're being ridiculous."

But Solange was on a roll. "Is Ali Marks your real name? Hell, maybe you're a terrorist or something and you have to leave the area in a hurry."

"Girl," he said, obviously pissed, "you have lost your damn mind."

"All you had to do was to go in to work today and sign up to take the detective test again. Ask for special accommodations. Did you do that? Hell no! This is just a way for you to not have to deal with your disability. You'd rather totally uproot your life, our lives," she stressed, "instead of facing your fears."

Ali stood immobile. Then he grabbed his coat off the chair where he'd thrown it earlier and stormed out.

After he left, Solange wearily walked into the bedroom, lay face down on the bed and wept.

Hours later, Ali walked into the darkened room.

Solange lay on her side with her back to him, but he knew that she was aware of his presence because of the rigidity of her form.

Slowly he sank on the side of the bed. He cleared his throat and said softly, "Solange, I'm sorry that I didn't discuss things with you before I accepted the job. I was so excited that I didn't think about the effect this would have on you, on us."

The air hung heavily between the two of them. "The fact that it didn't even cross your mind as to my feelings, that's the scary part. I don't want someone in my life who is so selfish that I have to take a back seat to his desires and whims of fancy."

Ali cringed at Solange's unspoken threat. "This isn't a whim or fancy. I've wanted this since I was a teenager. It just never occurred to me that it would happen. And certainly not like this."

"Then this is something else you've hidden from me," she said, and a deep hurt was reflected in her voice. "Since when did you crave the career of a sniper?"

"Since they wouldn't let my father in," he said resentfully.

Solange's body jerked in surprise when she heard Ali's words.

"My dad's dream was to be a sniper. They wouldn't even let him apply to be on the SWAT team in order to make sure he never got the chance. When he got home I could tell he felt beaten by some unknown force. My father wasn't dyslexic, but he was born in Iraq, and deep inside he knew that he had a snowball's chance in hell of getting invited in to that elite circle. But still he kept trying. Then today," Ali took his index finger and placed it on his chest, "today they invited me in. Things have changed."

"I didn't know about any of this." She turned over on her side and faced him. Tears of worry and frustration had formed frown lines on his forehead, and she started to take her hand and soften them with her fingertips, but in mid-air she stopped her movement and let her hands fall onto the mattress with a thud.

"I went for a long walk and thought about things." He added doggedly, "I will go in tomorrow and decline the offer."

"But you said that you had already filled out the paperwork."

Ali grimaced and said, "I think I can wiggle my way out of it. There are plenty of other men out there willing to take my place." Ali took his hand and ruffled Solange's hair. "I'm going into the den and watch the news."

For hours Solange lay in the darkness before eventually drifting off to sleep. She awoke to daylight streaming through the blinds. Without opening her eyes, she reached for Ali and realized that his side of the bed was empty and felt a stabbing pain in her heart.

Solange turned over onto her stomach and, unable to go back to sleep, she flopped over on to her back again. Without giving it any more thought she padded barefoot out into the den.

Ali lay on his back asleep, with his arm across his forehead. Even in repose, his face was frowned from concentration.

Solange sat on the edge of the sofa and jostled him. Then she took her forefinger and gently smoothed his frown lines. He slowly opened his eyes, and she saw reflected in them the deep love that he had for her.

She sat on the edge of the cushion. "I want you to go," she said.

"No," he flatly stated. "I don't want to lose you. I choose you."

She smiled and said, "That's very big of you, Mr. Ali Marks. But you don't have to choose. You won't lose me."

"Long-distance relationships are very hard."

"I know that, but I think that we can withstand the pressure. How about all of these women who are alone while their husbands fight overseas? They make it work, and so can we. I'll just pretend that you're a soldier at war."

He shook his head negatively. "I don't want you to feel abandoned."

"I won't. We'll be jet-setters," she said in a quirky voice.

There was a long silence in the room, and then Ali asked, "Are you sure?" He searched her face to see for himself that she really felt it was okay for him to go.

"I'm sure," she said. "A happy man makes a happy husband."

Ali breathed in a deep sigh of regret, and when he spoke, penitence was evident in his voice. "I promise that I will never make such an important decision without your input again."

Solange took two fingers and placed them on his lips stilling his words. "We need to postpone the wedding."

"No," Ali said adamantly.

She smiled gently at him. "You said that it was important for you to be involved in the planning of the wedding, and that'll be just too hard with you in Florida."

"But we'll be seeing each other as much as possible. Either I'll catch the red-eye up here or you'll come down."

"I know, but with the wedding being at my mother's church and all, it would be just too difficult. The love we have is not going to change because we postpone the wedding."

"Then when will we be getting married?" Ali asked in a mournful tone.

"The minute you graduate from sniper school, we'll set the date," she said and pressed her lips to his.

# *CHAPTER 14*

Solange scrutinized the Excel sheet with deep concentration. She highlighted several entries that required investigation. Suddenly her phone rang. She grinned when she saw that it was Ali. "I'm packed to go and I'm leaving for the airport right after work."

"Solange," he said, sounding overwrought, "I just got some bad news. I'm being sent to the Everglades this weekend. They want us to do some field training in marshy terrain."

A burning anger ignited in her. "This is the second time you called me and cancelled. I can't get my money back for my plane ticket."

"Solange, I'm just as pissed off as you are," Ali growled.

"Wanna bet?" she countered. "It's Valentine's Day weekend."

"It can't be helped," Ali said, frustration evident in his voice. "Hey, you're not the only one suffering. I haven't had sex in a month."

"Are you sure?"

"Yes, I'm sure," he drawled. "Doing it alone doesn't count. Solange, please try and see if you can change the plane ticket for next weekend. If Delta won't credit you the flight, put your next ticket on my spare Visa card that

I have in the nightstand. I know they won't be sending us out in the field two weekends in a row."

"I'll think about it," she snapped and slammed down the phone.

Ali stomped out to the deserted gun range. He put on safety goggles and, picking up a .308 rifle, he aimed and shot the mock target criminal in the middle of his forehead. Then he hit a lever on the right panel and when another target flipped into position, he shot it in the heart.

Solange sat with her chin on her hand, pouting.

Her telephone rang, and when she heard it, her heart skipped a beat. She stubbornly refused to pick up the receiver. *It's probably Ali calling to apologize, but I don't feel like hearing it. And if it's anyone else I don't want them to even know I'm here. I told everyone I care about that I was going to Orlando, and I don't feel like answering any damn questions.*

Frustrated, she stood and went to go and take a shower. Then her doorbell rang. Solange peered through the peephole and she saw a brown uniform. "Who is it?"

"It's a delivery for Miss Solange Montgomery. She has to sign for it."

Solange cracked open the door, and when it appeared as if the man actually did work for UPS, she opened it wider and took the box. Then with the pen he handed her, she quickly scribbled her signature.

The man tipped his hat and then walked down the driveway and drove off with a roar.

Curiously Solange walked into the kitchen, got a pair of scissors out of a drawer and quickly sliced open the packing tape. Once she opened the box she found a pretty flowered box. Opening it she laughed out loud when she saw a honey-colored teddy bear with a mask on its face. *Bear.* He was dressed in a black shirt and was holding a bag of heart-shaped candies. Picking it up, she clutched it to her chest and when she did the smell of Ali's signature cologne wafted to her nostrils. Then she picked up a small card.

'You stole my heart the minute I saw you. Love, Ali.'

Tears moistened her eyes and she felt mortified at the way she'd acted the previous day. Picking up her phone, she called Ali's cell.

He immediately answered. "Hello."

"Hey," she said softly.

"I can barely hear you, Solange," he shouted.

"What's all that noise?" she shouted over the static of the connection and gunfire in the background.

"Nothing," he said. "We're doing a mock exercise and I'm in a marsh trying not to be seen."

"Why did you even answer the phone?"

"Because I knew it was you. You're in danger. Get down," Ali shouted.

Solange swung her head around and surveyed her den to see if she really was in danger and then she realized that he was talking to someone in Orlando.

"Call me when you have a chance."

"Don't hang up. I tried to call you earlier, but you didn't answer the phone. Will you come down next weekend? I miss you."

"Yes," she answered without hesitation.

"Good," Ali said. "I love you, Solange."

Then the phone disconnected and she didn't know if he'd dropped the line on his cell or if he was being captured by the opposing team, but she'd heard enough. She'd be on the plane Friday going to Orlando, Florida.

That night she lay in bed with a small smile on her lips. Next to her lay the teddy bear lay on the side where Ali usually slept.

The plane rocked through the sky and a feeling of nausea rose in her throat. Solange undid her seat belt, hoping that she could make it to the bathroom before the bile she was valiantly trying to keep down spilled out of her and embarrassed her in front of a plane full of people.

The minute she undid her seat belt a stewardess appeared. "I'm sorry ma'am, but the captain says everyone must remain seated until we get through this turbulent weather."

"I'm sick," Solange replied haltingly.

"What's wrong with you?" the stewardess asked in genuine concern.

"I feel as if I want to vomit," Solange could barely say.

"I'm sorry to hear that, but if the plane was to take a sudden dip while you are in the lavatory you could become physically injured with the space being so small and all. You're better off having vomit on you than a broken rib."

Suddenly the plane tilted and the stewardess looked fearful. "I have to go back to my seat. Do not get up," she ordered and then disappeared.

With sheer willpower and a love for the Calvin Klein designer dress she was wearing, Solange managed not to let go of the contents of her insides. After about another thirty minutes, the plane leveled off and the passengers on it heard the captain's voice for the third time on the trip from New York to Orlando.

"This is Cpt. Washington. I'm sorry that the inclement weather has made our flight so uncomfortable. We've had a rocky flight, but we are now twenty-three minutes outside of Orlando, Florida, the home of Minnie and Mickey Mouse."

Solange heard some disgruntled passengers muttering, "Who gives a damn?" and, "I'll never get my ass on a plane again."

The captain's voice continued smoothly over the intercom. "Those of you journeying to Orlando only on business should take a day and go enjoy the theme parks."

Next, Solange heard an older man mutter, "Is he going to pay for it? After this lousy trip Delta should give everyone on this flight a free ticket."

"You deserve it. Please, do not unbuckle your seat belts until we are safely landed and the safety sign is on," the captain concluded.

Once Solange entered the passenger waiting area, she spied a man holding a large sign with a name on it. Still suffering from nausea, she slowly walked up to him. "I'm Solange Montgomery," she said feebly.

"Hello, my name is Santiago," he said with a slight Brazilian accent, and when he smiled, she saw a set of perfect white teeth. "The limousine is waiting for you outside. Your luggage will be in baggage claim F." He pointed to a vehicle that looked like a go-cart. "I'll take you to where we can get your luggage and then take you to the hotel."

"Thank you." It was all Solange could manage to say.

Santiago made short work of getting her luggage and ushering her outside to where the taxi van was waiting at the curb. The blast of heat that hit Solange made her almost stumble. "I can't believe it's so hot in February," she said to Santiago.

"It's the greenhouse effect. We have no cushion from the sun. You think this is bad, I hear we're in a ten-year hurricane cycle. We are already bracing ourselves."

They crawled along in the bumper-to-bumper traffic and Solange swung her head around in amazement. "There's no train or anything around here to ease the congested traffic?"

"No." Santiago sadly shook his head. "We're at the mercy of the gasoline companies. There's no real public transportation and the bus system is horrible. You have to transfer at least three buses to get from one destination to the other and they have a stop at every major crossway road. But at least we have Disney World."

"I know," Solange said carefully because she didn't want to offend Santiago, who probably had love in his heart for the place where he lived. "But how many times a year can a person go to Disney World?"

"Disney is only the beginning. MGM, Universal and especially Islands of Adventure employ a lot of families, and the kids buy season tickets and hang out there every weekend."

"I guess if you're a kid, then this is the place to be," Solange said graciously.

Santiago veered the truck to the right. "We're here at La Quinta Suites. Oh, I almost forgot." He handed her a key. "Your husband instructed me to give you the key to your hotel suite. You don't even have to go by the desk."

Solange didn't bother to correct him in his assumption that Ali was her husband. As far as she was concerned it was a moot point because she felt as if he was.

Santiago pulled the van around to a side entrance and backed it up the ramp.

Solange viewed a group of businessmen in the process of getting their belongings off a van very similar to the one she was riding in. She noticed one man very pointedly staring at her and checking her out from head to toe. She averted her gaze and deliberately focused her attention on Santiago.

"Your suite is on this side of the hotel. It's a shorter walk to the elevator if we go through this way," he said.

"Thank you," Solange said.

"There's no need to wait in the heat, ma'am. You can go to your suite and I'll be up as soon as possible with your luggage."

Solange wiped the sweat off of her forehead and grimaced in disgust when she saw the greasy streak marks on the yellow sleeve of her dress.

When Solange entered the suite, she was overcome by the beauty of the beige and mahogany décor. She subsided feebly down on the bed and clutched her stomach. "What is wrong with me?" Then she lurched forward and stamped down her desire to vomit. Rushing into the bathroom, she missed the toilet, instead spattering what was left of her breakfast on the floor.

Dropping to her knees, she slid away from her spillage and dropped her head over the toilet. Heaving, she rid herself of the rest of the breakfast burrito she'd purchased from a cart in the White Plains airport. Feeling immediate relief she looked up she saw Santiago staring at her.

"Miss, is there anything I can do for you? Would you like me to have the desk call a doctor?"

Embarrassed, Solange struggled to her feet and grabbed a washcloth from a rack. She wiped her mouth and then bent down and cleaned up the floor. Feeling humiliated, she avoided Santiago's eyes. "No, thank you. I feel much better now. I think that there was something wrong with the breakfast that I purchased from a sandwich cart," she said.

"That's why I don't eat outside food." He wagged his finger at her. "My wife cooks every day and packs my lunch."

Disgusted, she threw the washcloth in the sink. Crossing over to where her purse was, she withdrew a bill, folded it, and handed it to him. "Thank you very much for everything, Santiago."

He shone his bright smile at her, dipped his head and said graciously, "Enjoy your stay in Orlando, ma'am."

Once she was alone, Solange went to her suitcase, took out her toiletries and went to the bathroom. After brushing her teeth she scrubbed, polished, and applied lotion to herself from head to toe. Once finished, she weakly crawled naked under the plush hotel sheets and waited for Ali.

Solange awoke to the feel of a hand gently gliding from her waist to her thigh. "Ali," she said in a voice groggy from sleep.

"Were you expecting anyone else?" He kissed the side of her neck.

Solange felt a fluttering in her stomach and she turned over on her side to face him.

She looked for a clock in the darkened room. "What time is it?"

"A little after six o'clock." Ali folded her into his embrace. "How was your flight?" he asked.

"Horrible," she said, "but it was totally worth it." Solange slid her hand under the cover and clutched his penis. It was hard and pulsated in her hand.

"I'll make sure that it was," Ali promised.

He gently positioned her on her back. Then he lowered his mouth to hers and slowly parted her lips with his tongue. Their tongues explored each other as if it was they first time they'd met. Then he turned her on her stomach.

Solange felt Ali's mouth kissing the base of her neck and then her shoulder blades, and all the while he was caressing her with the palms of his hands. Next she felt his hands on her waist anchoring her as his mouth made a trail down to her spine. Then he cupped her buttocks with his hands and spread her cheeks. Out of surprise she clenched them, but he gently parted them and she felt his tongue. First he probed her and then he licked her until she felt dizzy. He went from top to bottom and as he did so, Solange felt an oozing of desire escape her. Wet and ready, he entered her and she screamed her desire.

An exhausted Solange let herself into her office. It was still dark outside and she hit the switch for the fluorescent light. Sinking into her leather chair she took her set of keys and stuck it in the keyhole. The drawer opened without her turning the key. *I know I locked this door before I left on Friday.*

Solange sifted through the papers that were inside the drawer and couldn't figure out what was missing. Then suddenly it hit her. The Excel sheet she'd been working on for weeks was missing. She picked up the telephone and dialed Seth Dickerson's office.

When he answered and it didn't go to voice mail, Solange got flustered. She'd thought that she'd be able to leave a message that something was amiss, and hadn't prepared herself for a conversation with him.

"Dickerson here."

"Hello, Seth. This is Solange Montgomery."

"Good morning, Solange. You're at work early this morning."

"Well, I was out of the office yesterday because I went to Orlando for the weekend."

"Yes, I know. I called you and your secretary told me you were out."

"I'm sorry, but I haven't checked my messages yet."

"You've been missing quite a lot of days lately."

"I've only been taking vacation days that are owed to me," she answered carefully. "Did you need anything?"

"It's what I expected. Keep this under wraps for the time being, but it seems as if you're going to have to let another twenty people go at the end of the quarter."

Her heart dropped. "Oh, no."

"It can't be helped. Now you're barely staying afloat and everyone is cutting back. All our branch managers are asking to do the same. We're also going to have to get rid of some of the fluff management. But you don't have to worry. You're so competent we want to keep you in place. Now what did you need from me this morning? Not a requisition for another office party, I hope."

Flustered, Solange pondered what to say. "Of course not," Solange said and grasped for something to say. "I just wanted to give you my cell in case you tried to reach me and I was out of the office."

"Good idea," Seth Dickerson said. "What's the number?"

"It's 203-255-7517," Solange recited.

"Got it," he said.

After she hung up, she cradled her head in her hands and then, with determination, she booted up her computer and searched the web for the nearest locksmith.

"What do you want to do this time?" Ali asked, smiling at Solange in her silk kimono housecoat.

"What I'm doing right now. Absolutely nothing."

"I have tickets for Islands of Adventure. Want to go?"

"What's there?"

"It's the best theme park in town. They have The Hulk roller coaster."

Solange's stomach became queasy at the thought. "Maybe next time. I'm too tired. Last week I had another bout with my stomach, and I'm still just getting up to speed."

"Your immune system is probably low. You work very hard, and then you have to travel down here to see me. It's your fourth trip in four months," he said sympathetically.

"You're right," she said only half-jokingly. "I didn't sign up for this."

Ali looked guilty. "I didn't know that I would be practically held hostage at the barracks. You don't know what red tape I have to go through in order to get furloughs over the weekend to stay at the hotel with you."

"Well they wouldn't let me stay at the barracks with you. Not that I'd want to. I'm sure there are a lot of hungry men out there in the wilderness."

"Not as many as there were when we started," Ali said disappointedly. "We started with twenty-five and now there are only fourteen of us."

"I know one guy lost his wife and had to leave, but how about the others?"

Ali held out his hand and ticked off reasons one by one. "One couldn't stand the heat. Another guy couldn't handle the rigorous training. Another guy got kicked out for insubordination with one of the trainers. It just goes on and on."

"Gee, you didn't sign up for the military behind my back, did you?"

"Of course not," Ali replied teasingly. "Remember you made me promise no more important issues without your permission."

"Not permission," she corrected him, "but input."

"Let's go and check out a movie," Ali said, picking up the Sunday paper and looking at the entertainment section.

"What's out?' she asked.

"I don't know. We can go to the cineplex and see what they have. If we're too early for the show we want, we'll get something to eat and go back."

"It sounds like a plan," Solange agreed.

Solange was sitting on the couch watching the news until Ali finished getting dressed. *What the hell!* Her eyes bored holes into the television screen as the news story unfolded. "Groom shot five times the night of his bachelor party as he stood in front of a nightclub in Manhattan. No weapon was found on the slain man."

"Ali," she said. "Come out here and listen to this!"

As Ali entered the suite area, he was buttoning his shirt. "What is it?" he said, staring at the television headlines.

"Five cops shot an unarmed black man in Manhattan last night."

A cloud settled on Ali's face. "That's terrible."

"I'll say. How the hell do five cops shoot to death an unarmed man?"

"They probably didn't think that he was unarmed."

"Then they should have checked, dammit," she sputtered angrily. "Today was his wedding day."

"That's horrible." Ali shook his head sadly.

"Those losers are on administrative leave. Why the hell are they getting paid? They should be fired."

"They deserve due process," Ali quietly admonished her.

Solange turned to Ali with fire in her eyes. "Think about how I would feel if you were killed the night of your bachelor party. The night before our wedding," she said, stressing her last words.

Ali stared at her and said, "There's no fight here, Solange. It's a terrible mistake, but we don't know all the facts."

"We know that they riddled his body with bullets. They deserve to lose their badges."

There was edginess in the room and the air surrounding them was stifling. Ali watched Solange with narrowed eyes. "Do you think that I deserve to lose my badge?"

"Whatever are you talking about?"

"I killed a man," he spoke harshly. "Do you think that maybe instead of killing him, I should have shot him in the leg or something and just stopped his flight?"

"Where'd this come from?" Solange shook her head in confusion.

"Do you think that I should have lost my badge?" Ali asked again. "The mother of the victim certainly did. Or even more importantly, do you think once I'm a sniper, every time I kill my target I should be investigated?"

"Don't be ridiculous," she scoffed.

"Why is it ridiculous? It's still loss of life. There's a mother who will never see her son again. Children who will never see their father."

"Ali, I don't know what you're tripping on, but that has nothing to do with this and is nothing like what those cops did to that young black man last night! You and four other policemen didn't shoot an unarmed man."

"You don't know what the hell happened. No one but the people that were there know, and maybe they don't. Don't you sit in judgment about how we do our jobs."

Solange digested this for a moment, and when she finally did speak, her tone was acidic. "I do know that if five men shoot an unarmed man, they are not experienced enough to be on the police force and the city needs to pay for their mistake. What the hell ever happened to shooting someone in the leg and taking them down? They do it in the movies," she sneered.

"You just don't how difficult it can be to make split-second decisions. At your job, you have all day to decide what to do about things and your life is never in danger."

That afternoon they didn't go to the movies, and that night they slept with their backs to each other.

The next morning neither spoke on the short drive to the airport. Ali stared straight ahead and Solange kept her head turned to the right, staring impassively out the window. Once they reached the airport, Ali pulled up to the curb in front of the departure terminal. He climbed out of his SUV, opened the trunk and beckoned a zealous skycap.

He said to him in a brusque voice, "Please check these two bags in for Delta flight 1685 to White Plains." Then he handed the skycap a ten-dollar bill.

Once they were alone, they each stood silently staring at each other, waiting for the other to make the first move.

Airport security pulled up next to them and a uniformed man spoke to them. "Unloading time is over. You need to move your vehicle."

Ali and Solange glared at him and he drove off in a huff.

Then they stared each other down in a measuring way, waiting for the other to blink.

"Have a safe trip," Ali said and then stormed off, got in his Explorer and pulled out into the lane of traffic.

With head held high, Solange picked up her carry-on case and stalked into the terminal.

# *CHAPTER 15*

The ringing of the telephone made Solange groggily turn over in frustration. *It's six o'clock on a Saturday morning.* With eyes shut, she fumbled for the receiver in the dark room. "Hello," she whispered, sleep clouding her voice.

"Solange, it's Grace," her friend said, and her voice cracked. "Ebony is sick."

Solange sat straight up in bed and exclaimed, "What's the matter with her?"

Grace's voice trembled. "We don't know. First it started off with her being lethargic and having pain in her legs. You saw the beginning of that when you and Ali were here. By the time we'd get her to the doctor she'd feel fine, so the doctor assumed that it was growing pains.

"Her legs are growing so long we thought that the joints in her legs were having a hard time keeping up," Grace said and began to whimper. "Then her hands and feet began to swell. That's when the doctor told me to bring her to the hospital for tests."

"Oh, no," Solange said and reached for the lamp on her bedside. Once she turned the knob, the room was flooded with a light so bright the shock of it made her flinch for a second.

"She's in the hospital in Florence. I'm so afraid. She's in so much pain, and I can't do a thing to help her."

Solange could tell her friend was desperately trying to hold back hysteria. "You are doing the only thing that you can do. She's getting medical attention and you're there for her. I'm flying down on the next plane out."

"I'm not going to even pretend that I don't want you to come. I need you," she said with a catch in her voice. "Ebony needs you."

"I'll fly into Florence Airport. What hospital is she in?"

"McLeod Health on Cheves Street."

"Okay," Solange said decisively. "I'll take a cab from the airport."

"Thank you, Solange."

"I'll see you soon," Solange said and hung up.

Solange went to her computer and pulled up the search engine Google and then searched for airplane flights.

Solange stood at the reservation desk of McLeod Health Center. "Can you please tell me what room Ebony Newman is in?"

The pretty receptionist quickly typed something on the computer keyboard and then handed her a visitor's badge. "She's located on the children's wing, room thirteen."

"How do I get there?" Her voice was high from nervousness.

"Just go through those double doors and take the elevator to the fifth floor. You'll see it."

"Thank you," Solange said nervously before pinning the visitor badge to her shirt and riding the elevator up to the fifth floor. She was alone and she took this opportunity to talk to God. "Lord, please make everything all right." The door to room thirteen was closed, and she quietly pushed it open.

Grace was sitting next to the bed in a chair with her head bent. Ebony was asleep and she looked so peaceful, Solange was afraid to make the slightest noise and wake her.

Feeling her presence in the room, Grace lifted her head, revealing a face filled with anguish.

Grace put her fingers to her lips, noiselessly got up, and motioned for Solange to meet her in the hallway.

Without speaking they held each other. Grace clung to her and began to softly cry into Solange's shoulder.

Grace held her until her tears subsided.

"Thank God you're here," Grace said.

"Thank God I'm here," Solange whispered.

This made Grace give a slight chuckle, and she broke their embrace.

"Where's Jet?" Solange asked softly.

"He went to get me a cup of coffee," she answered, exhaustion evident with every word she spoke.

"Where's Livingston?"

"I took him to Liza's house. This hospital is too cold, and I don't want him getting sick."

"Do the doctors have any idea yet what's wrong with her?"

"They're narrowing it down. They just finished running more tests, which is why she's asleep. She's still sedated."

"Oh," Solange said.

"I'm glad that she's asleep. That's the only time she seems to be free from pain. Here comes Jet."

Grace looked at Jet striding down the hall holding two cups of coffee. His serious expression brightened when he saw Solange standing with his wife. Once he reached them, he handed Grace a cup of coffee, and leaning over kissed Solange on the cheek. "Thank you for coming," he said in a somber voice.

Solange gave him a look that clearly stated, "Are you kidding me?"

Jet handed her the other coffee, and before she took it, Solange asked, "Are you sure you don't want it?"

Jet gave her a look that spoke volumes. Then he turned his attention to Grace. "How's my munchkin doing?"

"She's still asleep."

"Good," he said with relief. "Let her sleep through as much of this as she can." He turned to Solange. "Ali's plane will be in later this afternoon around three."

Solange gave a start of surprise. "Who called him?" she asked with a little apprehension.

"I did," Grace said, watching her closely. "Right after I called you, because I figured that you might be too overwrought to remember."

She looked at the floor in order to hide her expression.

"Here comes Dr. Ginsberg," Jet said in a voice filled with trepidation.

Dr. Ginsberg stood about five feet, five inches tall and had small, beady eyes hidden behind a pair of large-framed spectacles. He walked up to them and gave Solange a look. Then he turned to Jet. "May I discuss your daughter's case in front of her?"

"Yes, she's Ebony's godmother. She just flew in from New York."

Dr. Ginsberg gave her a brief nod. "I think that your daughter has sickle cell anemia, or at least the trait. We have to run more tests to see how severe it is."

Grace's knees buckled, and she would have fallen had Jet not grabbed her and hoisted her upright.

"I'm aware from Ebony's personal information sheet that she's adopted," Dr. Ginsberg said.

"Yes," Grace said in a taut voice.

"Do you know either of her parents' history?"

"Her mother is dead and her father is unknown."

Jet's body froze and Grace felt the sudden hardening of his body as she leaned on him.

"That is unfortunate," Dr. Ginsberg said as he jotted down something on the notepad he was carrying.

"We're going to start treating her as if she has the disease, which is more severe than the trait. I've cut off the air-conditioning in the room, because she needs to be kept warm, and the nurse is setting up a liquid drip in order to pump fluids into her."

Jet looked at Dr. Ginsberg. "I might know who Ebony's father is," he said.

"Jet," Grace shrieked in a shocked voice, moving her body away from his.

Jet looked overwrought and he held his hands out helplessly. "A man came around at Christmas and said that he might be her father. He really just wanted money, so I gave it to him and he took off."

Dr. Ginsberg spoke in a no-nonsense tone as if hearing these sorts of revelations was an everyday occurrence. "I know that her mother is deceased, and I'd like to know the medical history of this man. Do you think that you can find him?"

"I'll do my best," Jet answered bleakly.

"There's no need for you to stay the night. Once the antibiotics filter into her system, she'll sleep for at least another twelve hours." Then he gave a look of encouragement that included everyone in the room. "Now I have to go and order more tests for Ebony," Dr. Ginsberg said and turned around and strode off.

The minute she lost sight of his retreating back, Grace turned on Jet. "Why didn't you tell me?"

"Tell you what? That some con artist left a note on our front door Christmas Day saying that he could be the father of our daughter?"

Solange watched them and she wished that she was standing anywhere but where she was.

"But . . ." Grace stuttered.

"I didn't want to needlessly worry you," he explained in a ragged voice.

"I thought we told each other everything," she said testily.

"I just wanted it to go away."

Grace folded her arm, looked him squarely in the face. "But it didn't."

"No, it didn't," he responded. "I need to go and get Ali from the airport. We'll meet you at the house."

Solange and Grace sat in chairs by Ebony's bedside. "He was just trying to protect you," Solange felt compelled to say.

"I know," she agreed softly. "I just wish . . ."

"Wish what?" she interrupted her. "Be honest with yourself, Grace. You wouldn't have really wanted to know Christmas Day that all this was going on, and Jet didn't know that this would crop up the way it has. As far as he was concerned, he was saving you heartache."

"That's Jet," she acquiesced with a soft smile. "He has always tried to protect me. That's one of the reasons why I love him so." Her next words had a tinge of warning. "When I go get Livingston, I want to ask Liza if she knows any of Naomi's medical history."

The drive to Lake City was grueling. Solange could barely contain her impatience as Grace carefully obeyed the myriad signs on the side of the road. It seemed as if every quarter of a mile there was a speed sign. The speed limit as they passed through the farmland area ranged from 20 mph to thirty-five and one really had to watch out for it or you'd miss it all together. Then all of a sudden the zone was a 50 mph stretch of road. They passed through Coward and then Scranton before they saw the sign for Lake City.

"Liza lives in the heart of town. That way she can keep up with what everyone is doing," Grace explained.

When Grace pulled her BMW into the yard of a small gray house with a fence, three or four children playing in the yard stopped to look and see who was in the shiny blue car. One took off running into the house and, before they could get out of the car, Liza appeared. She was wearing a day dress and house shoes and Livingston was clad only in a diaper and a T-shirt. "Let me get my baby," Grace muttered in a disgruntled voice.

They walked up the dirt driveway and Livingston held his hands out. Grace grabbed him and nuzzled his neck, making him emit gurgling sounds.

"Hey, you back again?" Liza peered at her with her round, large eyes.

"Yes, ma'am," Solange answered quietly.

Grace asked in a too-nonchalant tone, "Liza. Do you remember any of Naomi's medical history?"

"Whatcha mean by that?" Liza Taylor asked, interest immediately piqued.

"I mean, did she ever have to go into the hospital because she wasn't feeling well?"

"Nope. Not that I remember. She was just unhappy here in Lake City." Liza rolled her eyes. "She felt it was too slow for her. She was always dreamin' of big-city life, thinking she was too glamorous for Lake City. You see what happened. She couldn't handle it and got run over by a bus her first week there." Liza shook her head in mild disgust. "She shoulda stayed right here and kept her baby. Not that you and Mr. Jet ain't good parents and all."

"So you're saying that Naomi was a very healthy girl?"

"She used to complain that her legs used to hurt her when she came in from the field. So they tested her for that blood disease."

Solange's heart constricted and she looked away.

Grace looked like she needed a minute to gather her wits about her.

"The doctors tested her for sickle cell disease?" Solange asked.

"Yeah, they said that she had the trait. She was always laying down, saying she was tired. I say that she was just lazy. Why you asking all these questions? Is something going on with Ebony?"

"No," Grace lied. "The doctor just wanted some medical history on her. How about her father? Do you know anything about him?"

"No, just some guy in the military." By the curiosity of Liza's face she obviously didn't believe Grace's answer, but she knew that was all she was going to get. "I know she never told him. He was married."

Solange reached for Livingston and said to Grace, "I'm going to go and strap him in his car seat."

"Good," Grace said gratefully. I'll get his overnight bag."

On the drive to Grace's house, Solange looked at her out the corner of one eye. "Why didn't you tell her what's going on with Ebony?"

"I don't want it all over town," she answered shortly. "This will be Ebony's business to tell if she wants to when she's old enough."

When they got to Grace's, they saw Jet's car, and she knew that Ali must have arrived. Nervously, she wiped her hands down the side of her pants.

Grace cut off the engine and turned to her. "I don't exactly know what's going on with the two of you, but fix it. Life's too short to argue about worthless things."

Grace made short work of unbuckling Livingston and then strode off with him into the house.

Solange took Grace's key out of the ignition and walked to the back and unlocked the trunk. She looked up and saw Ali walking over to her. She swallowed the lump in her throat. "Hey," she croaked.

"Hey," he said and planted himself in front of her.

Then she reached for him. She grabbed the tail of his shirt and drew him close.

Once he was only inches away, Ali took his hand and lifted her chin.

She closed her eyes when she saw his mouth descending towards hers, and she lost herself in the pleasure of his kiss as he hungrily devoured her mouth with his. When he was finished ravishing her and withdrew his mouth from hers, she was breathless. "I'm sorry," she managed to say.

"So am I," he murmured throatily and buried his face in her hair. After what seemed to be an endless time, he broke their embrace and said, "Let's go into the house. They need us." And with her suitcase in one hand and his other one clasped around hers, they walked into the house.

They sat around the kitchen table. There was an unfinished bucket of chicken with the fixins' from KFC. "What are we going to do?" Grace asked in a tone filled with dread.

"I've been thinking about this ever since Jet called me in Orlando. I think I have a solution."

All eyes turned on him. He looked at Jet. "You said that this Sidney Mack said that he was going to L.A.?"

"Yes," Jet said. "He said that he wants to be a rapper."

"Oh, my God!" Grace ejaculated.

"Give me a break," Solange said.

"I called a friend of mine and they're running a check on him to see if he's used his credit card in the last day or so. They way we can probably trace him."

"What if he doesn't have a credit card?"

"I also have someone checking his military status. You said that he was in Iraq, right?"

"That's what he said, and that's where Naomi said that Ebony's father was."

"But Liza said that he's married," Grace interjected. "Did this Sidney mention a wife?"

"No," Jet said, "but why would he? We didn't exactly have a pleasant conversation."

"I'm scared to find him," Grace whispered fearfully. "What if he *is* Ebony's father?"

"We need to know," Jet said quietly.

Ali said, "If he is ex-military the army will have all of his medical records, and we'll be able to find out for sure if he is Ebony's father."

"How will we do that?" Solange asked.

"That's easy to do. The government has a file on every person in this country that has either attended school here or filed an income tax return. If you know the right people, it's not hard to get. If he wasn't military, we'll drag him back here and have him take all the necessary tests that the doctor needs. If he refuses to come, I'll threaten him with prosecution for extortion. Do you have a record of that money transaction?"

"My lawyer has a written statement from me about withdrawing the money, and the reason why, along with a transaction number. It was for insurance against future problems out of him."

"That's all the leverage we need," Ali said with certainty.

Suddenly a new respect for Ali and what he did for a living overwhelmed Solange. She didn't realize it, but it shone brightly from her eyes.

That night, after a hefty bout of makeup sex, they snuggled in bed. Solange lay with her head on Ali's shoulder and played with the wavy hair on his chest. "This week without speaking to you was the longest week I've ever spent in my whole life," she murmured.

"Ditto," he answered.

Solange could tell by his voice that he was more than satisfied with the outcome of their evening and she hid a smile.

"Solange, I don't quite understand this whole sickle cell thing. Explain it to me."

Solange answered him in a sober voice. "It's a blood disease that minorities have. Mainly African-Americans suffer from it. It's when the red blood cells in your body clump up and don't flow freely to nourish other parts of your body. There are basically two kinds. There's the sickle cell trait, which in essence is a milder form of the disease, and then there's the actual disease."

"How do you cure it?"

"You can't. Everyone is supposed to be tested. If you have the trait and your mate has the trait, you're advised not to have children because they'll have the disease. But, on the other hand, if one person has the trait and the other doesn't, their offspring will most likely have the trait. It runs in families. That's why we need to find out if this shyster Sidney Mack has the trait."

"What difference does it make if he is the father?"

"We need to know what Ebony is up against. Grace and I talked to Liza Taylor today, and it's a pretty well-known fact that Naomi had the trait."

"Why isn't there a cure?'

"I don't know," she responded in a disgruntled voice. "There should be a more aggressive effort to find a cure because the medical community has known about it for over fifty years. Their answer seems to be not to have kids with someone that has the trait."

"I know that's not a cure, but I think that should cut down on the amount of people who will suffer with being ill in the future," Ali said.

"The problem is a lot of young people today don't ask questions. They have children by people they're not married to or don't know their mate's medical history." Solange's voice trembled from fear tinged mixed with anger, "Because of the devil-may-care attitude of others, a beautiful little girl like Ebony has to suffer."

Ali took the palm of his hand and rubbed her back consolingly. "Grace and Jet will do the best they can for her, and then she also has us."

"Yes, she does," Solange said.

"Now go to sleep, honey. I have a feeling that tomorrow's going to be a long day."

"Hug me, Ali," she whispered.

Obligingly he tightened his hold around her and his arms were like bands of steel.

"Tighter," she whispered.

And if possible, he hugged her tighter, and eventually they drifted off to sleep in each other's arms.

The next morning they were all dressed and on their way out the door when Jet said, "I'll meet you guys there. I need to stop by the clinic for something."

"What is it that can't wait? Dr. Ginsberg said for us to meet him in the delivery room at nine, and it's almost eight o'clock already," Grace said.

"I want to go to the clinic and take a look in the medical archives at Naomi's medical history."

"Can you do that, not being a doctor?"

"Yes, I can. Before she passed, Naomi used to visit the free clinic for treatment, so this morning I called Jesse and asked him to dig up her medical files. Since I co-founded the clinic with him, I can look at her medical records. I want to know if Naomi had sickle cell anemia, or if it was just the trait like Liza told you guys," he said.

"Good," Grace responded with feeling. "It'd rather have our information confirmed instead of relying on hearsay."

Jet looked at Ali. "Man, are you riding with me?"

"Yes," Ali said. "Then we need to go and get that fax that I'm waiting on from the FBI."

After they departed, Solange looked doubtfully at Grace. "Are you going to bring Livingston to Liza's house again?"

Grace sighed in resignation. "Yes. I hate to, but I really don't want him at the hospital. I've heard cases of adults actually getting sick from the hospital," she said and shuddered in revulsion. "I'd hate to think of what could happen to a baby."

They were in Ebony's hospital room and watched her carefully as she finished her bowl of cereal. "Godmomma," Ebony said in her usual chipper voice, "I got an A on my paper."

Solange smiled at her gently. "I'm not surprised to hear that. You're a very smart girl."

"Mommy, when can I go home?" Ebony asked in a plaintive voice.

"I don't know, pumpkin. The doctor will be here any minute and then maybe we'll know."

"I have to go to school, Mommy. Our teacher is taking us to a petting zoo."

"When is that?" Solange asked.

"I don't know, but I have to go," Ebony wailed.

"It was on Friday. She doesn't realize how long she's been in here. She has lost the concept of time," Grace said quietly.

Solange whispered back, "But I can't believe she's this alert. This has to be good news."

"My legs don't hurt anymore," Ebony said and pushed back the covers, attempting to get up.

"Settle back down, young lady. No one gave you permission to get up," Grace said firmly.

Ebony immediately pulled the covers back over her, but now her bottom lip was thrust out. "Where's Daddy?"

"I'm right here," Jet said and walked through the open door with Ali right behind him.

"Godfather!" she shrieked and held her arms out.

Ali walked over to the bed, bent over and gave her a big hug and a squeeze.

"Well, look who's starting to look like my little girl again," Jet said.

"When can I go home? I want my brother," Ebony whined.

"I don't know, little lady." Dr. Ginsberg had noiselessly entered the room from behind them.

All the adults whipped around.

"May I talk to all of you in the waiting room in five minutes?" he said.

"When can I go home?" Ebony reiterated with a thrust-out bottom lip.

"Let me talk to your parents outside and I'll come back and let you know," the doctor said. Then with a tender smile aimed at Ebony he departed as noiselessly as he'd entered.

They were seated in the waiting room when Dr. Ginsberg arrived.

Dr. Ginsberg pulled up a chair and positioned it in front of the couch.

"First of all, things could be worse. Ebony has the sickle cell trait. That means from time to time she'll have what we call crises, which is what she's just recovering from now. These crises come out of nowhere and can withdraw just as quickly. You'll know when she's having an episode because she'll get either a headache or feel dizzy, and she'll probably experience shortness of breath. She shouldn't overexert herself. She should be kept warm."

He gave a wry smile. "She can't be a high school cheerleader, but the fact that she has only the trait means that if she takes proper care of herself, she can live a reasonably healthy life. She won't be needing blood transfusions. Make sure to give her a healthy dose of folic acid every day." He paused before saying, "Do we have any family history on her father yet?"

"No. I have a picture that Jet confirms is him, but we're waiting for his medical records."

"You say that he was in the army?"

"Yes," Jet said, handing a folder to Dr. Ginsberg. "Here's his picture with his enlistment file."

"If he was in the military he wouldn't have sickle cell or the trait. They don't allow people in the army with the condition. They test for that before they are allowed to join," Dr. Ginsberg said. He swiftly read the file. "Also, Ebony's blood type is AB and this Sidney Mack's isn't O. He is not the father."

A dawning realization hit all the adults at the same time and everyone exhaled. For the first time since Solange had arrived in South Carolina she saw a relaxing of Jet and Grace's facial expressions.

"Thank God," Grace breathed and tears formed in her eyes. Jet pulled her close and hugged her.

Then Ali turned to her and did the same.

Silently, Dr. Ginsberg watched them and then said, "I'm going to release Ebony in this evening. There's nothing that we can do for her here that you can't do for her at home."

# *CHAPTER 16*

The next day, Solange and Ali sat in the terminal holding hands. Solange felt a deep sadness that they were parting company again so soon. She knew that horrible circumstances had brought them to Lake City, but Solange was a huge believer in God working in mysterious ways.

Ali was afraid to ask, but he was not going to let Solange get on her plane without an answer. "When will I see you again?"

"I'll fly down in two weeks," she said.

"Promise?" He sounded like a wounded soldier away far too long on a mission.

"I promise," she said, smiling gently at the almost apprehensive expression on his face.

"I love you, Solange," he said quietly.

"I love you, too, Ali."

When they heard the airport intercom system announcing Solange's flight, Ali took her in his arms and kissed her. As their tongues danced, a sudden thought hit her.

When Ali released her mouth from the prison of his, Solange stepped back, picked up her carry-all and walked to the flight attendant, who scanned her ticket. Just before she entered the corridor that led to the plane, she turned around and blew Ali a kiss that he returned with a wink. Then she disappeared from view.

As Ali watched his woman disappear from sight, he felt bereft. For the first since he'd started sniper school, he felt that he'd made a mistake.

Solange viewed the list of personnel profiles of employees at Microsystems Computers. She picked up Arnold Benedict's file and began thumbing through it. He'd been late six times in the last six weeks and he called in two times. After another three hours, Solange had managed to find twenty employees that she felt she could do without. She'd decided again to talk to each employee one on one and she felt nauseous at the thought of it.

She looked up and Jane stood in the doorway staring. "It's after five o'clock. I'm getting ready to go for the evening, if you don't need anything else."

Since she'd been back to work from Lake City, she'd sensed an undercurrent from Jane and she didn't like it.

"Yes. I wanted to ask you where the files are that I asked for over an hour ago."

"They're in the storage area in the basement. Since you had the locks changed, I didn't have a way to get them," Jane said in a slightly offended tone.

"Then you should have said something before now," Solange responded shortly. "I'll go and get them."

When Solange entered the dank supply room, an unusual odor permeated the air. She wished that she had a handkerchief to cover her nose. She flicked the light switch and, still finding it difficult to see, she gingerly held her hands out in front of her, feeling her way over to the boxes grouped together on a shelf. Squinting in the dimness, she read the labels on the outside of each carton. "September, October, November." All of a sudden the steel door slammed behind her and she heard a decisive click.

Solange stumbled over to the door, gripped the doorknob, and twisted it, but it wouldn't budge. Then she began beating on the metal door. *Why is no one hearing me?* Feeling overwrought with fear in the closed area, she began to shiver in the ninety-degree room.

*Ten-year-old Solange Montgomery was playing hide and seek with her friends in an old abandoned house. She scurried into a bedroom on the second floor and found a door that led to a dark attic. She slid her narrow body inside and hid. Solange smiled to herself at how clever she'd been. Her friends would never find her there. After waiting for over twenty minutes, Solange's body ached and her legs were cramped from stooping. "I'm hungry," she complained aloud to herself. Solange began to back out of her hiding place and when she pushed against the door, it had no inside handle and she couldn't open it.*

*Solange began screaming, "Natasha, Toni, help!" When no one came to her aid, she started banging on the door. Suddenly she was paralyzed with fear when no one came to release her from her prison. A bat flew by her head and then circled around and darted at her. Solange began to hyperventilate and then suddenly blackness overcame her and she passed out.*

*When Solange opened her eyes Natasha and Toni were standing over her. Someone had thrown water on her and her face was wet.*

*Toni was weeping and tears were streaming down her face.*

*Natasha, the older of the two girls, was staring at Solange with a look of intense fright on her face. "Are you okay?"*

*Solange's breathing was labored, so all she could manage to was to shake her head.*

*"Why did you go in there?" Toni asked.*

*"I wanted to win," Solange managed to choke out.*

*Now Toni stopped crying, but, sniffling, said, "You did."*

*Natasha said, "When you tell your momma, we're all gonna get a whooping because we ain't supposed to be in here."*

*Solange struggled to sit up and her friends grabbed her by the arms and hoisted her up. She whispered, "We ain't gonna tell. I don't want no whoopin' either."*

*"I won't say anything," Toni gulped.*

*"I won't, either," Natasha promised. "Now let's get out of here."*

*The three friends ran out of the house and never went back.*

Solange began beating both fists on the door, and out of the dimness something darted at her head. The residue from her childhood phobia overcame her, and she slid into unconsciousness.

Hours later, Solange woke to a flashlight being shined in her face.

The custodian, Roland Masterson, stood watching her with an expression of grave concern. "Miss Montgomery, what happened?"

Solange struggled to sit up. "The door slammed shut behind me and I got locked in." She took her hand and pushed it through her long, disheveled hair. Her throat was dry. "What time is it?"

"It shouldn't have because there's a safety catch on it," Roland said in confusion. "After I finished cleaning the bathroom down the hall, I was passing by and thought I heard someone in the records room."

"Thank God," Solange said, blinking back tears.

"It's after nine o'clock, miss. Ain't nobody at home missing you?"

Ali's face flashed in front of her eyes and a deep, flaring resentment consumed her. "No one is looking for me," she answered in a cold voice.

"Well, that just don't seem right. A fetchin' lady like you should be missed." He held out his hand. "Here, let me help you up."

Solange gratefully grasped Roland's hand, and he practically lifted her to her feet. Once she was standing, she brushed the dust off of the legs of her pantsuit.

"Miss, you're bleeding."

Solange took her hand and touched her temple where there was a trickle of dried blood and grimaced at the feel of it.

"It's late," Roland said solemnly. "I'll walk you to your car to make sure you're safe."

Solange nodded gratefully. "First, I have to go to my office and get my pocketbook."

In silence, they walked up the steps and down the corridor to her office and she went inside her office.

Quickly, she opened her desk drawer and pulled out the list of names of the employees she felt compelled to lay off. She took out a red pen and crossed off the name of Roland Masterson. Then she replaced the pad in her desk, grabbed her purse out of her file cabinet and met up again with Roland, who was in the hall patiently waiting for her. As Solange got in her car, neither she nor Roland Masterson saw the shadow of the tall man as he hid in the darkness.

Solange revved up her car and her tires screeched as she tore out of the parking garage.

Right before she got ready to go to bed, Solange swallowed three Advil tablets in an effort to still a headache. She massaged her throbbing temples with her fingertips and stared at her reflection in the mirror. Her fair skin had a bruise right above her left cheek. The telephone rang for the third time since she'd been home. Solange stomped over to the receiver. "Hello," she said.

"Hey, baby." Solange could hear the teasing quality in Ali's voice. "Where the hell have you been? I've been calling you for hours. Come on now, give account of yourself."

"None of your damn business," Solange spat out angrily and slammed down the telephone receiver. It immediately started ringing again and she took the receiver off the hook.

That night, as was her habit, she lay on one side of the bed. In the darkness she slid her hand over to the spot Ali used to sleep. When she felt the vacant spot, a huge lump became lodged in her throat. An overwhelming feeling of loneliness consumed her, and Solange Montgomery wept.

When her telephone rang early the next morning at work, she knew intuitively it was Ali. "Solange Montgomery speaking."

"What in the hell is going on with you?" Ali's angry voice resonated through the phone line.

"Hold on a minute," Solange said brusquely. She put the receiver down and went and closed her office door from Jane's prying ears.

"I got locked in the storage area yesterday, and it scared me to death."

Now genuine worry replaced hostility in Ali's tone. He said in an exasperated tone, "Why didn't you let me know?"

All of her anger suddenly tumbled out of her and she said in an icy tone, "How am I supposed to do that, Ali? You're down there in Orlando chasing some damn dream."

"You told me that I could come, Solange."

"I had no other choice. It was either allow you to go or end up having you resent me."

"Allow is the wrong word," he stated.

"You know what the hell I mean." She ground out the words, "No, I mean exactly what I did say. Allow is the apt word. I mean, you did in the end ask me, didn't you? Or did you ever honestly intend to give it up?"

"I was going to give it up, Solange, and now I wish I had," Ali said quietly, and his regret resonated through the phone line.

"No, you don't," she whispered, her anger cooling.

"Now you resent me, so what was accomplished by you lying?"

"I didn't lie. At the time I felt you should go, but I didn't know that I was going to have to do all of the work. I've made six trips in six months. When the hell are you graduating, anyhow?"

"I don't know," he answered morosely. "I'll have more to tell you about that his weekend."

"I'm not coming," Solange said after a long silence.

"What?" Ali shouted. Then again he lowered his voice and said sadly, "So you're trying to punish me because you got yourself locked in a storage area. That's very passive-aggressive, Solange. I thought more of you."

"That's not why I'm not coming, Ali. There's a lot going on up here at Microsystems Computers, and I can't get away. I've worked very hard to get where I am today, and I love my job."

"More than you love me," Ali said, and he sounded like a hurt little boy.

"No," she said. "But I can't keep flying up and down the coast. Something has to give."

Her phone line beeped. "Now I can't talk about this anymore because I have a scheduled conference call with Seth Dickerson, and this is him."

Her last statement was met with harsh silence and the air hung heavy between them.

"I'll call you later," Solange stated briefly before hanging up and pressing the intercom button.

"Hello, Mr. Dickerson."

"Hello, Solange," he said with severe asperity. "I called yesterday and didn't get you or anyone else in the office."

"My secretary must have gone home," she answered smoothly.

"I also left you a message the other week and didn't get a return call. Jane said that you were out of town visiting your fiancé."

"I'm sorry, but she didn't tell me that you'd called."

"It seems as if you're out of town an awful lot. Are you interviewing at other companies?" Seth Dickerson asked suspiciously. "Maybe in Orlando, since your fiancé is down there in sniper school?"

Flustered, Solange stammered, "Of course not. I'm very happy at Microsystems Computers."

"Then maybe you ought to start acting like it and spending more time in the office," Seth Dickerson said curtly. "Now is not the time to do as little as possible, but as much as possible."

"Yes, Mr. Dickerson."

After Solange hung up, she felt a knot in her stomach.

Late Friday afternoon, Solange watched the nineteenth employee be escorted to the gate by the security guard, Rodney Willis.

Arnold Benedict walked out the gate through the turnstile and turned around.

Suddenly, Solange felt the violent glare from his eyes as they locked with hers. She stumbled back, shocked that he'd been able to zero in on her position through the tinted glass.

He continued to stare for a minute before he walked off and got into his truck and drove away.

Remorse for what she'd done that day flowed through her, yet she felt in her heart that she'd made the right decisions. Deep down inside she knew all of her decisions were those of a thoroughly trained manager and were not based on any kind of partiality. She pressed the intercom button. "Jane. Will you come inside please?"

Jane didn't answer for a minute, and then she said in a sullen voice, "Of course, ma'am."

When Jane knocked and then unceremoniously entered Solange's office, she was taken aback when she saw a folder on the desk with her name on it.

Solange stood and held her hand out. "Please take a seat, Jane," Solange said.

Jane plopped down into the small leather chair with a thud.

"Let me start by saying that I like you, Jane."

Now Jane's eyes bulged wide with horror.

"I've had to cut staff, and it was a hard decision, but I've decided to let you go."

"Me?" Jane said in disbelief.

"Yes," Solange said. "You disappear at ridiculous times during the day and don't say where you are. You leave the phones uncovered and you are indiscreet."

"Indiscreet?" Jane choked out.

"Yes. Without going into detail, it is not up to you to discuss my business with anyone."

"I didn't mean to, Miss Montgomery," she stuttered.

"Your work has slacked off, and I find that you have a bad disposition many days. No boss likes a moody secretary," Solange said.

"You bitch!" Jane hurled the words at Solange.

"Thanks," Solange replied drolly. Then she stood and, with dignity, walked to the door and opened it.

Rodney Willis stood on the threshold, waiting.

"Please escort Jane Tillman off the premises, and then ask Celeste Manning to come and see me."

"Yes, Ms. Montgomery," he said quietly.

Solange had her head cradled between her hands. She mustered up all of the willpower she could to keep from bawling right then and there. She lifted her head when she heard the sound of someone coughing for her attention.

Celeste Manning was standing nervously in the doorway.

"Can you type?"

"Yes, ma'am," Celeste said.

"How fast?" Solange asked directly.

"About sixty words a minute."

"I'll take your word for it. Would you like to fill in as secretary to me until I get someone permanent?"

Celeste hesitated as she grappled for words.

"Don't feel bad about stepping into someone else's shoes. I can't do without a secretary, and it might as well be you. The hours will be from eight-thirty until five o'clock with an hour lunch. It pays $4 an hour more than what you're getting now."

Still Celeste hesitated.

"If you don't work out, I won't fire you. I'll let you return to your position on the assembly line," Solange said with a soft smile.

"In that case, thank you for the opportunity, Miss Montgomery."

When Solange stared at Celeste Manning with a critical eye, she saw loyalty and gratitude.

# *CHAPTER 17*

Solange stared at the rain as it pelted the sides of the sliding glass door in their suite in La Quinta Inn and Suites.

Ali sat perusing the Saturday paper. As he did so, he absently drummed his fingers on the wooden table.

"Stop it!"

"What?" He looked up, perplexed.

"Your fingers tapping on the table. It's driving me crazy," Solange said irritably.

"Oh." He looked genuinely sorry, and Solange felt bad about how sharp her tongue had been.

"I'm just upset that we can't go to the theme parks today. I was really looking forward to it," she apologized.

"We can still go. They're not closed, and we shouldn't let a little rain stop our fun. Come on," he said cajolingly, "be a trooper."

Solange ran her hand through her streaked tresses. "You must be out of your mind. I just got my hair done. When I got back to New York, I'd have to go back to the hairdresser and I just don't have the time," she said plaintively.

"You can always wear that wig thing you have for emergencies."

"You're crazy after all the money I just paid. Besides," she said as she looked in a frustrated manner out the window at the torrential rain, "I can't afford to get sick. I have a meeting Monday with Seth Dickerson and I feel that I need to look my best."

"How you look on the outside should have nothing to do with how well you do your job," Ali said.

"You know that's not how the real world works. They expect you to do a dog and pony show no matter what."

"As a matter of a fact, I do know. Another trainee got kicked out this week. Now we're down to six."

Solange walked away from the depressing view outside and sat down across from Ali. "What happened?"

"Andrew started arguing with the colonel." Ali looked shamefaced. "They were asking him to do things that they weren't asking the rest of us to do."

"Like what?"

"Cleaning the rifles after we finished practice."

"That doesn't seem so horrible."

"But he'd already done it twice this week, and it should have been this other guy's turn."

"Well, was it an honest mistake on the part of the colonel?"

"I don't know. All I do know is that you don't interfere with Col. Amsterdam when he's having a battle of wits with someone. It's best not to get involved," Ali said.

"How does that make you feel when you see unfairness like that?"

"I think it sucks." Ali shrugged his shoulders in a self-deprecating way. "But I'm just a peon so there's nothing I can do about it. If I ever get in a position of power over a group of people I promise not to let it overcome my sense of fairness."

"I know you will," she said. "You're such a good man, Ali."

They sat together companionably, watching television. Suddenly their program was interrupted with a special bulletin.

"Oh, no," Solange said in a worried tone. "Now this rain is listed as a tropical depression."

"It's that time of year. Hurricane season is right around the corner."

"I'd hoped that you'd be out of here before then."

"I have only a month to go," he said soothingly.

"How about my plane? I hope I don't have a problem getting out of here tomorrow."

"I doubt that. These pilots fly above the clouds. You're probably safer in the air than you would be driving in traffic."

"But to get the plane up over the clouds, that's the problem." Solange got up off the sofa and walked over to the plate glass window and looked outside. When she saw the onslaught of harsh weather, she hurriedly pulled the drape back into position and blocked out the sight.

"Well if they did ground the planes, you'd have to stay and I get to spend more time with you," Ali said.

"You don't care anything about my job, do you? If I can't get back to White Plains this week I'll miss my meeting and be in big trouble. I'd be in jeopardy of losing my job. You know, Ali, you're not the only one with a life," Solange said, miffed by his insensitivity.

"You need to relax," he said. Frowning his displeasure, he turned back to the television.

Solange tapped Ali on the shoulder as he took an afternoon nap in their bedroom. "Wake up. I'm bored," she complained, standing over him in the darkness with her arms folded.

Feeling disgruntled, Ali peered at her. "You said that you didn't want to do anything because of the weather."

"I said that I didn't want to go outside in the rainstorm. I didn't say that I didn't want to do anything."

Ali patted the empty space next to him. "Why don't you lie next to me and keep me company?"

"I kept you company all last night," she said in an abrupt tone. "Find something else for us to do."

Ali got a contemplative look on his face. "There's a pool table downstairs. Why don't we go and play a couple of games?"

Solange's face brightened. "That sounds like a good idea," she said.

Ali slid off the bed. "I'm going to freshen up before I go," he said.

"Okay. I'll meet you downstairs. I want to make sure that there's an available table."

"Do you know where to go?" Ali asked, still somewhat groggy from his afternoon nap.

"Yes, the basement. Hurry up!"

"I will," Ali said to Solange's retreating back.

Solange rode the elevator down to the basement and was relieved to see that the recreation room was empty. Just in case, she went and signed her name on the chalk board that hung on the wall.

She heard a slight noise and whirled around, yet saw no one. Cautiously, she walked out to the hallway and looked around. She still saw no one and, instead of waiting for the elevator, took the side stairs.

She was a little breathless when she entered the lobby and the flashing light that indicated that the bar was open beckoned her. Solange walked to the counter and gave a small smile to the bartender. “May I have a double martini?”

“Sure.” The young man quickly fixed her a drink and slid it on the counter to her.

“I don't have my card. May I run a tab? I'm Solange Montgomery in room 2569.”

“No problem,” the bartender said affably.

Thirty minutes and three double martinis later, Solange's temper rose to the point that it began to bubble over like a volcano. “Where the hell is Ali?”

Suddenly a short man in a business suit sat in the chair opposite her. Solange put her empty glass on the counter and glared at him.

“How much?”

“Excuse me?” Solange said, her eyes bulging out of her head, not quite sure that she heard him right.

“I asked how much,” the man said, darting his eyes from side to side.

“How much for what?”

"An hour," he whispered. "I see you here in the lobby all the time. I come here from my country on business."

"I'm not a hooker," Solange said. "How dare you!" She bolted from the bar.

When she reached the second floor, she was out of breath from her sprint. Their suite door was open, and, pushing it open, she became more incensed when she saw Ali. He stood with his back to her and she walked around him, snatched the phone out of his ear and slammed it on its cradle.

"What the hell!"

"I'm downstairs waiting for you in the bar and some man thought I was a hooker."

"What the hell were you doing waiting in the bar?"

"Waiting for you," she screamed.

Ali went and slammed the door to the room shut. "Be quiet," he ordered.

"No, I will not be quiet. I want everyone to hear how damn disrespectful you are to me. Who the hell were you talking to?"

"Col. Amsterdam called me when I was on my way to meet you."

"Then you should have told him that you'd call him back and not kept me waiting," she spat out.

"I had no way to call him back," Ali said in a thoroughly disgusted voice. "He's in the Everglades."

"You shouldn't have answered the phone anyhow."

"I need to try to reach him. I won't bother to explain to him how rude my woman is. Hell, I'll just pretend that my cell phone dropped the call." He bent to pick up the phone.

All of Solange's pent-up frustrations spewed out of her. "You keep putting everyone and everything in front of me. I'm so tired of waiting for your ass. I'm tired of doing all the damn work." She slammed her hand on the table. "I'm tired of this fuckin' hotel, and most of all I'm tired of you."

Ali put the phone down, and when he spoke his tone was hard and cold. "And I'm tired of your tirades."

"Good, because I'm not coming back," she said resolutely. "If you ever see me again, it will be in White Plains and it will be your damn money spent on the plane ticket. But for today, now matter what it costs, I'm going to change my flight for this evening and get as far away from you as I possibly can."

Ali stormed to the couch, sat down and stared stonily at the television, ignoring Solange's presence.

She felt the need to drive the stake home. "And I hate this sniper bullshit."

A couple of hours later, there was a knock on the door, and when she opened it, she saw Santiago. Without preamble she pointed. "There are my bags. I'll be down in a minute."

Santiago cast a knowing look at Ali's severe profile as he kept his head turned, not looking in their direction. He quickly picked up the bags and disappeared.

Solange spoke in a disheartened tone. "There's three double martinis on the hotel bill."

Ali didn't answer her.

Solange stared at his stern profile before she stormed out.

The next evening via telephone Solange poured her heart out to Grace. "My job is a nightmare. I had to let more people go, and now I have to retrain a secretary. My boss has started sniffing around, and sometimes I feel as if my American dream is going up in smoke."

"You're not in danger of losing your position, are you?" Grace asked in a fearful voice.

"I don't think so, but I have to work twice as hard to keep it, and I don't even get a damn thank you for burning the midnight oil."

"Unfortunately, when there's a recession people are always saying, 'You're lucky to have a job,' " Grace said.

"That's bullshit! They use that as an excuse to take advantage of you," Solange exclaimed bitterly. "And now Ali and I are having problems. I walked out on him in Orlando and haven't heard from him since. I'm about ready to throw in the towel on us," she said. "I think he already has."

"You can't mean that, Solange," Grace said in an appalled voice.

"Yes, I do. I feel as if I'm doing everything. I don't want to be my mother," she wailed. "Ali changed the rules of the game after we were halfway through it."

"So you think that Ali deliberately made you fall in love with him with the intention of later hurting you?"

"Yes," Solange said, beginning to sob.

"So you think that Ali deliberately made you fall in love with him with the intention of hurting you?" Grace reiterated, pausing between each word in order to give Solange enough time to absorb what she was saying.

"No," Solange admitted, "but in the beginning we were partners and now I'm the one who is having to change every nuance of her life in order to have a relationship with him."

Grace expelled a long sigh of understanding. "Solange, there is always someone in a relationship who gives more than the other. That's just the way things work. All that equality, fifty-fifty relationship rule stuff is crap. It's something that sounds good in theory, but it doesn't work in the real world. Take me and Jet, for example."

"You and Jet? Jet does everything for you."

"That's how it looks to someone on the outside looking in. I run the household. Now, I have it better than a lot of housewives because we have a lot of money, so it's not that big an issue. I pay everything by Internet and that also makes it easier. But if I worked outside the home or we were struggling financially, it would be a big issue that he never sits down and does it. He doesn't even know when things are due. I do all of the grocery shopping and the majority of the housecleaning. And now I have to monitor Ebony all the time to make sure she doesn't do too much and stays as healthy as she can. If I worked a nine to five, I'd be exhausted. Hell, I'm tired anyhow," Grace said.

Solange's tears were now drying up as she listened to her friend. "I would think that Jet would help you if you asked him."

"When?" Grace asked. "After one of his numerous city council meetings that last until after nine o'clock at night, or how about after he stops by the clinic and does the books there in order to make sure that people in Lake City get as much free health care as legally possible? These are things that I don't want him to stop, and I don't think that he would even if I asked him to. Jet can be as stubborn as the next man when it comes to following his dreams."

"But the two of you are together. I don't even have Ali with me."

"He'll be back."

"I don't know if we can weather the storm," Solange said miserably.

"My suggestion to you is for you to be the bigger person through this trying time. Then if things don't get better you have no guilt and you can let it go. But remember, Solange, I've known you for over ten years and have never seen you as happy as you have been since Ali entered your life. I'd think very carefully before I walked away."

"But I'm so lonely," she whispered.

"You need a friend. What haven't you called Isabel? You said that she moved to the area."

"I dunno," Solange said. "She said something negative about Ali."

"She didn't say something racist, did she?"

"No," Solange said a little sheepishly, because in reflection it seemed like an innocent comment. "She said something to the effect that policemen are known for being abusive."

"Oh, good grief. That's such a stereotype."

"I don't think that she meant it the way I took it."

"Then call her up to meet you out for a luncheon or something. How about asking her to go to the Alvin Ailey show, since it seems as if Ali won't be able to make it because he's being held hostage in Orlando?"

"I'd completely forgotten about it. But that's a little while away."

"Well, start doing a few things with her, and if you guys get along better, you can give her the extra ticket."

"I'll think about it. I never realized it because I've been so wrapped up with Ali since he came into my life is that I have no girlfriends except you. And you live too far to be of any real use," she added only half teasingly.

Grace attempted to soothe her friend's ruffled feathers. "If things don't work out and you have no one else to go with, I'll fly up that weekend and go with you," she said in a cheeky voice.

"And leave the kids?" Solange asked in mock horror. "I'm shocked."

"Well, Ebony hasn't had an episode since you left, and Livingston is standing up straight, so I might be able to sneak away."

For the first time since the start of their conversation, Solange's spirits lifted. "Then that sounds like a plan. Now I have to go because I have to be at work early in the morning. The head honchos are coming this week for a visit, and I need to get my work house in order."

"Okay, honey. I'll talk to you soon," Grace said.

"Yes," she answered.

"Remember what I said about Ali. No relationship is perfect."

"I'll remember," Solange promised before she hung up.

The next morning Solange nervously ran her hands down her sides, rubbing the moistness. She stood outside the open door to the storage area.

"Do you need me to help you with this?" The question by someone behind her startled Solange. She whirled around. It was only seven-thirty in the morning, and Celeste stood in a navy blue pencil skirt, low black heels and white ruffled blouse.

After giving a quick onceover, Solange smiled her pleasure at Celeste's dignified appearance.

"Well, I need to take inventory of what we have and match it with what we're supposed to have," Solange said.

"I saw that scribbled on your desk calendar, so I thought that I might come in early to see if you needed any help." Celeste held up a manila folder. "Jane's Excel sheets are in here."

Solange stamped down her fear of enclosed places and said gratefully, "In that case, I'll count boxes and you can check off everything as I call it out."

For the next several hours, Solange methodically read the serial number of each box that was stacked in the storage area and Celeste drew with a highlighter through each entry. There was little small talk.

Celeste sat perched on two stacked boxes and occasionally sipped from one of the cans of soda that Solange had purchased for them during one of their short breaks. The smell of the highlighter, combined with the dank smell, made her feel a little queasy at times, and if it were not for Celeste she would have given up an hour earlier. Yet they persevered and eventually Solange gingerly stood up. She brushed the dust off her hands and knees. "That's it," she said.

"But it can't be," Celeste said.

"Why not?" Solange asked with a frown.

"Because there's a lot of inventory missing. Actually about two pages' worth."

Solange walked over and looked at the Excel sheets with white areas that hadn't been highlighted. She squinted and saw that on every page that held a month's inventory, there were boxes of product that couldn't be accounted for. Solange swallowed nervously when the full impact of what was going on hit her.

"I need to call Corporate."

As Solange drove in the drizzle, she spoke her thoughts aloud in frustration. "Now that the weather has broken, instead of snow up to my kneecaps, I have to battle with the daily onslaught of rain." She pulled into her driveway and with consternation saw that once again the newspaper wasn't on the front porch being kept dry and shielded by the overhang, but instead was on the grass in a puddle of water. She parked her car and ran out to fetch it, her feet sinking into the mossy grass. "Oh, my goodness!" she exclaimed, almost toppling as she picked up the newspaper.

Suddenly the hairs on the back of her neck rose and she slowly turned around. Staring into the cluster of trees, she thought she saw a sudden movement and at the same time a flash of silver. Then it was gone. A dog started barking somewhere down the street and Solange steadily walked to the garage, staring in the direction that she'd thought she'd seen the movement. She couldn't see anything. Once inside the garage, she hit the button to close the door. Her eyes never wavered from watching the opening and a feeling of relief swept through her when the door closed. She shook her head in an effort to clear her thoughts.

That night Solange sat on the sofa drinking a glass of her favorite wine, Chateau Ste. Michelle. *Did I really hear something out there in the yard or is my mind playing tricks on me?* After her third glass of Riesling she picked up the phone. She pulled up her call list and hit Ali's number. Then before there was a dial tone, she disconnected it. *At this point, what's the use?*

# *CHAPTER 18*

Solange sat at her desk across from Seth Dickerson and his boss, Alexander Russert. Dickerson and Russert looked like carbon copies of each other. They were both dressed in khaki slacks, blue shirts and ties. The only difference was that Seth looked like he'd just walked out of a tanning bed, and Russert was about twenty years older and balding.

"I've gone over the Excel sheets time and time again and I can't find an entry when those goods were shipped out of the warehouse."

Dickerson spoke, and his voice had a tinge of accusation in it. "How about an entry as to when they disappeared? Was it when you were out of town?"

"I don't know," Solange answered honestly. "If I knew when the merchandise disappeared, then I would probably know when and where it went."

The tension in the room was heavy. Russert cleared his throat. "Who else knows about the missing merchandise?"

"Only my secretary Celeste Manning."

"Can she be trusted? That's not who I've been bandying telephone conversation with when I call," Dickerson asked.

"I had to let Jane go."

"Why?"

"Her work was not up to par," Solange responded smoothly. "So since I had to lay off so many people, I felt it was in the best interest of the company to not keep her. Celeste Manning is doing an excellent job. She's the one who helped me to identify the missing inventory."

Russert leaned back in his chair. "It's obviously an inside job. It could be someone who worked here and had access to the storage area or gave someone else keys and access to everything."

"I've never lost my keys, so that's out," Solange said decisively. "Maybe if the company hadn't cut down on security, we would have been able to catch the thief on camera." She slid Seth Dickerson a sidelong look. "A picture is worth a thousand words," she added.

"I think that we should have the place dusted for fingerprints," Dickerson said.

"I already had that done, and the only fingerprints that were found belonged to me and Celeste."

"They probably wore gloves. This is bad press for us, and we have to keep it on the down low about what's going on. I don't want to tip anyone off. I'd rather lose product than the whole government contract. Our microchips are used in spy satellites. But there's something that I know that they don't know," Russert said.

"What is it?"

"If anyone tries to sell our merchandise on the black market, every one of our chips has a serial number that can only be seen with special laser equipment. Let's see if our stuff surfaces and then we'll know," Russert said.

"What about the inside person? Can you trust this Celeste Manning to keep her mouth shut about what's going on?" Dickerson asked.

"Yes," she answered unequivocally.

"Good, because your job may depend on it," Dickerson said in a deceptively quiet voice.

Solange chose to ignore the threat. Instead she turned her attention to Russert. "I've had to lay so many people off. What if this person no longer works here?"

"Then we're pretty much up the creek without a paddle." Alexander Russert rubbed his chin thoughtfully. "We don't want to scare off the thief. We'll install cameras and wait to see if we're hit again. I have a contact in the FBI. He'll make discreet inquiries about any 14-karat-gold-plated chips being sold on the black market. Maybe we'll get lucky."

After Dickerson and Russert left, Solange went to her private bathroom inside her office and vomited up her lunch.

Ali Marks sat exhausted in the sweltering bunkhouse. *I miss Solange.* Beads of perspiration ran down the sides of his face and he carelessly wiped them away with one hand. His head was bent as he looked at the concrete slab floor, and he was so deep in thought, he didn't hear anyone come in.

A sudden tap on his shoulder startled him, and he was surprised to see Col. Amsterdam because he never entered the barracks where the three remaining snipers in training were housed.

Col. Amsterdam gave a brief smile at the nonplussed expression that crossed Ali's face when he saw him.

Ali started to struggle to his feet, but the colonel stilled his movement with a hand on Ali's shoulder. "Don't get up. You're not in the military yet," he said.

"I was going to stand as a gesture of respect," Ali rumbled in his low, throaty voice.

"I appreciate that, but you need to conserve your strength. Tomorrow's a big day for you guys."

"Yes," he said. "It's the start of our field day exercises."

"Yes, and if you make it through next week, all you need to do is pass your written exam."

Ali felt the familiar curl of trepidation inside his stomach, but he brushed it away.

Col. Amsterdam interrupted his thoughts. "Are you nervous?"

"Very," Ali answered without hesitation.

"You should be." Then without another word he turned around and left as quickly as he'd appeared.

Solange watched Isabel polish off her second slice of cheesecake.

"I know that I shouldn't have had two pieces, but I rarely treat myself like this. I won't have any more for a long time."

"I didn't say anything," Solange laughed lightly.

"No," Isabel said dryly, "but you were thinking it."

"Ahh. Believe me, I have better things to worry about other than what you eat."

"Yeah. I bet you do. When you told me the other night about all the trouble at work, it seemed as if you were on the edge."

"Everything that goes wrong over there ultimately falls on my shoulders. 'It was the best of times, and the worst of times . . .' " Solange said.

Isabel gave a long sigh. "Even though they say that we're coming out of this recession, my business hasn't picked up. People aren't throwing parties. When it comes to weddings, most people don't have a big one, much less a wedding planner, but instead go to the courthouse and have a cheapie reception."

Solange grimaced. "The best news I've read is that the divorce rate is down because people can't afford to split their assets, much less get a divorce."

"When are you and Ali getting married? I'll give you a half-price rate for the party planning and the wedding."

Solange looked away, hiding her expression. "We've put the wedding off indefinitely."

Isabel leaned forward with a glassy look in her eyes, obviously wanting more info. "You didn't tell me that."

"It doesn't matter about the wedding. I can't wait for him to get back so he can protect me," Solange said effusively.

Now Isabel's eyes widened. "Protect you from what?"

"I don't know." She shrugged her shoulders in an attempt to appear nonchalant. "Sometimes it feels as if I'm being watched."

"Watched!" Isabel exclaimed, looking over her shoulder.

"Not right now, silly." Solange laughed at the look of sudden look of fear that crossed Isabel's face. "There have been more than a couple of times. One time I was in the garage at work. Another time I thought that someone was outside my bedroom window," Solange confided.

"When did all this happen?"

"Not one after the other. But it's been going on for a while," Solange said.

"Where was Ali during all of this? Didn't he go and check things out with his gun?"

"He was never around when it happened."

"Maybe it's him,' Isabel said.

"What?" Solange's eyes narrowed into mere slits.

"Maybe he's a mad stalker."

Solange was consumed with so much anger, she could barely choke out a response. "Explain."

"If he was never around when this happened, how do you know it's not him?"

"Because he has no reason to stalk me. He already has me," Solange said.

"Hell, maybe he's a freak and stalking gets his juices going." Isabel burst into laughter and her eyes began to tear. Once she saw that Solange was not amused, she made an effort to stop. She wiped the tears with the back of her hand. "Seriously. I'm just kind of funning you, but is there ever a time when Ali showed up right after you felt you were being watched?"

The time Solange was frightened in the stairwell surfaced, but she pushed that memory away. "No," she said.

Isabel studied her for a minute, noticing Solange's discomfiture. "Okay. I'm sure you know your man best."

The rest of the lunch date was sprinkled with desultory conversation, and when Isabel waved at her as she got in a taxi cab en route to Ali's mother's house, she knew that she wouldn't be spending any more time with that insidious troublemaker.

When Solange rang Amira Marks's doorbell, it was immediately flung open. Amira looked her usual graceful self. The designer dress she wore fit her to a tee, and her hair was pulled back into a chignon.

"Thank you for coming, Solange," Amira said as she welcomed Solange into her home.

"It wasn't a problem. I had a lunch date in Manhattan."

"With a man?" Amira looked at her in horror.

"Of course not."

"Good," she said with obvious relief. "I know that absence does not make the heart grow fonder."

Solange decided to cut to the chase. "I guess Ali told you that we've been having difficulties."

"Yes, but I do understand, even though he is my son that he is the one who decided to follow a dream. A dream that may not have been yours, am I right?"

"You're right," Solange said. She choked back tears. "In the beginning I was against it and then I understood. But things are not what I expected them to be."

"He is trying to get redemption for his father. His father's dream has become his dream."

"I understand that, but it doesn't change the fact that I feel abandoned."

Amira took her hand and placed it on top of Solange's. "He will come back to you, and when he does, he will be a better man because he will have the resolution, will and determination of his father combined with his own."

"But he hasn't called me since I left Orlando," Solange wailed.

"He's giving you a chance to feel what life will be like without him. Do you like it?"

"No, I don't," Solange replied shortly.

Amira nodded her head in relief. "Then when you see him again, things will right themselves."

"Are you sure?"

"As sure as I am that I will finally right things with my father."

"Your father!"

"Yes. He is coming next month with Anah. They want to tour the university here."

"Congratulations," Solange said as she leaned over and gave Amira a hug that was returned with love and affection. "I hope that you and your family will mend your differences."

Amira spoke, and even though her lips quivered there was a determination in her eyes and hardness in her voice that Solange had never heard before. "I have to. It will be my only chance to set things right."

Ali hid in the marshes of the Everglades. He looked at the mock target through his sniper rifle, and with a steady index finger, slowly squeezed the trigger. The target fell to his feet and sank into the water hidden from his eyesight.

When the computer monitor in the operation booth, over a mile away, showed that the target had been hit, Col. Amsterdam nodded with complete satisfaction.

Ali turned and with a feeling of supreme confidence waded out of the water and began his five-mile trek back to headquarters.

The next morning at the gun range, Ali sat with the two remaining snipers that had been his roommates for the last six and a half months. He, Jeffrey Gates and Frances Calhoun sat anxiously waiting for their next instructions.

"My hands are torn to shreds," Gates said in a disgruntled voice. "I don't know why they didn't let us use gloves. I would if I was out in the field on a mission."

"We would if we had access to them, but what if we didn't? They give us the worst-case scenarios here to see if we can cut the mustard."

"Hell, as far as I'm concerned the fact that we're sitting here means we did that," Calhoun declared in a tight voice.

"I get the feeling that they want one more of us to quit. Since we didn't do it today, it might be the written exam that knocks one of us out," Gates said.

"How ready do you think you are?" Calhoun asked Ali.

"I'm as ready as I'll ever be," Ali replied, his voice barely a whisper.

Late that night, Ali was unable to sleep. The snores of his comrades only worsened the matter. Looking at the clock he saw that it was midnight. Ali grabbed his cell phone, which he kept on in case Solange called and padded barefoot outside. He dialed her number, but before it could ring, he severed the call and dropped it in his pajama bottom pocket.

Looking up at the sky he saw that the moon was a huge golden orb, and a sudden peacefulness enveloped him. Ali slowly walked back into the barracks, settled into his bunk and fell into his first peaceful sleep since he'd been in Orlando, Florida.

The next morning, Ali, Calhoun, and Gates were seated outside the examination room. Colonel Amsterdam strutted towards them, and behind him a young bespectacled man held a manila folder clutched tightly in his hands.

"Marks, you'll take your exam in the room down the hall with Mr. Jones. Gates and Calhoun, you'll take your test with me in here," Col. Amsterdam said to the trainees.

Immediately Gates and Calhoun looked suspiciously at each other and then Gates turned to Col. Amsterdam. "I don't mean any disrespect or to question your authority, sir, but why is Marks taking his test in a separate room? The three of us have been together all along through everything else."

Before Amsterdam could reply, Ali spoke. "It's because I'm dyslexic and I get extra time. I also have requested an oral interpreter on some of the questions if I need it."

"Oh, I'm sorry, man." Gates looked genuinely sorry and Calhoun averted his gaze. "I didn't mean to put you on the spot like that."

"I know you didn't, Gates." Ali shrugged his shoulders in an attempt to appear unruffled. "I was born with this disability and I have learned to do the best I can with what I have." Then he bumped fists with Gates and Calhoun before, with a proud tilt of his head, he strode to the end of the hall and the classroom Amsterdam had pointed to.

Solange was taking a midafternoon nap when suddenly she sat bolt upright in the bed. "Ali," she murmured. She looked around the room for a minute, not understanding where she was. Then she reached for her phone and quickly dialed Ali's cell. It went straight to voice mail. Without leaving a message she disconnected and, turning over, punched her pillow and laid back down, willing herself to sleep.

Four hours after he started the exam, Ali Marks gestured to Jones, who sat at the desk in the front of the room.

Immediately he rose and walked over to him. "Yes," he said.

"I've finished every question but eighty-three. I can't decipher what it's asking me."

Jones picked up the test and read it. Then he handed it back to him. "There's a typo on it. It's merely asking you from what distance can a .308 rifle hit its target?"

"Thank you." Ali took the test from him and filled in the answer, "C." Then he handed it to him. Nervously he asked, "When will I get the results?"

"In the morning there will be a meeting and you'll know then whether or not you made it." Jones patted him on the shoulder. "Best of luck to you, Mr. Marks," he said.

"Thank you," Ali said gratefully and strode out of the room.

Once he got to the barracks, he stood outside and opened his cell phone. He'd cut it off during his exam, and when he flipped it open, he saw that no one had called. With resolution he walked into the barracks and started packing his belongings. He was almost done when Gates and Calhoun entered with a bucket of fried chicken.

"Damn, you look like you're ready to get the hell out of here," Calhoun said.

"Rain or shine, I'm on a plane tomorrow afternoon."

"Me, too," Gates said with a sheepish look at Ali. "Hey, look, man. I'm really . . ."

Ali interrupted the apology that he knew was forming on Gate's lips. "Let it go, man. I'm not ashamed of it anymore. It can only cripple me if I let it."

Calhoun plopped down on his bunk. "My sister's dyslexic."

"She is?" Ali asked in surprise.

"Sure. I know the signs, but you certainly do hide it well. I would've never known had you not said it."

"What does your sister do?"

"She's a lawyer. In fact, she's thought to be one of the best in Atlanta."

"Hells' bells. She sounds like a catch. Is she married?"

"Nope," Calhoun said, grinning.

"Call her and ask her if she wants to meet a single, good-looking sniper." Gates laughed. "Don't tell her I'm white, though."

"So you're sure that you're going to make it?" Ali asked.

"I'm sure that we're all going to make it," Gates said with certainty.

"I hate that I can't come up and go to the show with you," Grace moaned.

"So do I, but your family needs you. I'm scared to death about Ebony."

"I was at first, but the doctor said that all she has is the flu. But because of her condition we have to be extra careful with her."

Solange tried to keep the forlorn tone from creeping in her voice so that Grace didn't feel guilty. "I wouldn't dare have you come under those circumstances."

"I hate the thought of you going to the show alone," Grace said and groaned.

"As Beyonce said, I'm an independent woman. I'm perfectly capable of going to a show without a man hanging on my arm."

"It's too bad you can't seem to get along with Isabel."

"Now that she's an unattached woman, I see just how nasty she can be. My life is complicated enough, and I don't need any more drama. I'd rather sell my extra ticket to someone in front of the theatre and buy myself a shirt or something with the money."

"I hear you," Grace said. "Look, I don't mean to cut you off, but I hear Ebony calling me."

"I'll let you go then." After Solange hung up the phone she felt more alone than ever.

The next morning Ali Marks, Jeffrey Gates, and Frances Calhoun were outside the examination room waiting for Col. Amsterdam.

When Ali saw him striding towards them, his eyes automatically went to the three large folders in his hands. Once he was abreast of them, he nodded in their general direction and indicated that they were to follow him inside his office. In a subdued manner, Frances led the way, followed by Gates. Ali brought up the rear. Once inside he saw that there were three chairs stationed in front of the desk. After closing the door, Ali slid into the vacant one.

Col. Amsterdam handed each man a folder. Clearing his throat he spoke with sincerity. "I'm very happy to inform you that all of you have passed the field test and written exam. Congratulations," he said.

Gates and Calhoun slapped high fives while Ali sat there in stunned silence.

A sudden flashback of him sitting in a desk in grade school and shoving his failed test into his backpack surfaced, and he had to fight back tears of joy. *I finally did it.*

"Man, why are you so quiet?" Gates clapped him on his back. "I told you last night that you would make it."

Ali still sat immobile, afraid to speak because he knew that if he did, his voice would quiver and that the lump in his throat would turn into tears.

Noticing Ali's loss of composure, Amsterdam stood and walked around his desk. Instinctively they all stood and he held his hand out and shook each one of theirs. "I have enclosed all of your credentials in your envelopes. You are hereby certified as the first to graduate from the U.S. Sniper Academy. I've included all of my numbers for you to use on any forms as you seek positions that will enable you to use your talents."

"Thank you, Col. Amsterdam." Gates smiled before he walked to the door.

"Yes, thank you, sir," Calhoun echoed, following him out.

Ali gave Amsterdam another hard shake, and when he did he felt Amsterdam's firm clasp.

"I need you to stay behind, Marks," Amsterdam said.

Once they were alone, Amsterdam pointed to the middle chair that had been occupied by Calhoun. Ali subsided into it with a questioning look at Amsterdam.

"We didn't graduate with as many snipers as we'd hoped. Because of that I've been asked to run another course similar to this one. I watched you the whole time you were here. The focus that you showed was, to say the least, like nothing I've ever seen. I am offering you a position as a field supervisor for the next group of recruits."

Ali felt the blood rush to his face and he thought that he might burst from pride. Then Solange's face flashed in front of him. "Your offer has been one of the best things that has ever happened to me. I'm very grateful and I will never forget it, but I have no choice but to turn it down," Ali said humbly.

"Why?" Amsterdam asked in a forthright manner. "Because of your fiancée?"

"Yes," Ali answered.

"People love Florida, and Orlando is one of the more beautiful cities. Hell, everyone's trying to get out of that rat race in New York and come down here for an easier life," Amsterdam said.

"Not my Solange. She has a career and she loves where she is and what she's doing. I've already asked her to give up too much, and I can't ask her to give up any more."

"It's a six-figure income," Amsterdam said, shocked that Ali was not taking him up on his offer.

Ali felt his heart drop at the thought of what he was passing up, but he knew in his heart that there was no price tag in the world that was worth more to him than his relationship with Solange.

"I want the job, but it's in the wrong city. If you ever run a training camp within 100 miles of New York City, I would greatly appreciate you giving me another shot at the position."

Amsterdam shook his head in bewilderment. "I hope you know what you're doing. Lightning doesn't always strike twice in the same place."

"I'll pray that it does." Then Ali stood and once again held his hand out.

Amsterdam shook it with a look of disappointment on his face.

Once Ali got back to the deserted barracks, he walked over to the bunk bed that he'd slept in for over seven months and fell to his knees. Clasping his hands in front of him he bent his head. "Thank you, God, for your blessings."

Then he stood and grabbed the three duffel bags that held his belongings. An eerie feeling came over him. "It's time to go. My woman needs me," he said and headed to the airport.

# CHAPTER 19

Solange had found an empty seat in the back of the train. She stared vacantly out the window at it sped past a combination of gray buildings, green foliage, and barren countryside before she recognized the outskirts of the city. The train ground to a halt to pick up more passengers and, as was her custom, she reached inside her purse and pulled out the latest issue of *Essence* and deliberately started flipping through it.

She kept her head bent when she felt a body slide into the seat next to her. Refusing to look up, she was suddenly startled by an eerily familiar aroma. It was Cool Water. Solange had to quell a sudden desire to burst into tears and instead decided to move her seat. Without looking at the person, she stood in order to distance herself and sit across the aisle. Her attitude soured even more than it already had.

She felt compelled to glare at the person disapprovingly, and when she looked up, her eyes locked with Ali's. Her jaw dropped.

The golden embers of his eyes stared at her with such an intensity that she quivered. Her breasts strained against the fabric of her silk dress that stopped mid-thigh. She swallowed hard.

Ali was dressed in a black and white French-cut shirt and black dress slacks, and his hair was combed back from his face. It looked as if he'd applied gel to it while it was wet and combed it.

Ali stared pointedly at the expanse of thigh that she was exposing and she found herself automatically trying to pull her dress lower to cover more skin.

Solange realized that several occupants of the train were watching them. The tension in the air between them was so tangible, she was at a loss for words. He appeared to be satisfied for them to not enter into conversation until they reached a place where they could talk in private.

It felt as if decades passed before the train stopped at her destination. She stood and Ali slid behind her, effectively blocking any man's way who might want to get close to her. Once they got on the landing, Ali cupped her elbow and guided her towards the stairs that led to the city. "I heard that you need a date for the Alvin Ailey Dance Theatre of Harlem."

"Yes," she said unsteadily.

"Well, now you have one." His tone was resolute and Solange felt a surge of happiness that for the first time in what seemed to be eons someone else had taken the reins and was making her decisions for her.

"If we hurry, we'll just make curtain."

"We just might," she whispered.

The first act of the performance flew by, and as breathtaking as it was, Solange had a hard time concentrating on the exotic nature of the dancers with Ali's thigh touching hers. That was the only physical contact he'd made since they were together and Solange was a little fearful as to what he might be thinking. She hadn't talked to him since she'd stormed out on him in Orlando. She had a million questions churning inside her head.

Ali felt Solange's gaze on him in the darkened theatre and he turned to her. Without uttering a sound he took his hand and lifted the hand that should have held her engagement ring. He put it to his lips and kissed it. Then instead of letting her hand go, he kept in encased in his strong, warm grip.

The feel of his grip felt so comforting that she mentally sent up a prayer to God.

At intermission, Ali managed to secure a small booth, and, signaling to the waiter, he ordered two glasses of Chateau Ste. Michelle.

Sipping it gratefully, Solange she studied him over the rim of her glass. "How long are you staying in town?"

"How long do you want me to stay?"

"I never wanted you to go," she answered solemnly.

"If I promise not to go back to Orlando can we put all of this behind us and resume our life together?"

From out of nowhere, Solange found herself blurting out her innermost feelings. "Sometimes I feel as if I don't know you. It's as if you're hiding a part from me that I never knew existed." She gave a self-deprecating shrug. "I don't want to be the reason why you don't finish sniper school and miss out on your passion."

His eyes held hers a prisoner. "Why aren't you wearing my ring?"

"Only because I didn't want to get robbed." She saw an easing of his features and his nod of agreement. "Also, I did call, but your phone went straight to voice mail." Her eyes moistened as she struggled to keep her emotions in check. "But then I didn't call back because I didn't know what to say. Ali, when did you get back in town?"

"Last night. My stuff is at Randolph's house. He's generously offered his spare bedroom to me until we got a chance to sort things out."

"Oh." She hung her head, avoiding his gaze.

"I didn't want you to go to the theatre alone tonight or I would have called you tomorrow and asked you out on a date or something. But since that didn't seem like a plan, I felt that if maybe I could recreate the scenario of how we met, you'd see that I'm still the Ali Marks that you fell in love with."

The sound of the bell and the fluorescent lights blinking three times was their cue. Ali stood to his feet and held out his hand. "Let's go back and enjoy the show and we'll finish our conversation later."

It was after eleven-thirty at night when they stood on the train platform. There were very few people around, and Solange swung her head around, taking particular notice of who was in the vicinity. "My Cadillac is at the depot station in a secure parking lot."

"I figured as much," Ali said. His hands were in his pockets and she could see that they were balled into fists. "I'm going to ride the train to White Plains with you and then come back to Randolph's."

Solange started to say something, but he cut across her words and his tone brooked no argument.

"I'm not letting you ride the train alone this time of night."

"I was going to say that you don't have to go back to Randolph's tonight," she said, avoiding his eyes. "We're both tired. You can sleep in the spare room. Tomorrow's another day."

With the sound of her words, Ali's stormy countenance cleared as the train made a rumbling sound as it ground to a halt. He held his hand out in a sweeping gesture. "Ladies first."

As they sat close on the almost deserted train, the jostling motion felt comforting and Solange soon drifted off to sleep. Later, she was awakened by Ali gently nudging her. "We're almost home," he whispered.

Groggy from her sleep she opened her mouth and closed it several times, trying to rid herself of the taste of cottonmouth before giving Ali a soft smile. She spied her car illuminated under the light in the open garage and, once they reached it, Ali held his palm out. Solange gratefully handed him the keys.

Her house was a ten-minute ride from the station, and for some reason, Solange felt nervous now that she was alone with Ali. But once they were in the house, all of her fears dissolved and for the first time in a very long time, she felt safe.

Ali turned to her and planted a warm kiss on her forehead. "Goodnight," he said. "I'll see you in the morning." Then he disappeared down the hallway and went into the spare room.

Solange slowly walked into the kitchen, and because her throat was dry, poured herself a glass of water. Solange walked stealthily down the hall and when she got in front of the room where Ali had disappeared, she stood hesitantly.

She heard the sound of the shower running in the adjoining bathroom, and with a knowing smile of satisfaction, she went into the master suite and crawled between the sheets and waited.

Solange awoke in the night and blinked several times, giving her eyes a chance to adjust to the darkness. She took her hand and swept it under the covers to find the other side of the bed vacant. *Ali didn't come to me.*

She lay in the darkness and mulled over the troubles that they'd had over the last few months. With determination, she slid out of bed and strode to the shower. Solange stood under the spray as hot as she could stand it and scrubbed her body from head to toe. Then she quickly dried and oiled herself before spraying Amber Romance from *Victoria's Secret.* Naked, she left the room and walked across the hall. She quietly opened the bedroom door and tiptoed over to where Ali lay sleeping. He was on his back and his arm was held across his face. She couldn't fathom his features in the darkness.

"Are you sure?" Ali's voice reverberated in the night.

"Yes," she said quietly.

Ali took his hand and lifted the sheet, and when he did, Solange could see from his erection that he'd been impatiently waiting for her.

She slid into bed next to him and encircled his waist with her arm and buried her face in his chest. Then Solange started crying, and once she started the deluge seemed to be everlasting.

Ali soothed her by rubbing her back with his hand in small, circular motions. Then he shushed her. "There's no need to cry, Solange. The worst of it is over. You'll see."

Once her tears subsided, Ali gently eased her onto her back and began to cover her body with his.

Solange wriggled from underneath him, and, instead, turned him onto his back. She slid her body on top of his, and when she planted herself on his stomach, she flanked each one of his thighs with hers. The wetness between her legs excited him, and his penis moved until it was vertical and was nestled in the crease of her vagina.

Solange moved her legs and lay flat on top of him. Lowering her mouth to his, she leisurely explored his mouth with hers and each one of their tongues reacquainted themselves with the other's. Then, pulling away, she began to feather kiss along the side of his neck, making a trail down to his navel. There she sank it and probed the small crater, loving the smell of oil, soap and pure manliness.

Hungry for more, Solange scooted herself down until her face dipped just below his navel. Taking his manhood in her hand, she gripped it as if he was a rope that she clung to for survival. Solange turned on her side, and guiding him, she turned him on his. With her lips she lightly teased him by making circular motions around the tip of his head before taking his penis fully into her mouth.

The feel of her moist cavern made him flinch and he began to move, but she swatted him gently on his buttocks, willing him to stop his movement and be patient. Once he did, she began to suck him.

Ali cradled her head with his hand, firmly pushing her more and more roughly until he gasped, "Solange."

The impetus of him calling her name made her hungrier and she pleasured him for an eternity. The next time when he began to move, she didn't stop him, and when he came she didn't flinch. Instead she drank him in and then, exhausted, fell asleep, her limbs intertwined with his.

The next morning she awoke when she felt Ali's eyes on her. She felt suddenly shy and pulled up the sheet, making sure their nakedness was covered from the harsh glare of the morning.

"What are you going to do today?" she whispered, breaking the silence.

"I don't know," he said and smiled. "What am I going to do today?"

"I hope you're going to go and get your things from Randolph's."

"It would be my pleasure, wifey."

She smiled. "When does your plane leave for you to go back to Orlando?"

"I have no plane reservations back to Orlando."

Astonished, she pushed herself up on one arm. "Why not? Nothing went wrong down there, did it?"

"No," he said gratefully. "For once everything went right. I am a certified U.S. Sniper."

"You're done! You passed the test!"

"I'm done," he replied, his eyes dancing with pleasure.

"The oral and the written?"

"With flying colors," Ali replied with a touch of smugness.

Solange jumped out of bed and, forgetting her nakedness, started dancing around the room.

Ali sat up and rested his back against the headboard and laughed. "Be careful. With you bouncing around like that, you're apt to give yourself a black eye."

Solange dove on the bed and Ali made a grunt from her impact before grabbing her and hugged her close.

"You are so good-looking, brave, and smart, Ali Marks."

"I am kind of smart, Solange Montgomery. Look how I've managed to hang onto you."

Ali was leaving the precinct when his cell phone rang. Answering it he said, "Hello, Mother."

"Son!"

Ali smiled at his mother's exuberant voice, which couldn't be disguised even with a bad cell phone connection.

"Will you come over to the house? I have some wonderful news."

"Okay," he replied. "I just finished my shift, so I'll be there as soon as I can."

As Ali sat at his mother's kitchen table, he bit into one of the cookies that was on the dessert plate she'd put in front of him.

He smiled approvingly at her. "These cookies taste delicious. What are they?"

Amira watched her son with a pleased expression on her face. "I'm glad that you enjoy them so much. They are Hadgi Badah. I used to eat them all the time when I was a young girl in Iraq. You better get used to Iraqi food."

"Why is that?"

"Our family is arriving tomorrow."

Ali put a half-eaten cookie down on the plate. "And they're staying here?"

"Of course, son," Amira Marks said in a slightly confused voice. "Where else would they stay?"

"Mother," he said seriously, "I don't want you to get too excited about their visit."

"Why not?" Her eyes were open wide with anticipation. "My father would not make such a long trip if he didn't want me to be his daughter again."

"After years of neglect," Ali said fiercely.

"I am at fault also. I should not have married without his permission. I disobeyed the rules and embarrassed the family."

"Are you saying that you wished that you didn't marry my father?"

"Of course not, son. But I knew the ways of our world and I made a choice. I chose your father. Now I have a second chance to regain my family, and I will do everything in my power to accomplish this."

"Well, leave me out of it," Ali said in a no-nonsense tone.

"I cannot leave you out of it. You are my son and are a reflection of me. My father, your grandfather, will be paying attention and judging me as a mother by your behavior."

"I need something to drink."

"I have tea," she offered.

"I don't want any of that," he said in a disgruntled manner. "I'll take a beer."

"I have none."

"How about some water, Mother? Do you have any of that?"

Frustrated, Ali started to rise, but Amira stopped him. "I will get it."

Ali watched his mother as she glided to the refrigerator and poured him a glass of water from a jug. He looked at her accusingly. "Why don't you have anything decent to drink?"

"I have rid the house of alcohol. Your grandfather wouldn't approve."

"You have been in America for over fifty years, and you are now changing your whole lifestyle for people who you don't even know and haven't had the desire to know you or me," Ali said harshly.

Droplets formed on Amira's long eyelashes, and she blinked them away before they fell. "Ali, I need you to help me mend fences with my family."

"But I don't want . . ."

"But I do want. If I can have my father back in my life, I can leave this world in peace knowing that I righted a wrong."

Ali looked at the almost childlike expression of neediness on his mother's face. "I will try to help you, Mother."

"Promise me, son," she pressed him.

"I promise."

They sat in Ali's Explorer outside his mother's house. "Ready?" Solange said with a quirky smile.

"As ready as I'll ever be," he replied. Taking a deep breath they exited the SUV and, hand in hand, walked up to the front door. "I could let myself in with a key, but I'd rather not, since I feel like I'm visiting the house of a stranger."

"That's a bad attitude," Solange lightly admonished him. "Have you forgotten our little talk already?"

Ali merely grimaced and plastered a smile on his face when he heard the front door being opened.

Solange's mouth fell open at the sight of her future mother-in-law. Amira wore a long black cloak from head to foot and a black veil.

Out of shock, Ali dropped Solange's hand. "Mother, is that you in there?"

Ali's mother stepped aside and made a sweeping gesture for them to enter the foyer. "Thank you for coming. Your grandfather has been asking for you for days and has been getting impatient."

"Oh, yeah? I've been waiting for him for thirty-four years, so I think that he is the rude one."

Solange hit Ali in his back with her fist.

Amira saw the gesture and gave Solange a look of gratitude. "Everyone is in the den. The food is almost ready."

As Solange followed Ali and his mother, a feeling of foreboding encompassed her. Inside the den, a man who was obviously Ali's grandfather sat in a chair. He was clad in a white, ankle-length shirt-like garment and a white square scarf folded into a triangle covered the top of his head. He had black eyes and his hands were folded in his lap. He gave Ali a long, hard, appraising stare.

"Father, this is your grandson, Ali."

Without speaking or rising, Ali's grandfather held out his hand.

Ali walked towards him and shook it.

"He has a firm grasp," he said to Amira.

"Hello, Grandfather," Ali said.

"He looks like you. Let's just hope that he listens better than you did."

Solange saw Ali's body stiffen in anger, so she quickly intervened. "Hello, I'm Ali's fiancée."

Hakim Abraham looked at the proffered hand before he held his out. Their fingers barely touched before he withdrew his. Then he turned to Amira and spoke rapidly in Arabic.

She replied with a soft voice that quivered.

Hakim interrupted her with another flow of words, and she didn't respond with words, but only nodded her head in assent.

"What did he say?" Ali asked suspiciously.

Amira answered with averted eyes. "He only asked what time we would be eating, and I told him now."

Then the woman, dressed identical to Amira, who'd been watching the whole exchange, rose gracefully from the couch, walked over to them and held her hand out to Ali. "I'm your cousin, Anah." She nodded in the direction of the young woman who was dressed like her. "And this is my daughter Farrah."

Farrah looked up briefly, and when she did, Solange was taken aback by the most beautiful set of doe-like eyes that she'd seen on a human being.

Amira Marks spoke, and her accent was thicker than Solange had ever heard before. "Our meal is ready."

Not knowing what to do, Solange stood quietly, but everyone remained still until Hakim Abraham rose. Then they followed him to the dining room.

The table was set with what Solange knew to be Amira's finest china, and as Hakim sat at the head of the table, she saw him studying her. Glancing at the other women at the table she felt suddenly underdressed in her button-down dress that stopped at her knees.

Farrah, who hadn't yet spoken, filled every person's bowl with some kind of soup. Making sure that she wasn't the first to eat, once she did she was pleasantly surprised because it was so good.

Astutely reading her mind, Anah offered, "It is Shorbat Rumman. You would call it pomegranate soup. My daughter makes the best in all of Baghdad."

"It's quite tasty," Solange said. "Isn't it wonderful, honey?"

Before Ali could reply Hakim Abraham began speaking again in Arabic, and no one interrupted his spiel.

Her eyes locked with Ali's and he gave her a slight negative shake of his head.

Finally Amira spoke. "The next part of the meal is Khinta."

"What is that, Mother?"

"Khinta is wheat porridge with stuffed beef pocket."

When Solange dug into her plate of food she thought to herself, *I'd rather take mine to go so I can get the hell out of here. And by the look on Ali's face he'd make a dash for the door with me.*

After dinner they had returned to the den and Hakim studied Ali. "What is your occupation?"

"I'm a police officer, like my father."

He nodded approvingly. "That is a good occupation."

Amira said in a boastful manner, "He just finished getting his sniper's license."

"Sniper?" Hakim's lips pressed together in annoyance. "They miss many times. American snipers come to my country and shoot civilians."

"I never make a mistake," Ali retorted. "If I shoot a man, he's the intended target."

The next week, Solange heard her doorbell ring. She looked through the peephole and recognized by all the black that it was Ali's relatives. Scurrying to the kitchen she took the frying pan of smothered pork chop off the stove and sprayed Glade in the air, trying to camouflage the smell of pork in the house. Then she opened the door.

Farrah stood there with a small suitcase, and Solange looked at Amira questioningly. Then she looked around them and saw Hakim sitting in the backseat of a car in the driveway.

"I tried to call, but you didn't answer the phone."

"I'm sorry, but Ali isn't here. You're welcome to come in, though," she lied.

Amira, Anah, and Farrah entered the foyer.

Solange leaned over to give Amira a hug, and her response was lukewarm, to say the least. "I have already spoken to my son, and he said that it is okay for Farrah to stay here."

"What! I mean, why?"

"She has several tours and meetings at Purdue University, and there is a van picking her up so that she can be with the other girls from her school. They will not come to Brooklyn to get her, and I cannot drive because of my sickness. One of the girls is staying not far from here, and they will pick Farrah up and drop her off."

"Oh," Solange stammered. "For how long?"

"Not more than a week."

*A whole week. I'm going to kill Ali.*

"We were very grateful when Ali said that she could stay here. Otherwise our trip from Baghdad would be a waste."

"Well, of course she can stay. Farrah, take your suitcase down the hall to the first room on the right."

Farrah's eyes twinkled and she quickly walked the direction that Solange had pointed to.

"Thank you, Solange. Now, we must go because my father is waiting."

After they left, Farrah sat on the couch, carefully watching Solange. Then she spoke in a clear voice that held just a tinge of an accent. "Hakim is telling her to stop Ali from marrying you. It's a secret, so don't tell anyone that I told you."

Solange stared at Farrah.

"Would you like to hear more?"

Solange mutely nodded.

"I heard Amira asking her father if he would stay in the United States if she could get Ali to back out the marriage, and he said maybe."

"He's a racist," Solange uttered in disgust.

Farrah nodded her head and said sadly, "That, too. He told Amira that if you were, what do you say, white, that you could help Ali go far, but you are black and of no use to him."

"Haven't you ever heard not to tell family secrets, especially to a stranger?"

Farrah shrugged her shoulders awkwardly. "I do not like Hakim. He is sullen like my father."

"So you don't like your father?"

"No. My mother is not so lucky. My father, Yusef, beats my mother because she cannot have any more children, and I am a girl. He screams at her that she is not Amira. That is why we aren't going back."

"What!"

"My mother and I are going to stay in the United States. That is why we came. We kept putting the trip off until my father said that he couldn't come because it is his busy part of the year with the business. He would have been hard to stand up to, but now we don't have to worry."

"I don't like me or Ali being caught in the middle of this family drama."

"You are not caught. You do not know anything. You promised that you would not say anything, and if you tell Ali, he would tell his mother to save her the embarrassment. She would tell Hakim and he would call Father. He would have my mother and I killed before we could execute our plan. As a student at a college in the United States, I would be protected and in turn will give a safe haven to my mother."

"So Amira knows nothing of the real reason why you came to the States?"

"No, but she will help in the end," Farrah added in a hard voice. "My mother helped her and was forced to take her place because of it. Amira owes her."

When she heard her garage door open, she hurriedly got to her feet and went to get Ali.

She started talking before he could get out of his Explorer. "How could you agree to have Farrah come here for a week without telling me?"

"A week!" he said. "Mother told me that it would only be overnight."

"Then they changed the game plan since they talked to you."

"Shit!" Ali ejaculated. "What are we going to do?"

"There's nothing that we can do. But out of all of them, I'd rather have her stay than anyone else."

"Including my mother?"

"Including her," she stated clearly, storming back into the house.

# *CHAPTER 20*

Farrah smiled at a sleepy Solange when she entered the kitchen. Like a blind woman, Solange went to the coffee pot and poured a steaming mug of the drink in a mug that Farrah already had ready and waiting for her. Lifting it in gratefulness she said, "Thank you, Farrah."

"It was no problem." Farrah sat with her legs Indian style and, uncrossing them, stood and sashayed over to Solange. "I want to thank you and Ali so much for your hospitality."

"You have been no problem, Farrah. As a matter of fact, I've enjoyed your company, even though you did get into my house with subterfuge."

Farrah's tinkling laughter made Solange smile.

"I think that you will make my cousin a wonderful wife," she said, sliding onto a bar stool. "When is the wedding?'

"Good question. Since Ali got back from sniper school, we haven't set a date. I really would like to go to the courthouse, but I know that he won't have it."

"His mother will not approve of that."

When Amira Marks's name was mentioned, Solange's face looked like a thundercloud.

"I see your face. You do not like her anymore?"

"It's hard to like people that don't like you," Solange answered tactfully.

"She likes you," Farrah said with certainty. "But she is under Hakim's thumb. That is not the life that I want for me."

"I don't think that you'll have it, either, Farrah. Where did Ali go?"

"He said that he was going to the grocery store. I did not want to get dressed."

"Obviously," Solange said and she studied Farrah's appearance. She wore a striped day dress that showed off her long legs. Her shiny black mane hung loose down to her waist, and large oval eyes reflected a freedom and satisfaction that had not been there the afternoon that Solange had met her at Amira's house. Gone was the young girl with the subdued personality of a young deer. The time Farrah had spent on the college campus had already changed her, and she had begun to blossom into a fashionable young coed.

"Did he bring in the paper before he left?" Solange asked.

"No, I will go and get it out of the driveway."

Solange sat at the table sipping her drink and while she was refilling her mug, she heard a commotion outside. There were screams and language in Arabic and English. Hurrying outside, she saw Hakim standing in the driveway, and he was shaking a hysterically crying Farrah.

"Stop it," she yelled and hurried towards them.

Amira and Anah stared helplessly at Farrah as she tried to keep herself from falling from the violent way she was being manhandled.

"I said to let her go," Solange said when she reached them, and her tone was lethal.

Hakim stared at her with a malevolent look and said, "Mind your own business."

"Oh, so now you have something to say to me?" she said, her voice dripping sarcasm. "You came to my house three times this week, yet I never heard you utter a word. How dare you try to snub me."

"You're beneath me," he said.

Solange gave a snort of derision. "You come to someone else's house and make a scene and you have the audacity to make a judgment about me? Now, if you like you may come inside, and we can discuss whatever the problem is, but you won't be making a ruckus outside for all of my neighbors to see. I have to live here."

"I'm not leaving without Farrah. She is indecent and behaves like a street woman." He pointed his finger at Farrah. "Why are you outside dressed like this?"

"I came for the paper," she mumbled, continuing to cry softly.

He released her arm as if he was repulsed by her mere touch. "Go inside and get your things."

Farrah shuffled inside and Solange followed her.

Amira and Anah mutely followed suit.

"I'm already packed because I knew I was leaving today," she sniffled in a tragic tone.

"They should have called and then we would've been warned," Solange said.

"Warned about what?" They turned around and saw Hakim standing in the doorway. He pointed an accusing finger at her and said, "This is your fault. You and your ways have made Farrah crave a life that is unseemly. You are unclean. You sleep and live with a man you are not married to. You have mesmerized him with your dark skin."

Solange said in a deadpan voice filled with disgust, "Get out of my house!"

Hakim's eyes narrowed until she nearly couldn't see them. He looked her up and down in an insolent manner.

"How dare you come into my home and denigrate me. You're a stupid old man with stupid old ways. Get the fuck out of my house and stay out!"

"Don't talk to my father that way," Amira said in a nasty voice.

Solange turned on her. "You shut up. You're nothing but a phony. And you can get the hell out, too."

"Solange!"

Ali had come in the house and observed Solange first screaming at his grandfather and then his mother.

Now Farrah entered the room with tears streaming down her face. She was dressed in a hijah and abayah.

"Don't talk to my mother like that," he said, his eyes shooting daggers at Solange.

"But she . . ."

"But she's my mother," he brusquely reprimanded her.

Then he turned to his mother and said, "What's going on in here?"

"Tell him, Amira," Hakim said. "Tell him what you want."

"I do not want you to marry this woman," she said tremulously. "She is disrespectful."

"Mother," Ali said with tiredness in his voice. "We'll talk about this later."

Solange whirled around and gave him an icy look. "Is this the first time that your mother told you not to marry me?"

Ali didn't reply. She could tell by the look in his eyes that he was doing some hard thinking as to what to say that would douse the fire in her eyes.

"Well, we all finally agree on something. I don't want to marry you, either. Now everyone," she looked pointedly at Ali, "especially you, get the hell out of my house."

Solange went to her bedroom and slammed the door.

When she crept out hours later and saw the house was empty, she went to the Internet and Googled a locksmith.

Next she dialed Verizon Wireless and changed her cell phone number. Then she got up and started packing Ali's belongings.

Hours later, after she'd gathered her wits, she called Grace.

"Hey, kiddo," Grace said, answering the phone. "What's cookin'?"

"Ali and I are over," she declared without preamble. "I called to give you my new telephone numbers."

"Are you serious?" Grace exclaimed. "What happened?"

"I can't talk about it yet. I trust you and Jet. Under no circumstances are you to give him these numbers." She said in a tone full of warning, "I mean what I say, Grace."

"Okay," Grace acquiesced in a subdued voice. "I'll abide by your wishes, Solange. You're my girl."

After Solange hung up from Grace, she turned onto her stomach in bed and let go of all of the hurt because she couldn't keep it bottled inside for fear of losing her sanity.

The next morning, she was awakened to the sound of her doorbell ringing. She got up and stumbled to the door. When she saw it was Ali, she stomped over to the window, unlocked it, and raised it. "What do you want?" Solange asked through the screen.

Ali walked over to the window and stood on the grass, staring at her in amazement as she glared at him through the screen. "I want to talk to you. And why in the hell don't any of my keys work?"

"You don't live here anymore."

"Solange," he said, exasperated. "You can't be serious."

"Go home to your momma, momma's boy," she yelled.

He face turned beet red from anger and embarrassment. "Momma's boy?"

"Yes. Where did you stay last night?"

"I stayed at my mother's house in order to give you a chance to cool off."

"See, I told you," she jeered. "You ran straight home to your momma and those ingrates that you claim you don't want anything to do with."

"You told me to be nice to them," he shouted.

"I didn't tell you to choose them over me," she screeched.

"I didn't choose them. You kicked me out right in front of them."

"Because you were taking their side," she continued to screech.

"Solange, all I know is that when I got into the house you were yelling like a banshee at my grandfather and my mother."

"No one talks shit to me in my house," Solange countered fiercely.

Ali tried to reason with her. "How would you like it if you caught me cursing your mother out?"

"My mother doesn't act like your mother. She doesn't turn on people who love her and always treated her with respect." Solange swallowed the lump in her throat. "And only wanted the best for her."

"And your mother doesn't have an identity crisis. I can't fix my mother, and it's wrong of you to blame me for not being able to control her behavior," he countered, trying to reason with her.

"But you left with them," she said, lowering her voice. It was filled with hurt.

Ali felt his insides wrench at the sound of her obvious pain. "You gave me no choice. All I wanted to do was to calm the situation and give you time to cool off and think about how ridiculous this is."

"Did your mother tell you not to marry me before yesterday?"

"Yes," Ali said with brutal honesty. "But it was only after Hakim came. I knew immediately that he was pulling the strings."

An onslaught of tears cascaded down her cheeks and dribbled to the bottom of her chin. "Why didn't you tell me?" Solange hiccupped as she tried to control her breathing.

"Because I didn't want to hurt you," he said with a pang of regret in his voice. "It's you and I, Solange. What anyone else in the world thinks doesn't matter."

"But we can't shut the world out, Ali. We can't live in a vacuum, and if it's not one thing, it's another. Either you following a dream of your father or satisfying one of your mother's. It's obvious to me that we're not meant to be. I've packed your clothes, and I'll leave them outside tomorrow morning before I go to work so you can get them when I'm not here."

"You can't be serious," Ali said, aghast.

"I've never been more serious about anything in my life." Solange pulled down the window and locked it. She took one last look at Ali's forlorn face before she went into her bedroom and slammed the door.

Solange sat at her desk, staring vacantly into space. There was a knock on her door, and when she asked her secretary to come in, her voice was lethargic, the result of three sleepless nights.

Celeste entered the room with a worried look on her face. "Mr. Dickerson called again."

"What does he want?" Solange asked irritably.

"Now you know that he's not going to tell me. He doesn't even speak when he comes."

Solange turned her head to stare outside her large glass window. "Tell him I'm busy and that I'll call him as soon as I get a chance."

"Will do," Celeste said gently, again noticing the absence of an engagement ring on Solange's hand as she left the room.

Once she was alone again, Solange picked up a pencil and started wiggling it in front of her face. Quickly bored with that, she rearranged the papers on her desk. Suddenly feeling cabin fever, she stood, grabbed her purse and walked past Celeste. "I'm going to get some lunch."

Solange decided to take the stairs down to the bottom street level where her car was parked. Once she got outside, the scorching heat of August in White Plains hit her. Loving the unaccustomed feel of the steamy weather, she decided to walk to the corner deli. The clicking sound of Solange's heels made her notice that there was another sound of footsteps behind her.

She warily looked over her shoulder and saw Ali striding towards her. She stopped. Isabel's haunting words surfaced—"Maybe he's a mad stalker"—but she brushed them aside.

"Don't you get the message, Ali?"

"No, I didn't get the message, and you couldn't get mine since you changed your phone numbers." His hostile eyes pinned hers.

She looked around the empty garage. "What are you doing, stalking me?"

"I'm here to try to talk some sense into you one more time. If you don't want to listen, then that's it for us."

"I don't like ultimatums any more than I like being stalked."

Ali stared at her for one long minute. "Solange, grow the hell up," he said before he stormed off and disappeared from her sight.

That night Solange sat at her desk trying to accomplish some of the things that she should have taken care of that day. Her red light indicating that she had voice mail made her draw in her breath in annoyance and press down the message key. She heard Seth Dickerson's voice and there was an obvious note of urgency in it. "Solange, someone tried to sell our goods on the black market yesterday, and I think that we have an idea who the thief is. Call me when you get this message."

Solange looked at the clock on the wall. Her call to his office went straight to voice mail. "Seth, this is Solange Montgomery. I just got your message and I'm leaving for the night. My new cell number is 914-254-1853. I'll have my cell on tonight if you need to reach me." Hurriedly she grabbed her keys and purse and dropped her cell phone in it. As she locked her office door, she felt a cloth cover her face right before she lost consciousness.

When Solange regained consciousness, she was sitting in a small chair and her hands and feet were bound. Her eyes focused into the dimness of the room, and immediately she became aware that she was being watched. "It's about time your ass woke up. I was getting ready to throw some damn water on your face." She immediately recognized the voice of Arnold Benedict. She tried to twist her body around to see him, but she couldn't budge.

"You can't move," he said and came around to stand in front of her. His belt buckle was the height of her face as he stood in front of her in a threatening stance. "I got you trussed up real good like the pig that you are."

"So you're the one who's been stalking me?" She felt horror building inside her.

"Not stalking," he said. "That would mean that I want you or something. I've just been waiting for the right moment. I almost got you that night in your driveway, but some dog started barking and ruined it."

"Why? What did I ever do to you?"

"First you with your high-falutin' ways fired my mama. Then you fired me. Have you no feelings for anyone?"

"I kept you as long as I could."

"Everyone ain't smart like you with your equal-opportunity affirmative action bullshit getting all the breaks from this government," he screamed.

Solange made sure she spoke in a soothing voice. "What is it that you want, Arnold? We don't keep any cash on the premises."

"Oh, I know that. If you had any, I would have gotten it already."

"How did you get in here? I know that the building was locked at five because I made sure of it."

"I let myself in with a damn key. How the hell do you think I got in?"

"But where did you get a key from?"

Arnold pulled a chair up close to her, and when he did, he reeked of alcohol. "I got in from my girlfriend, of course," he said with a smirk.

"Your girlfriend?" Solange asked in a confused voice.

"Well, she's not my girlfriend anymore," Arnold said with a snort of derision. "Since you fired her, too, she's of no use to me."

A look of confusion that Solange didn't attempt to hide crossed her face. She could see that Arnold was playing cat and mouse with her, but she just had to know who hated her to such a degree she was willing to put her life in jeopardy and maybe have her killed.

"I've been doing that lardo Jane for months. I was pleasantly surprised. I didn't think that she'd be such a freak. It was so easy," he said with an air of superiority. "All I had to do was to give her a compliment here and there. A cheap dinner and a promise that if I got money, we could get married and have a life. Of course she'd help me rob you blind while she moved the data around on those damn inventory sheets. But then you got nosy."

Solange had difficulty digesting this information, but once she processed it, a lightbulb went off in her head. She was disgusted with him, and also with herself for not seeing what had been going on right beneath her nose.

"So where do we go from here, Arnold? What do you want me to do to help you get yourself out of this mess?"

"You still trying to come off superior to me? It reminds me of those damn employee meetings when you wouldn't shut the fuck up." Arnold suddenly reached into his back pocket and took out a .38 revolver.

Solange closed her eyes, not wanting to see what was next. When the barrel of the gun hit her temple, once again she slipped out of consciousness.

The next time she awoke, it was because Arnold had thrown water on her. Gasping for air in the storage area, she could barely breathe, but she pushed her phobia back because she knew her life was on the line.

"Why did the feds come to my house today?" He leaned in close to her, and she had to stop herself from gagging from the stench of his breath.

"I don't know," she answered honestly.

"Do they know that I tried to sell stuff on the black market?"

"No," Solange lied.

"Well, I need you to call somebody. I need some money wired to the Cayman Islands, and I need it now."

"No one in my life has any money," she stated tremulously.

"Call that damn cop boyfriend of yours. His ass was panting after you in the parking garage today. He'll get someone to pay."

"I need my cell phone to call him. It's in my purse."

"I'll call him." Arnold reached into the purse and, after he retrieved her phone, he threw it in the corner.

Randolph Vernon's telephone rang at three o'clock in the morning.

"Hello," he whispered so he didn't wake his wife.

Ali sounded so different that he wasn't sure that it was him.

"I need you, man. Solange is in danger." Briefly Ali told Rudolph what was going on.

"I'll call the police and then meet you at her job," Randolph said.

"He said no police. He doesn't want to attract attention."

"They always say that. Think clearly, man. We have to call them. It's the only chance we have of saving her life. While they try and talk him out, we'll come up with a backup plan."

The shining lights and barricade that police cars were behind lit up the dark sky. Cpt. Heath looked at Ali. "Let me handle this. You're too emotionally involved." Then with the megaphone he shouted to the building, "We're willing to negotiate with you, but you have to let her go."

"That cop you screw doesn't give a flying flip about your ass," Arnold said. After looking out the window, Arnold turned to Solange. "I told him no cops." He stuck the barrel of his gun in her face. "He must want me to kill you."

"His phone is hooked up to headquarters," she lied. "They probably intercepted the call."

"I'm going to up the ante from $100,000 to $200,000 for him being so damn smart. Get on the damn phone and call him and tell him that. If you call my name," Arnold said before he hit the redial button, "I'm going to kill you."

When Ali's cell phone rang, he gave Randolph a look and followed him away from the other officers.

"Ali," she said weakly.

"Yes, Solange, how are you holding up?"

"I feel like I'm suffocating because of my phobia."

"Shut up with that extra bullshit," Arnold whispered.

"He said that because you called the police he now wants $200,000 wired to the Cayman Islands."

Ali said, "I had to call the police to get the money. They're working on it. I'll tell them and get to work on it," he promised.

After he hung up, Ali looked at Vernon. "She gave me a clue. He has her in the storage area, and I have her spare key to that on my chain."

Ali and Randolph let themselves in the building through a side door. Stealthily planting their bodies against the wall, Ali on one side and Randolph on the other, they felt their way into the darkness. Once Ali saw the storage area, he pointed it out to Randolph, who raised his revolver in readiness.

Ali picked up an empty bottle of chloroform and threw it against the wall. Crouching, they saw the handle of the storage area being slowly opened.

Randolph faced the door, his body half hidden by an empty shelf that should have been thrown into the dumpster. When the door opened, Ali's heart plummeted when he saw that Arnold was using Solange as a human shield and had a revolver pressed to her temple.

"She don't go with you. Where the hell is that Arab she . . ."

From the shadows, with a menacing stare, Ali took his revolver and aimed it at Arnold.

Arnold screamed like a wounded animal when he was hit as the bullet pierced his hand. His gun clattered to the floor.

With lightning speed, Randolph ran to Benedict and put his face on the floor while he handcuffed him.

Ali ran to Solange where she had fallen to the floor and scooped her into his arms, "Honey, are you okay?" He gently touched her bruised cheekbone and ring of black and blue under her eye. "Solange, are you okay?" He stared into her dazed honey-colored eyes.

Solange looked at Ali, then Randolph and Arnold Benedict who he was dragging to his feet. She stared deeply into Ali's eyes. "Ali."

"Yes," he said, his throat clouded with fear and love.

"I thank God you went to sniper school," she said weakly before she fainted.

Labor Day weekend, Solange stood in a white wedding dress in the vestibule of Deep River Holiness Pentecostal Church. Grace, clad in a light blue matron of honor dress, clucked around her like a mother fussing over a newfound chick.

Finally satisfied, she stood back and looked at Solange appraisingly. "I've never seen you look better," she teased.

"I hope not." Solange chuckled. "I'm supposed to look like the happiest woman in the world on the happiest day of her life."

"Well you certainly look the part," Grace conceded.

"And I feel the part," Solange confirmed. "Marrying Ali is a dream come true." She gulped back tears. "I see nothing but joy on the horizon as his wife."

Grace scrutinized her best friend's countenance. Carefully she asked, "So in your heart you've really moved past Amira's harsh treatment of you when her father was in the States?"

Solange drew in a long sigh. "It was hard," she admitted. "But with Farrah's help I was able to forgive her."

Grace raised her eyebrows in query. "How did Farrah manage to do that?"

"After Hakim left, she facilitated a meeting between the two of us, and we sat down and had a long talk. I agreed to it because I didn't want to start my marriage off at odds with my mother-in-law. So in the end I forgave her for me and Ali. Besides, I feel sorry for Amira. Not having the support and love of a parent is something that

I've never had to deal with, because mine have always been there for me."

A faraway look settled on Grace's face, and Solange knew that she was thinking of her own lack of parental support, so she hurriedly changed the subject not wanting her friend to become morose from memories. She asked hastily, "Where is Daddy?"

"He said that he was going to the men's room one last time," Grace said and grinned.

"Good." Solange returned the smile. "Once I start my vows, I don't want to be interrupted by my father saying, 'I'll be right back,' and taking off out of the church."

Their banter was interrupted when Amira quietly entered the foyer. Her eyes glistened at the vision Solange made. "I wanted to see you before the wedding because Anah and I have to leave for our trip immediately after the reception."

Solange gave her a smile of genuine love. "So your plans are all set?"

"Yes," Amira breathed. "In the van, Farrah is going to drop me, Anah and your parents off at Myrtle Beach. Then she is going to drive to meet her friends from school."

"I'm glad that the doctor gave you something to quell the motion sickness you have when riding in a car."

"Even if he hadn't, nothing in the world could have kept me from this wedding." Amira looked at Grace and then refocused her attention back to Solange. "I want to thank you for forgiving me," she said.

"It was something that I had to do for me and for Ali," Solange replied quietly. "I love him very much and I will do everything that I can to make him happy."

"You will," Amira said with confidence. "Sometimes second-chance relationships actually do turn out right." Amira gently touched Solange on the arm, careful not to mar her wedding dress, and then slipped back into the church.

Frank Montgomery approached her and Grace in his black tux and held his arm out to his daughter. "Let's get this show on the road," he said with twinkling eyes.

Grace winked at the two of them. "I'll meet you at the altar," she said before she took off the same manner Amira had just done.

When the ushers opened the double doors to the church, Solange and her father took in a minute to survey the small crowd of people. Their families hadn't separated themselves on opposite sides of the church, but instead the small gathering was seated together in the first pews.

Her mother, Rosemary, with Tiana on her lap, and Rufus sat in the front. Right behind him were Farrah, Anah and Amira, who sat next to Randolph, his wife Madison and the kids.

At the altar Ebony, holding a bouquet of flowers, stood next to Grace, who held Livingston's hand. Finally her eyes rested on Detective Ali Marks as he stood next to Jet. She stared at him in his black tux with tails, and she knew that he was the right man for her. "Let's go, Daddy," she whispered, and together they walked towards her destiny.

## 2010 Mass Market Titles

**January**

Show Me The Sun
Miriam Shumba
ISBN: 978-158571-405-6
$6.99

Promises of Forever
Celya Bowers
ISBN: 978-1-58571-380-6
$6.99

**February**

Love Out Of Order
Nicole Green
ISBN: 978-1-58571-381-3
$6.99

Unclear and Present Danger
Michele Cameron
ISBN: 978-158571-408-7
$6.99

**March**

Stolen Jewels
Michele Sudler
ISBN: 978-158571-409-4
$6.99

Not Quite Right
Tammy Williams
ISBN: 978-158571-410-0
$6.99

**April**

Oak Bluffs
Joan Early
ISBN: 978-1-58571-379-0
$6.99

Crossing The Line
Bernice Layton
ISBN: 978-158571-412-4
$6.99

How To Kill Your Husband
Keith Walker
ISBN: 978-158571-421-6
$6.99

**May**

The Business of Love
Cheris F. Hodges
ISBN: 978-158571-373-8
$6.99

Wayward Dreams
Gail McFarland
ISBN: 978-158571-422-3
$6.99

**June**

The Doctor's Wife
Mildred Riley
ISBN: 978-158571-424-7
$6.99

Mixed Reality
Chamein Canton
ISBN: 978-158571-423-0
$6.99

## 2010 Mass Market Titles (continued)

**July**

Blue Interlude
Keisha Mennefee
ISBN: 978-158571-378-3
$6.99

Always You
Crystal Hubbard
ISBN: 978-158571-371-4
$6.99

Unbeweavable
Katrina Spencer
ISBN: 978-158571-426-1
$6.99

**August**

Small Sensations
Crystal V. Rhodes
ISBN: 978-158571-376-9
$6.99

Let's Get It On
Dyanne Davis
ISBN: 978-158571-416-2
$6.99

**September**

Unconditional
A.C. Arthur
ISBN: 978-158571-413-1
$6.99

Swan
Africa Fine
ISBN: 978-158571-377-6
$6.99$6.99

**October**

Friends in Need
Joan Early
ISBN:978-1-58571-428-5
$6.99

Against the Wind
Gwynne Forster
ISBN:978-158571-429-2
$6.99

That Which Has Horns
Miriam Shumba
ISBN:978-1-58571-430-8
$6.99

**November**

A Good Dude
Keith Walker
ISBN:978-1-58571-431-5
$6.99

Reye's Gold
Ruthie Robinson
ISBN:978-1-58571-432-2
$6.99

**December**

Still Waters...
Crystal V. Rhodes
ISBN:978-1-58571-433-9
$6.99

Burn
Crystal Hubbard
ISBN: 978-1-58571-406-3
$6.99

## Other Genesis Press, Inc. Titles

| | | |
|---|---|---|
| 2 Good | Celya Bowers | $6.99 |
| A Dangerous Deception | J.M. Jeffries | $8.95 |
| A Dangerous Love | J.M. Jeffries | $8.95 |
| A Dangerous Obsession | J.M. Jeffries | $8.95 |
| A Drummer's Beat to Mend | Kei Swanson | $9.95 |
| A Happy Life | Charlotte Harris | $9.95 |
| A Heart's Awakening | Veronica Parker | $9.95 |
| A Lark on the Wing | Phyliss Hamilton | $9.95 |
| A Love of Her Own | Cheris F. Hodges | $9.95 |
| A Love to Cherish | Beverly Clark | $8.95 |
| A Place Like Home | Alicia Wiggins | $6.99 |
| A Risk of Rain | Dar Tomlinson | $8.95 |
| A Taste of Temptation | Reneé Alexis | $9.95 |
| A Twist of Fate | Beverly Clark | $8.95 |
| A Voice Behind Thunder | Carrie Elizabeth Greene | $6.99 |
| A Will to Love | Angie Daniels | $9.95 |
| Acquisitions | Kimberley White | $8.95 |
| Across | Carol Payne | $12.95 |
| After the Vows | Leslie Esdaile | $10.95 |
| (Summer Anthology) | T.T. Henderson | |
| | Jacqueline Thomas | |
| Again, My Love | Kayla Perrin | $10.95 |
| Against the Wind | Gwynne Forster | $8.95 |
| All I Ask | Barbara Keaton | $8.95 |
| All I'll Ever Need | Mildred Riley | $6.99 |
| Always You | Crystal Hubbard | $6.99 |
| Ambrosia | T.T. Henderson | $8.95 |
| An Unfinished Love Affair | Barbara Keaton | $8.95 |
| And Then Came You | Dorothy Elizabeth Love | $8.95 |
| Angel's Paradise | Janice Angelique | $9.95 |
| Another Memory | Pamela Ridley | $6.99 |
| Anything But Love | Celya Bowers | $6.99 |
| At Last | Lisa G. Riley | $8.95 |
| Best Foot Forward | Michele Sudler | $6.99 |
| Best of Friends | Natalie Dunbar | $8.95 |
| Best of Luck Elsewhere | Trisha Haddad | $6.99 |
| Beyond the Rapture | Beverly Clark | $9.95 |
| Blame It on Paradise | Crystal Hubbard | $6.99 |
| Blaze | Barbara Keaton | $9.95 |
| Blindsided | Tammy Williams | $6.99 |
| Bliss, Inc. | Chamein Canton | $6.99 |
| Blood Lust | J.M.Jeffries | $9.95 |

## Other Genesis Press, Inc. Titles (continued)

|  |  |  |
|---|---|---|
| Blood Seduction | J.M. Jeffries | $9.95 |
| Bodyguard | Andrea Jackson | $9.95 |
| Boss of Me | Diana Nyad | $8.95 |
| Bound by Love | Beverly Clark | $8.95 |
| Breeze | Robin Hampton Allen | $10.95 |
| Broken | Dar Tomlinson | $24.95 |
| By Design | Barbara Keaton | $8.95 |
| Cajun Heat | Charlene Berry | $8.95 |
| Careless Whispers | Rochelle Alers | $8.95 |
| Cats & Other Tales | Marilyn Wagner | $8.95 |
| Caught in a Trap | Andre Michelle | $8.95 |
| Caught Up in the Rapture | Lisa G. Riley | $9.95 |
| Cautious Heart | Cheris F. Hodges | $8.95 |
| Chances | Pamela Leigh Starr | $8.95 |
| Checks and Balances | Elaine Sims | $6.99 |
| Cherish the Flame | Beverly Clark | $8.95 |
| Choices | Tammy Williams | $6.99 |
| Class Reunion | Irma Jenkins/ John Brown | $12.95 |
| Code Name: Diva | J.M. Jeffries | $9.95 |
| Conquering Dr. Wexler's Heart | Kimberley White | $9.95 |
| Corporate Seduction | A.C. Arthur | $9.95 |
| Crossing Paths, Tempting Memories | Dorothy Elizabeth Love | $9.95 |
| Crush | Crystal Hubbard | $9.95 |
| Cypress Whisperings | Phyllis Hamilton | $8.95 |
| Dark Embrace | Crystal Wilson Harris | $8.95 |
| Dark Storm Rising | Chinelu Moore | $10.95 |
| Daughter of the Wind | Joan Xian | $8.95 |
| Dawn's Harbor | Kymberly Hunt | $6.99 |
| Deadly Sacrifice | Jack Kean | $22.95 |
| Designer Passion | Dar Tomlinson Diana Richeaux | $8.95 |
| Do Over | Celya Bowers | $9.95 |
| Dream Keeper | Gail McFarland | $6.99 |
| Dream Runner | Gail McFarland | $6.99 |
| Dreamtective | Liz Swados | $5.95 |
| Ebony Angel | Deatri King-Bey | $9.95 |
| Ebony Butterfly II | Delilah Dawson | $14.95 |
| Echoes of Yesterday | Beverly Clark | $9.95 |
| Eden's Garden | Elizabeth Rose | $8.95 |

## Other Genesis Press, Inc. Titles (continued)

| | | |
|---|---|---|
| Eve's Prescription | Edwina Martin Arnold | $8.95 |
| Everlastin' Love | Gay G. Gunn | $8.95 |
| Everlasting Moments | Dorothy Elizabeth Love | $8.95 |
| Everything and More | Sinclair Lebeau | $8.95 |
| Everything But Love | Natalie Dunbar | $8.95 |
| Falling | Natalie Dunbar | $9.95 |
| Fate | Pamela Leigh Starr | $8.95 |
| Finding Isabella | A.J. Garrotto | $8.95 |
| Fireflies | Joan Early | $6.99 |
| Fixin' Tyrone | Keith Walker | $6.99 |
| Forbidden Quest | Dar Tomlinson | $10.95 |
| Forever Love | Wanda Y. Thomas | $8.95 |
| From the Ashes | Kathleen Suzanne<br>Jeanne Sumerix | $8.95 |
| Frost On My Window | Angela Weaver | $6.99 |
| Gentle Yearning | Rochelle Alers | $10.95 |
| Glory of Love | Sinclair LeBeau | $10.95 |
| Go Gentle Into That Good Night | Malcom Boyd | $12.95 |
| Goldengroove | Mary Beth Craft | $16.95 |
| Groove, Bang, and Jive | Steve Cannon | $8.99 |
| Hand in Glove | Andrea Jackson | $9.95 |
| Hard to Love | Kimberley White | $9.95 |
| Hart & Soul | Angie Daniels | $8.95 |
| Heart of the Phoenix | A.C. Arthur | $9.95 |
| Heartbeat | Stephanie Bedwell-Grime | $8.95 |
| Hearts Remember | M. Loui Quezada | $8.95 |
| Hidden Memories | Robin Allen | $10.95 |
| Higher Ground | Leah Latimer | $19.95 |
| Hitler, the War, and the Pope | Ronald Rychiak | $26.95 |
| How to Write a Romance | Kathryn Falk | $18.95 |
| I Married a Reclining Chair | Lisa M. Fuhs | $8.95 |
| I'll Be Your Shelter | Giselle Carmichael | $8.95 |
| I'll Paint a Sun | A.J. Garrotto | $9.95 |
| Icie | Pamela Leigh Starr | $8.95 |
| If I Were Your Woman | LaConnie Taylor-Jones | $6.99 |
| Illusions | Pamela Leigh Starr | $8.95 |
| Indigo After Dark Vol. I | Nia Dixon/Angelique | $10.95 |
| Indigo After Dark Vol. II | Dolores Bundy/<br>Cole Riley | $10.95 |
| Indigo After Dark Vol. III | Montana Blue/<br>Coco Morena | $10.95 |

## Other Genesis Press, Inc. Titles (continued)

| | | |
|---|---|---|
| Indigo After Dark Vol. IV | Cassandra Colt/ | $14.95 |
| Indigo After Dark Vol. V | Delilah Dawson | $14.95 |
| Indiscretions | Donna Hill | $8.95 |
| Intentional Mistakes | Michele Sudler | $9.95 |
| Interlude | Donna Hill | $8.95 |
| Intimate Intentions | Angie Daniels | $8.95 |
| It's in the Rhythm | Sammie Ward | $6.99 |
| It's Not Over Yet | J.J. Michael | $9.95 |
| Jolie's Surrender | Edwina Martin-Arnold | $8.95 |
| Kiss or Keep | Debra Phillips | $8.95 |
| Lace | Giselle Carmichael | $9.95 |
| Lady Preacher | K.T. Richey | $6.99 |
| Last Train to Memphis | Elsa Cook | $12.95 |
| Lasting Valor | Ken Olsen | $24.95 |
| Let Us Prey | Hunter Lundy | $25.95 |
| Lies Too Long | Pamela Ridley | $13.95 |
| Life Is Never As It Seems | J.J. Michael | $12.95 |
| Lighter Shade of Brown | Vicki Andrews | $8.95 |
| Look Both Ways | Joan Early | $6.99 |
| Looking for Lily | Africa Fine | $6.99 |
| Love Always | Mildred E. Riley | $10.95 |
| Love Doesn't Come Easy | Charlyne Dickerson | $8.95 |
| Love Unveiled | Gloria Greene | $10.95 |
| Love's Deception | Charlene Berry | $10.95 |
| Love's Destiny | M. Loui Quezada | $8.95 |
| Love's Secrets | Yolanda McVey | $6.99 |
| Mae's Promise | Melody Walcott | $8.95 |
| Magnolia Sunset | Giselle Carmichael | $8.95 |
| Many Shades of Gray | Dyanne Davis | $6.99 |
| Matters of Life and Death | Lesego Malepe, Ph.D. | $15.95 |
| Meant to Be | Jeanne Sumerix | $8.95 |
| Midnight Clear (Anthology) | Leslie Esdaile<br>Gwynne Forster<br>Carmen Green<br>Monica Jackson | $10.95 |
| Midnight Magic | Gwynne Forster | $8.95 |
| Midnight Peril | Vicki Andrews | $10.95 |
| Misconceptions | Pamela Leigh Starr | $9.95 |
| Moments of Clarity | Michele Cameron | $6.99 |
| Montgomery's Children | Richard Perry | $14.95 |
| Mr. Fix-It | Crystal Hubbard | $6.99 |
| My Buffalo Soldier | Barbara B.K. Reeves | $8.95 |

## Other Genesis Press, Inc. Titles (continued)

| | | |
|---|---|---|
| Naked Soul | Gwynne Forster | $8.95 |
| Never Say Never | Michele Cameron | $6.99 |
| Next to Last Chance | Louisa Dixon | $24.95 |
| No Apologies | Seressia Glass | $8.95 |
| No Commitment Required | Seressia Glass | $8.95 |
| No Regrets | Mildred E. Riley | $8.95 |
| Not His Type | Chamein Canton | $6.99 |
| Nowhere to Run | Gay G. Gunn | $10.95 |
| O Bed! O Breakfast! | Rob Kuehnle | $14.95 |
| Object of His Desire | A.C. Arthur | $8.95 |
| Office Policy | A.C. Arthur | $9.95 |
| Once in a Blue Moon | Dorianne Cole | $9.95 |
| One Day at a Time | Bella McFarland | $8.95 |
| One of These Days | Michele Sudler | $9.95 |
| Outside Chance | Louisa Dixon | $24.95 |
| Passion | T.T. Henderson | $10.95 |
| Passion's Blood | Cherif Fortin | $22.95 |
| Passion's Furies | AlTonya Washington | $6.99 |
| Passion's Journey | Wanda Y. Thomas | $8.95 |
| Past Promises | Jahmel West | $8.95 |
| Path of Fire | T.T. Henderson | $8.95 |
| Path of Thorns | Annetta P. Lee | $9.95 |
| Peace Be Still | Colette Haywood | $12.95 |
| Picture Perfect | Reon Carter | $8.95 |
| Playing for Keeps | Stephanie Salinas | $8.95 |
| Pride & Joi | Gay G. Gunn | $8.95 |
| Promises Made | Bernice Layton | $6.99 |
| Promises to Keep | Alicia Wiggins | $8.95 |
| Quiet Storm | Donna Hill | $10.95 |
| Reckless Surrender | Rochelle Alers | $6.95 |
| Red Polka Dot in a World Full of Plaid | Varian Johnson | $12.95 |
| Red Sky | Renee Alexis | $6.99 |
| Reluctant Captive | Joyce Jackson | $8.95 |
| Rendezvous With Fate | Jeanne Sumerix | $8.95 |
| Revelations | Cheris F. Hodges | $8.95 |
| Rivers of the Soul | Leslie Esdaile | $8.95 |
| Rocky Mountain Romance | Kathleen Suzanne | $8.95 |
| Rooms of the Heart | Donna Hill | $8.95 |
| Rough on Rats and Tough on Cats | Chris Parker | $12.95 |
| Save Me | Africa Fine | $6.99 |

## Other Genesis Press, Inc. Titles (continued)

| | | |
|---|---|---|
| Secret Library Vol. 1 | Nina Sheridan | $18.95 |
| Secret Library Vol. 2 | Cassandra Colt | $8.95 |
| Secret Thunder | Annetta P. Lee | $9.95 |
| Shades of Brown | Denise Becker | $8.95 |
| Shades of Desire | Monica White | $8.95 |
| Shadows in the Moonlight | Jeanne Sumerix | $8.95 |
| Sin | Crystal Rhodes | $8.95 |
| Singing A Song... | Crystal Rhodes | $6.99 |
| Six O'Clock | Katrina Spencer | $6.99 |
| Small Whispers | Annetta P. Lee | $6.99 |
| So Amazing | Sinclair LeBeau | $8.95 |
| Somebody's Someone | Sinclair LeBeau | $8.95 |
| Someone to Love | Alicia Wiggins | $8.95 |
| Song in the Park | Martin Brant | $15.95 |
| Soul Eyes | Wayne L. Wilson | $12.95 |
| Soul to Soul | Donna Hill | $8.95 |
| Southern Comfort | J.M. Jeffries | $8.95 |
| Southern Fried Standards | S.R. Maddox | $6.99 |
| Still the Storm | Sharon Robinson | $8.95 |
| Still Waters Run Deep | Leslie Esdaile | $8.95 |
| Stolen Memories | Michele Sudler | $6.99 |
| Stories to Excite You | Anna Forrest/Divine | $14.95 |
| Storm | Pamela Leigh Starr | $6.99 |
| Subtle Secrets | Wanda Y. Thomas | $8.95 |
| Suddenly You | Crystal Hubbard | $9.95 |
| Sweet Repercussions | Kimberley White | $9.95 |
| Sweet Sensations | Gwyneth Bolton | $9.95 |
| Sweet Tomorrows | Kimberly White | $8.95 |
| Taken by You | Dorothy Elizabeth Love | $9.95 |
| Tattooed Tears | T. T. Henderson | $8.95 |
| Tempting Faith | Crystal Hubbard | $6.99 |
| The Color Line | Lizzette Grayson Carter | $9.95 |
| The Color of Trouble | Dyanne Davis | $8.95 |
| The Disappearance of Allison Jones | Kayla Perrin | $5.95 |
| The Fires Within | Beverly Clark | $9.95 |
| The Foursome | Celya Bowers | $6.99 |
| The Honey Dipper's Legacy | Myra Pannell-Allen | $14.95 |
| The Joker's Love Tune | Sidney Rickman | $15.95 |
| The Little Pretender | Barbara Cartland | $10.95 |
| The Love We Had | Natalie Dunbar | $8.95 |
| The Man Who Could Fly | Bob & Milana Beamon | $18.95 |

## Other Genesis Press, Inc. Titles (continued)

| | | |
|---|---|---|
| The Missing Link | Charlyne Dickerson | $8.95 |
| The Mission | Pamela Leigh Starr | $6.99 |
| The More Things Change | Chamein Canton | $6.99 |
| The Perfect Frame | Beverly Clark | $9.95 |
| The Price of Love | Sinclair LeBeau | $8.95 |
| The Smoking Life | Ilene Barth | $29.95 |
| The Words of the Pitcher | Kei Swanson | $8.95 |
| Things Forbidden | Maryam Diaab | $6.99 |
| This Life Isn't Perfect Holla | Sandra Foy | $6.99 |
| Three Doors Down | Michele Sudler | $6.99 |
| Three Wishes | Seressia Glass | $8.95 |
| Ties That Bind | Kathleen Suzanne | $8.95 |
| Tiger Woods | Libby Hughes | $5.95 |
| Time Is of the Essence | Angie Daniels | $9.95 |
| Timeless Devotion | Bella McFarland | $9.95 |
| Tomorrow's Promise | Leslie Esdaile | $8.95 |
| Truly Inseparable | Wanda Y. Thomas | $8.95 |
| Two Sides to Every Story | Dyanne Davis | $9.95 |
| Unbreak My Heart | Dar Tomlinson | $8.95 |
| Uncommon Prayer | Kenneth Swanson | $9.95 |
| Unconditional Love | Alicia Wiggins | $8.95 |
| Unconditional | A.C. Arthur | $9.95 |
| Undying Love | Renee Alexis | $6.99 |
| Until Death Do Us Part | Susan Paul | $8.95 |
| Vows of Passion | Bella McFarland | $9.95 |
| Waiting for Mr. Darcy | Chamein Canton | $6.99 |
| Waiting in the Shadows | Michele Sudler | $6.99 |
| Wedding Gown | Dyanne Davis | $8.95 |
| What's Under Benjamin's Bed | Sandra Schaffer | $8.95 |
| When a Man Loves a Woman | LaConnie Taylor-Jones | $6.99 |
| When Dreams Float | Dorothy Elizabeth Love | $8.95 |
| When I'm With You | LaConnie Taylor-Jones | $6.99 |
| When Lightning Strikes | Michele Cameron | $6.99 |
| Where I Want To Be | Maryam Diaab | $6.99 |
| Whispers in the Night | Dorothy Elizabeth Love | $8.95 |
| Whispers in the Sand | LaFlorya Gauthier | $10.95 |
| Who's That Lady? | Andrea Jackson | $9.95 |
| Wild Ravens | AlTonya Washington | $9.95 |
| Yesterday Is Gone | Beverly Clark | $10.95 |
| Yesterday's Dreams, Tomorrow's Promises | Reon Laudat | $8.95 |
| Your Precious Love | Sinclair LeBeau | $8.95 |

# Order Form

**Mail to: Genesis Press, Inc.**
**P.O. Box 101**
**Columbus, MS 39703**

Name ________________________________________
Address ______________________________________
City/State ______________________ Zip ______________
Telephone ______________________

*Ship to (if different from above)*
Name ________________________________________
Address ______________________________________
City/State ______________________ Zip ______________
Telephone ______________________

*Credit Card Information*
Credit Card # ____________________ ☐ Visa ☐ Mastercard
Expiration Date (mm/yy) _____________ ☐ AmEx ☐ Discover

| Qty. | Author | Title | Price | Total |
|---|---|---|---|---|
| | | | | |
| | | | | |
| | | | | |
| | | | | |
| | | | | |
| | | | | |
| | | | | |
| | | | | |
| | | | | |
| | | | | |
| | | | | |
| | | | | |

Use this order form, or call 1-888-INDIGO-1

**Total for books** ______________
**Shipping and handling:**
**$5 first two books,**
**$1 each additional book** ______________
**Total S & H** ______________
**Total amount enclosed** ______________

*Mississippi residents add 7% sales tax*